CW00853791

Dorothy Fielding

The Tall House Mystery

e-artnow 2022

Dorothy Fielding

The Tall House Mystery

A Murder Thriller

e-artnow, 2022
Contact: info@e-artnow.org

ISBN 978-80-273-4251-8

Contents

CHAPTER 1

THERE is no pleasanter place in London after dinner than the large central hall of the Carlton Club, with its comfortable armchairs and its little coffee tables, that suggest both privacy and gregariousness.

For here a man may speak to a fellow-member without being introduced-perhaps because it has so large a number of young men among its members. Just now, the tables were almost empty. It was only a little past eight. Haliburton had dined early in that large dining-room where the portraits of Conservative statesmen look down tolerantly on morning-coats or full tails. Haliburton had had a friend, a saturnine, silent man called Tark, dining with him; and now Moy, a young solicitor, had dropped in for a few words.

Haliburton was talking at the moment.

"I think I'm a fatalist," he was saying. "Yes, on the whole, I think I am." He was a pleasant-faced young man, tall, thin, with a certain assured yet unhurried way with him which, some said, was due to the fact that he had never yet had to bestir himself for anything. He was the son of Haliburton, the banker, and grandson of Haliburton, the ship-owner, and through his mother alone had as an income what many would consider a handsome capital. He was Unionist member for some small country constituency until something better should be free.

Moy was about the same age, around twenty-five; small of stature, quick and eager in eye and movement. Tark, the third man, struck such a different note that at first glance one would have taken him for a foreigner. Moy liked Haliburton, but he did not care for his companion, whom he had met in his company a couple of times lately. But, though he did not like Tark, Moy was interested in the man. For the young solicitor was writing a play in secret, and was keenly interested in finding characters for it. Haliburton, he had decided, was no earthly good to a writer. Rich. Easy going. Kindly...but this other, the chap with the name that suited him somehow-because it rhymed with shark probably, Moy decided-he might be very useful. He turned to him now.

"You a fatalist too?" he asked. "But you can't be, or you wouldn't have fished Haliburton out of that weir as you did."

Everyone in their little world knew that Tark's punt and Haliburton's canoe had collided on the Thames, and that, but for Tark's swimming powers, the House of Haliburton would have had no heir, for Haliburton could not swim. Somehow you wouldn't expect him to, Moy reflected. Haliburton would naturally count on a motor boat turning up, or a submarine nipping along, or a seaplane swooping to his assistance.

"No." Tark's voice suggested that he had said all there was to say on the point. He was the most silent man that Moy had yet met.

"A fatalist doesn't necessarily mean a man of inaction," Haliburton explained carefully.

"He evidently struggled in the water!" Moy said with a laugh. Haliburton laughed too. Tark only gave a twist of his thin tight lips.

What a pity that his play was not on the Inquisition, Moy thought. Tark would do so splendidly for one of the inquisitors; a man without feelings, but with plenty of intelligence. Or had Tark intelligence? He looked at the low forehead, the high set ears, the something about the whole face that suggested stone, or wood, and was not sure. But his suitability for the role of inquisitor seemed to fit better the longer he studied him. Yet Tark had never shown him any eagerness, any intensity of emotion, and an inquisitor must be capable of both. It must be something hidden deep down in the man. Unless his ideas of him were all wrong, Moy reflected.

"Well." Moy roused himself from his discreet but intent contemplation of Tark. "Now for the reason for my coming in formal state this evening. I have a Proposal I want to lay before you, Haliburton."

"And I thought you a friend," murmured Haliburton lazily.

"You know that we-my father's firm-often have houses to let for our clients? Well, among these is a house in Chelsea called The Tall House."

"Sir Miles Huntington's?" Haliburton labeled it correctly.

"Yes. He's off to the Arctic for a year. The year's nearly up, but as he wanted such a high rental, the place has been on our hands all the time. A week ago, we got a note from him, which had evidently been months on the way, authorizing me to let it for whatever I could get for it. But by now, there's only a bare six weeks or so left. It's a beautiful old house. Angelica Kaufmann lived in it. Reynolds painted one of the ceilings, or may have done so —"

He saw Haliburton sit up with sudden interest, his large clear eyes fastened on Moy. Moy knew why and nodded to himself with an inward grin. The fish was rising.

"Of course, it's hardly ever that a house of that kind is to be had furnished for a bit over a month, five weeks to be exact. As a rule, I could do nothing with so short a time, but I happened to speak of it to Frederick Ingram yesterday morning." More interest in Haliburton's steady gaze. Even Tark of the impassive features seemed to be listening very intently. "Yes, I mentioned it to Fred Ingram yesterday. His brother Charles and he —"

"Half-brother," corrected Haliburton in a tone as though the detail mattered.

" —half-brother, then," Moy corrected, "are also clients of ours. We handle their father's estate."

"If you're going to take Frederick Ingram as a lessee!" Haliburton spoke with a contempt at variance with his usual placidity.

"Hardly!" Moy's tone matched the other's. "No, he doesn't come in to this except as the originator of the proposal, which is this: Miss Pratt, it seems, wants tremendously to stay in town in a really old house with genuine period furnishings, and, though the Tall House is shabby enough inside and out, it contains some magnificent old stuff. Entailed, of course, or it wouldn't be there. Well, bearing this in mind about Miss Pratt, Freddie wondered if his brother wouldn't like to take the house on for the few remaining weeks."

Haliburton's face flushed.

"But Ingram turned it down when I dropped in last evening," Moy went on, and Haliburton's flush died away.

"He thought it would be beyond him. It's not merely the rent, it's the servants, and all that sort of thing. Well, that seemed that, but this morning Frederick had another brain wave. The new idea is to form a sort of syndicate among ourselves, five of us, and each take the house and run it for a week. Mrs. Pratt and her daughter being the guests of each host in turn. Charles Ingram is quite keen on this amended form. He will be one of the five; a friend of his, Gilmour, who shares a flat with him at Harrow, will make two; I come in as third-my humble tenement is in the hands of the plumbers at the moment, and I assure you I shall be thankful not to dance to any more of their piping for a while. Ingram at once suggested my asking you to be the fourth host, and any friend whom you liked to nominate could be the fifth. That would make you and him all square, he seems to think."

"That's very decent of Ingram," Haliburton said warmly. "Of course, I accept with pleasure. And Tark, here, will come as the fifth man, I know. He's keen on getting to know Ingram better, since reading one of his books."

Tark's affirmative came at once. He moved for a moment so that the light fell full on him, and Moy thought again how unprepossessing his face was, with its narrow lips slightly askew, its narrow-bridged nose just off the true, and its narrow dark eyes that never seemed to dance or sparkle. But his lips were parted now as though he were breathing fast. Moy was surprised. That Haliburton should be interested, he could understand, or rather he had firmly expected, for he and Charles Ingram were suitors for the hand of Winnie Pratt, but that Tark should be stirred...he had had an almost wolfish look for a second...Fortunately Haliburton was vouching for him, otherwise Moy would never have let him come in. But at any rate, he, Moy, could now tell Ingram that the syndicate was complete. Just like chivalrous Ingram to have practically insisted that his rival should have an equal chance with himself. Probably by the end of the five weeks Miss Pratt would have made up her mind which of the two men she preferred. Haliburton had been prime favorite till a month ago, when Ingram had first met her, and had seemed to score with his talk of books and plays. Ingram was a highbrow, a writer of scientific books himself. Mathematics was his especial line, but he was a man of broad literary interests. Mrs. Pratt openly favored Haliburton, but then Haliburton's rent roll explained that, and in time he would succeed his shipping grandfather in the peerage. Moy was looking forward to the five weeks. He certainly ought to get good material for his play out of it. Take Winnie Pratt for instance...a lovely young thing, complexion all cream and roses. But with no character that one could get hold of, how could one catch her wonderful charm?

Tark was speaking again. Moy felt as though the man's vocal chords must creak with the unaccustomed work.

"Ingram's book on *Ciphers Past and Present* is positively monumental." He spoke with slow heavy emphasis.

Moy did not know whether Tark's praise referred to quantity or quality, but he nodded a cheerful assent.

"I take the first week, beginning next Friday," he told them. "So as to get things rolling smoothly."

"Friday!" broke in Tark, "why not Thursday or Saturday?"

Moy thought he was joking, but the wooden features did not show any indication of it being a jest. On the contrary, Tark repeated his question.

"It fitted in better," Moy said rather vaguely.

"He's superstitious as a cat," Haliburton said.

Moy burst out laughing. "You mean nervous —" and he laughed again, for any one less nervous-if looks could be relied on-than Tark, he had yet to see.

"Well, he's superstitious as a Solomon Islander, then," Haliburton amended. "That's because he's not a fatalist. But go on, Moy, you're going to take the first week —"

"I suggested that Ingram should take the second, but he thought you and he should toss for it."

"Certainly not! Of course Ingram must take the second week," Haliburton said definitely. "Any week after his will suit me. And I'll take one day less or more, Tark, so as 'to throw your week, when it comes, on to the most auspicious moment."

Moy reflected how easy it was to work with pleasant chaps like Ingram and Haliburton.

"All right, then, you take the third week —" he was jotting notes down as he spoke, "shall we put Gilmour in for the fourth, and Tark here for the fifth?"

But Haliburton suggested that as Tark seemed so fussy over days-his smile rid the words of all offense-perhaps it would be better for Gilmour to take the third week, which would bring his, Haliburton's, week and Tark's together at the end, when days could be added or omitted as preferred. It was settled like that, and Moy stayed a few minutes more to explain how he had arranged about servants-which was why it would have been very awkward to alter the date of taking over the house. Another client of his firm's had given her servants a holiday on board wages and had been groaning at the expense. He had wired her a suggestion that he could get them a five weeks' engagement *en bloc*, to which she had agreed with alacrity.

The servants, too, partly unable to help themselves, and partly taken with the idea of handsome tips, had agreed to start work this coming Friday if so requested by Moy. Everything promised to go without a hitch. He would be treasurer. Any man could invite any friends he wanted during his week, but Moy hoped that only the bedrooms on one of the floors would be used, as he wanted no trouble with the maids. The house had a couple of full-size lawn tennis courts behind it, and day-time friends of any, or all, of the five would be welcome. As for evening entertainments, he, Moy, would give an opening dance, and a dance would close the last of the five weeks, otherwise, again remembering the servants, the hosts would do their entertaining outside the house.

Moy left, after the two had signed a simple preliminary agreement. Haliburton turned to Tark when the young solicitor had hurried out to his little car.

"I had no idea until you told me, that you were interested in Ingram's line of work." Haliburton looked at his companion with friendly curiosity as they sauntered back to their table in the lounge.

"Numbers, the science of numbers, has always fascinated me." Tark was unresponsive as always, yet now there was something in the dark depths of his eyes like slumbering fire. "More so even than ciphers, and they're fascinating enough."

There were those who hinted that Tark was getting full payment out of Haliburton for having dived in and held up the other's unconscious body, but if so, his manners were certainly not those of a climber. He gave the impression of disliking everyone at first sight. Even Haliburton at times wished that someone else had saved his life.

Moy drove on to Harrow, where Ingram and Gilmour shared the ground floor of a pleasant rambling house. It was emphatically the flat of two young men who were workers. Ingram, as has been said, wrote on more or less mathematical subjects. Gilmour was a Civil Service First Division clerk. Both young men lived well within their means. At the moment, Moy found Frederick Ingram with his half-brother in the latter's book-lined writing-room. Frederick had dropped in to ask about some doubtful figures in an equation, he explained. Moy knew that he had gone in for that sort of thing during his short and inglorious career at Oxford, and also knew that the elder Ingram was giving him some proof-reading to do for him. But proof-reading would hardly explain the look on Frederick's face as he brushed past the solicitor, his beetling black brows knitted, his small, but thick-lipped, mouth set. And even in the room, usually so devoid of all stir, there was something that suggested a clash of personalities still in the air. Ingram himself had a firm will. He looked as much. His was a handsome face with its scholar's brow and deep-set passionate eyes with their direct gaze. A humorous mouth, a rather forbiddingly high-bridged nose, and a resolute jaw.

He now pushed some books away, and stretched himself as though he too had felt the tension, and was glad to relax.

"Gilmour out?" Moy asked after shaking hands and accepting a glass of light Australian wine. He learned that Gilmour was in his own den. So into the lounge Moy and his host now went. A door opened.

"Frederick gone?" Gilmour asked in a defensive voice, apparently prepared to shut the door instantly on a negative reply.

"Yes, some of my figures puzzled him," Ingram said slowly, and with a sigh of vexation, or weariness that could hardly be connected with figures.

His telephone rang, and he stepped back into his room.

"Figures of some sort are always the explanations of a fall from Frederick," Gilmour said under his breath, as Ingram closed his door. Moy grinned. None knew better than he how involved the financial affairs of the younger Ingram were, and he strongly suspected that Ingram had given him some work to do merely as an excuse for helping him out with money, though he claimed to have found Frederick unexpectedly careful and good at the job.

Ingram now came back, and the three discussed the taking over of The Tall House. Ingram was vastly entertained at the idea. He had an engagement, however, and had to hurry off, leaving Gilmour and Moy to finish working out the details on paper.

"I hope he'll get his money's worth," Moy said as they finished. "A rather vulgar way of putting it. But I hope Ingram won't be let down."

"You mean Miss Pratt?" Gilmour slanted his head on one side and looked doubtful. He was a smallish man, very good at games. He was not, and did not look, clever, but he did look companionable and cheery, which was all that was necessary in a stable companion of Ingram's, Moy reflected. The mathematician had brains enough for any two.

Moy now grunted that he did mean Miss Pratt.

"If she's any judge of character, she'll take Ingram and be thankful," Gilmour said warmly.

"Haliburton's a nice chap too," Moy reminded him a trifle impishly. He found himself looking forward to the coming five weeks at The Tall House from its sheer human interest. A lovely girl, two honest men in love with her...what more could any future dramatist hope to find laid out before him? Whom would she choose? Ingram had fame and sufficient means to live in quiet comfort. Haliburton could offer splendor and a title later on. Which would Winnie Pratt take?

CHAPTER 2

"WHY do you dislike me so?" Winnie Pratt smiled up at the young man beside her. Most young men would have been overcome with joy, for Miss Pratt made a lovely picture as she stood on the lawn of The Tall House in a white muslin frock with a soft green sash and a large hat. Her flower-like little face just now wore a bewildered, hurt expression that her delicately aligned eyebrows emphasized.

Gilmour laughed awkwardly. "Have I been rude, Miss Pratt? If so, it's only because I'm not accustomed to such visions of loveliness. I'm grown into a dull old hack." Now Lawrence Gilmour did look rather dull, but he was distinctly not old, and he was quite unusually good-looking in a fresh-faced, ruddy, rather countrified way.

"Is he a dull old hack?" she asked Moy, who was passing them at the moment.

"Do you want a standing opinion?" he asked with affected seriousness.

"If it's not too expensive," Miss Pratt returned, smiling at him.

"Nothing is too expensive for you!" he retorted with mock devotion. "Then merely as an opinion for the purpose of the discussion, and subject to the —"

"Help! Let me escape!" Gilmour edged away with mock fright, but with genuine eagerness, and walked back into the house.

"There!" Winnie waved a hand after him, "tell me, Mr. Moy, why he avoids me so. It-it's — most —" She seemed at a loss for a word.

"Unusual," Moy finished, laughing. She laughed too. But there was vexation in her lovely eyes. "It's so noticeable," she persisted petulantly.

Moy refused to take her seriously. "The absence of one worshiper among the multitude? Surely not!" But he went after Gilmour.

He found him in the square hall of the house drinking lemon squash.

"Look here," Moy began at once, "why make yourself conspicuous, old man?"

"In what way?" Gilmour's tone was wary.

"By insisting so markedly on having nothing to do with Miss Pratt," Moy finished. "What's wrong with meeting a lovely young thing half way? Most men would give half their fortune to be in your shoes."

"I'll do a deal with them, instantly!" Gilmour grinned back. "I loathe the girl, Moy, and that's the truth."

Moy stared at him. Yet he looked in earnest. But of course this was just a joke.

"Because of her cadaverous and withered appearance, I suppose," Moy asked. Even Gilmour laughed at that question.

"I know it sounds mad," Gilmour was speaking a little under his breath, slowly and very gravely. "She's infernally pretty. And yet —" He hesitated. "Oh, well, put it down to my not wanting to make a fool of myself-just now. Oh, damn, there she comes again!" And catching sight of a flicker of white muslin, he once more fled, this time into a farther room.

Moy's lips twitched as he watched him. From where he stood, he could see that the white muslin belonged to Mrs. Pratt, not to the daughter. He himself went back into the garden again, but he did not make for Miss. Pratt. Winnie was not for any solicitor. He wondered with a moment's amusement how Mrs. Pratt would take it if he entered the lists too. For Mrs. Pratt considered that Haliburton was the only possible choice for her beautiful daughter. Unfortunately Winnie, like many another spoiled beauty, seemed on her arrival at The Tall House to have suddenly set her heart on what apparently she was not to have, and that was Gilmour. He was evidently anchored elsewhere, Moy reflected. No man whose heart was free could withstand those smiles. Gilmour had been about to say as much just now. What did perplex Moy was the extraordinary fact of Gilmour's dislike of the girl, his almost open hostility to her. It was all really more amusing to watch and speculate over than he had expected. And few things in life are that. He was, of course, prepared to see the Haliburton-Ingram silent, well-mannered duel continue, but he had never hoped to see Miss Pratt fairly throw herself at the head of a third man, who would try his best to throw the enchantress back again. He wondered how Haliburton and Ingram liked it.

Fortunately they were such pleasant fellows, both of them, and Miss Pratt's attack was simply an acute form of wanting what she was not going to get, which would cure itself in time. Luckily it was Gilmour and not Frederick Ingram whom she had suddenly decided to capture. Frederick Ingram professed himself one of her victims, but Winnie refused even to look at him; which was as well, for Frederick was an utter waster. It was said that even Ingram had been so stirred by the cheek of Frederick daring to lift his eyes to the Beauty, that he had told him not to come near The Tall House while she was there. Moy watched Ingram for a moment, reflecting on the oddity that the scholar should be so captivated by a featherhead. Moy was still of an age to put a value on cleverness in women which he would not do in later years. Yes, he vowed to himself, Miss Pratt would be difficult to put in a play...apart from her beauty, there seemed so little to get hold of...Then how, in a play, to make it clear why two sensible young men were ready to count a day well lost if it brought them but one smile from her?

Haliburton came out of the house again, and stood a moment watching Ingram play. As a rule he was well worth attention. Turning his head, Haliburton saw that Tark was also watching the game.

"Had your talk with him yet?" he asked pleasantly. Tark started as though he had not noticed that anyone stood beside him.

"Not yet."

"I heard you talking to someone in the house just now. It sounded like Frederick Ingram. He isn't here, surely?"

Tark did not reply.

"I didn't know you knew him," Haliburton went on.

"I met him abroad," came the casual reply. Moy thought again how his voice suggested lack of use. Yet the man did not look an anchorite. Or did he? Moy, for one, had a feeling as though Tark lived in a cell-windowless, doorless, dark and utterly lonely.

"Probably through no fault of your own," Haliburton said excusingly.

Tark gave the half-smile, half-sneer that was his nearest to showing merriment.

"I didn't realize that he was a brother of the mathematician Ingram. By the way, isn't he coming to stay here at the house too?"

"Certainly not," was the instant rejoinder. "I believe Ingram has taken him on in a sort of semi-demi-secretarial position, but neither he nor Gilmour are fond of Frederick. Like most people." And with that Haliburton seemed to lose himself in the game again.

"What's the matter with Ingram's play!" he ejaculated after another moment.

"Miss Pratt," came the reply. Haliburton's eyes, following the other's, now saw Gilmour walking stolidly along, his eyes on the grass, like a worried owner thinking of re-turfing, and beside him, her face turned up to his downbent one, which did not even glance at her, pattered the little white shoes of Miss Pratt.

Haliburton frowned and watched Ingram serve another fault.

"Women always want what they can't get," Haliburton said at length, and for once his good nature sounded a trifle forced. "Miss Pratt has all the rest of us at her feet, and just because Gilmour holds out, she means to have his scalp."

Moy came closer. He overheard the words. "She's a dreadful flirt," he threw in lightly. Moy wanted to hear what Haliburton would reply. Motives and cross currents, just now, were to Moy what rats are to a terrier. He could not pass them by.

"I wouldn't call her a flirt," Haliburton said uneasily.

Moy laughed at him.

"You wouldn't call her anything but perfection." Haliburton reddened. He had a trick of that.

"Oh, I don't know," he spoke awkwardly, "I don't mind owning that I wish she would stop trying to sweep Gilmour off his feet. There's no harm in her trying, of course, but —" He stopped, not quite sure how he intended to finish the sentence.

"She'll soon tire of her effort," Moy now said soothingly, and in silence the three watched Ingram miss a ball that he could have caught with his eyes shut had he been his usual nimble-footed self. He won in the end, it was true, but the games he had lost he had given away. He now made for Miss Pratt, and Gilmour at once stepped back, waving them towards the house for drinks. Miss Pratt would have lingered, but Gilmour fairly swept them on their path and stood smiling a little as they went.

Mrs. Pratt touched his arm. She, too, was smiling, but her eyes were not gay.

"A word with you, Mr. Gilmour. Suppose we have a look at the malmaisons?" They turned a corner of the artificially intricate little garden. It cut them off from the courts. As they stood before the flowers she went on:

"Mr. Gilmour, I think I must speak plainly to you."

"By all means." His sunburned face smiled encouragingly down into her worn one. Mrs. Pratt had been as lovely as Winnie in her day, but no one would have guessed it now.

"I want you to stop throwing my daughter at Mr. Ingram's head." She lifted her chin as she spoke and looked him straight in the eyes. For the first time, Gilmour really noticed her. He saw energy and will power in that face-qualities that he always admired. He saw more-the determination that makes things come to pass-another of his own likings.

"I don't agree with your way of putting it," he said now, quietly, "but if you mean, that because Ingram is my friend, I want him to have the girl he loves, you're right. I do. He'll make her a splendid husband. Any mother could hand her daughter to Charles Ingram with confidence. I've known him for years, and I assure you that he — —"

She made an impatient snap with the fingers that hung down at her side.

"Winnie is going to marry Mr. Haliburton. That was why I got out of all our other engagements to come here for this month. But your friend, Mr. Ingram, is quite another matter. I do not think she would be happy with him."

He looked his dissent.

"Please, Mr. Gilmour," the mother said to that, "please don't try to encourage your friend. He hasn't a hope of marrying her. She really does love Mr. Haliburton. She told me as much herself."

"When?" he asked skeptically. "Months ago? But that's over, or nearly over."

"Winnie's affections have a way of circling round," the mother, too, spoke a trifle dryly. There was a short silence.

"As for your own conduct," she went on frankly, "it's splendid. But then, you're a born realist."

"What's that?" he asked.

"I mean by that, a person who goes for the substance and not for the shadow. Winnie is born to go for shadows. You have the good sense and cleverness to know that she's only making a fuss over you in order to tease poor Basil Haliburton."

Gilmour liked being thought clever. "Is that it?" he asked. He looked genuinely relieved-and was.

"It makes it damned awkward for me sometimes," he said honestly. "I wish she wouldn't!"

For a second the mother's eyes flashed. And Mrs. Pratt's eyes could shoot fire on occasions, he saw to his surprise.

"You're the first man who has ever complained about it," she said, and he grinned at once placatingly and ruefully.

"I don't suppose I would either, but for —" He hesitated. "I'm giving you confidence for confidence, Mrs. Pratt. There's a certain girl whom I hope very much will some day be my wife. I want her to come up to The Tall House for a couple of days —"

"That's just what I told Winnie!" she said almost jubilantly. "I felt sure there was something like that. I do congratulate you, Mr. Gilmour. What's her name?"

"Alfreda Longstaff. But it's not settled-unfortunately. It's only a hope," he put in hastily.

"Do have her up here," she begged. "I'll chaperone her with pleasure. But now to come back to my first, my only grievance," she smiled at him now with genuine kindliness, "please don't try to wreck your friend's life-for if he were really to fall in love with my daughter, it would be such a pity!"

"It's too late to say that," Gilmour replied gravely. "He is deeply in love with her."

"He'll have to get over it," she said bruskly.

"I still don't see why he should have to." Gilmour's face was that of a man who would not easily give up his chosen path. "I don't in the least see why he should."

There was no mistaking the change in Mrs. Pratt's look. For a second she stood pressing her lips together, then she said slowly:

"Does Mr. Haliburton strike you as a man of unlimited patience? He doesn't me."

"He's very good-natured..." he began vaguely. Gilmour hardly knew Haliburton.

"He has that reputation," Mrs. Pratt threw in, "but-well —I doubt his standing much nonsense. He's not been accustomed to it. Besides, why should he? And if he let Winnie go —" Her face seemed to grow pinched at the mere words. "No, listen!" she said imperiously, "I'll be quite frank. I'm living on my capital. I was a wealthy girl myself, and married a man who was believed to be well off. So he was-so we both were for a time. But we were both extravagant, and when he died I found that even his insurance had been mortgaged. I was left to struggle along with Winnie as best I could, for we neither of us had any relations. Bit by bit my capital has been eaten into, until-well, I can't keep the flag flying much longer. Now Basil Haliburton at the moment would settle half the world on Winnie. And she loves him. In reality." The last two words came defiantly. "Anything else is just play. I want the affair settled when we leave here. And so it will be if you head off your friend."

"But he's quite well to do," Gilmour urged.

"Not as Mr. Haliburton is!" was the unanswerable reply. "Let alone as well off as Basil will be when his grandfather dies."

"I know he has big expectations," Gilmour agreed, "but I assure you that Ingram's means —"

"Are not the kind that I want for Winnie," snapped Mrs. Pratt.

"But perhaps the kind that she wants for herself," came the reply with a smile that Mrs. Pratt called "positively fiendish" in its impudence.

"It's no good, Mrs. Pratt. I'm backing my friend to win."

There was a moment's silence.

"Do you suppose I've endured what I have to be thwarted now-when the struggle is nearly over?" Her tone startled him by its intensity. He saw that he had gone too far.

"Look here, Mrs. Pratt," he spoke in a more conciliatory tone, "give Ingram a trial. You talk as though he were a pauper. He's anything but."

Again came that snap of her fingers at her side, and suddenly Gilmour guessed-rightly-that Mrs. Pratt had borrowed money on the strength of her daughter's coming engagement to Haliburton. But she only gave him a rather fierce look and moved away. Gilmour looked after her ruefully. He very much disliked unpleasantness.

"Mrs. Pratt seemed peeved with me-just like you," he said under his breath to Moy.

"I don't wonder. You're a sort of involuntary dog-in-the-manger. And she looks a good hater."

"Well, if my corpse is found some fine day lying in the tool shed, you'll know where to look," and Gilmour broke off to watch with open pleasure Ingram capture Miss Pratt and lead her off to the house under the plea of some books having come from Hatchett's and wanting her help to choose a couple for his sister's children.

Ingram led the way into the library which had been handed over to him for his exclusive use all the more absolutely in that no one else wanted it. He was the only member of the five who had to continue his work at The Tall House itself, and it evidently was work that admitted of no putting off. During the day and early evening he might-and did-dance attendance on Winnie Pratt, but from ten onwards every night he shut himself into the library and let nothing disturb him. Sometimes it was long past midnight when he went up to his rooms. No one at the house got up early. Moy talked as though he let the milkman in on his way to his office in Lincoln's Inn, but a quarter to ten was the earliest that ever saw him running down the steps to his little car. At half-past nine Gilmour would have started for the tube. Half-past ten saw Haliburton off the premises. Moy sometimes thought that it was because Ingram could be with Winnie so many hours of the day, that he left suppers and the evenings to Haliburton. Certainly as far as the two men were concerned, the balance seemed only too even. Whichever one was with her appeared to be the favored man.

In the library she carefully selected the books whose bindings pleased her the best, and then stayed on listening to Ingram's eager words about the popular book he was planning on the arithmetical aspect of the universe. He was a charming talker and, as she listened, as she watched his rapt eyes, something of the fascination which he could exert over her came back again. No one but Ingram ever talked to Winnie as though she had a brain. He appealed to it, and Winnie's intelligence struggled forward to meet the appeal. Perhaps, too, something was due to Gilmour's flat refusal to be led on her string. At any rate, for the time being, Ingram regained something of his old ascendency over her. There had been a week or two when he had entirely eclipsed Haliburton.

That young man now strolled in and joined in the chat. He seemed genuinely interested in Ingram's talk and gave a little sigh when Winnie drifted out again in answer to Mrs. Pratt's urgent reminder that she and her daughter were due at a friend's cocktail party.

When she was gone Haliburton would have lingered, but Ingram made it clear that he wanted to write a few pages before the post left. As a rule he let no one inside his writing-room. By sheer personality he had established a sort of frozen line at the door across which no one stepped uninvited. The door had stood open just now and the room had been free to anyone who cared to step in, but, with the going of Winnie, Ingram changed, as he was wont to change, at his desk. For one thing he seemed to grow years older, for another he tolerated no time-wasters.

Moy was certain that Ingram often locked himself in. He had an idea that the scientist was working against time, or at least working on something where time counted. And apparently that something was to be kept a dead secret until publication. Ciphers, probably, he thought. Once he had heard a sound he knew well enough, the clang of the lid of a deed box and the turning of a key. That was just before Ingram had hurried out to join the others. Evidently Ingram kept his ideas well safeguarded.

———————————————

CHAPTER 3

ALFREDA LONGSTAFF was not happy, and did not look it. But there were possibilities in her pale, dark face. She looked the kind to break records, had she the chance, behind a wheel, or in a 'plane. If so, Fate had not given her much of a hand to play, so far. Alfreda was the only child of the rector of Bispham, and was expected to keep house for her father and mother. She rebelled, naturally, but as no money was forthcoming for any training that would enable her to earn her own living, she had rebelled in vain-though by no means in silence, or in secret. But this last spring she had hoped for a release. Chance had brought down to Bispham a young man whose good looks attracted her immensely. She thought that he cared, too...he had come to the rectory in the first place because he heard that the rector played a good game of chess-as he did-but after that Alfreda had flattered herself that Lawrence Gilmour came because of her. He was the only marriageable man of good position and of her own age who had come into her life so far. Alfreda went all out for his capture. He liked games-well, she had a one figure handicap and a magnificent service, and gradually the links and the lawn tennis courts seemed to oust the chess board. She had shown her hand quite openly, sure of her prize. But he had gone away with only the usual civil partings. Flowers and a box of chocolates had come-once. That was over a month ago —a month of the village's open and concealed amusement or pity.

She was thinking of Gilmour today, when the secretary of the golf club asked her to play a round with a London man whose partner had failed to turn up, as had Alfreda's. Men met on the links meant little, she had found, and this one wore a wedding ring. He had a clever face, she thought, and decided, with one of her inward sighs, that he had not lived all his life in Bispham, or he would never look like that. The rector's wife had just been rebuking her daughter that morning because the sugar basins had not been properly filled. Alfreda was expected to see to this. What a life, or rather what a death! thought Alfreda.

She never played better, and Warner, the man from town, was two down at the ninth hole.

"You ought to give me a stroke a hole," he said with a smile, "but then, I'm —"

"Oh, don't say you're feeling ill!" she interrupted almost fiercely.

"Feeling ill?" he repeated wonderingly.

"Whenever I beat a man, he's 'got a touch of liver,'" came the retort, "or he's 'coming down with the 'flu.' Or he's 'most fearfully knocked with the heat,', or his 'wrist is wonky,' or 'one of his knees is giving him trouble again.' It's the aim of my life to live long enough to beat a really well man."

Warner burst out laughing. "So a grouch against the world was steeling those wrists," he said placatingly. "Let's have a rest and a talk. You've got me sunk already." He held out his cigarette case.

"But haven't you come down for a game?" She hesitated, taking one.

He shook his head. "For quiet."

"Good Heavens!" She sat so as to face him, her lip curling. "Fancy coming for quiet! Fancy wanting the stuff! Well, you've chosen the right tomb."

"So that's the trouble," he murmured in a kindly tone, "ah, yes, you're straining at your bonds. We all do-did. I'm not sure —-"

"Don't tell me that you aren't sure we're not happier when toddling round in pinafores, or lisping our prayers at mother's knee than when sitting on the Woolsack, or hobbling into the House of Lords," she interrupted again, even more hotly than before.

Warner eyed her. He felt a bit sorry for mother. This young lady looked as though she might have an awful temper. There was frustration in her face-and bitterness. She was quite handsome in a hard, clear-cut way. He was not attracted to her. But she had arresting eyes.

"I'm on a newspaper," he said simply, "and naturally the idea of quiet appeals."

"On a newspaper!" She drew a long breath, and almost choked herself with her cigarette. "Heavenly job!"

"Hardly." His eyes twinkled. "Interesting, if you like. But hardly heavenly."

"What are you? An editor?" She regarded him with envy.

He nodded. "Something of that sort." He was a newspaper proprietor.

"How does one get newspaper work?" she asked breathlessly.

"By writing clever articles," he said vaguely. Suddenly he saw an abyss opening at his feet. "That is to say-for real genius, that's the way," he corrected hastily.

"Oh, genius!" she said heavily. "But-had you genius?" She spoke with an air of sincerity that took the rudeness out of the question.

His shake of the head answered.

"I suppose you had a tremendous lot of determination," she went on, looking thoughtfully at his shovel of a chin. "There's nothing like a will of one's own for getting on, they say."

In Warner's case it had been a will of his uncle's that had deposited him in one of the high places of the newspaper in question. But he nodded. She, too, had a forceful jaw, he thought.

"Tenacity of purpose is necessary, yes," he agreed. Then he changed the subject of his own arrival on the mountain top by saying, "But, besides genius, you know, the thing to do is to be on the look-out for a scoop. By that —" Her ironic gaze told him that even in Bispham that word was familiar.

"I'm afraid there's not much chance of a scoop down here," she said. "My father's sermons, and my mother's chats at meetings, hardly lend themselves to that sort of thing. As for crimes-well, it's true a policeman got drunk once, and we still shudder at the tale, but that was years ago, when my father was a boy. The only dramatic happening I remember was when a woman lost her purse on the station platform, and I lent her half a crown-all my worldly possessions. As it was in this part of the world, she returned the money next day."

He laughed too. Then he tilted his cap further over his eyes and said meditatively, "And yet, that's what first gave me my taste for newspaper work, and set me on my feet —a scoop. A body was found floating in the river. Well, it might have been suicide. I worked it up into a three weeks front page thriller." He spoke with pride.

"Was it suicide?" she asked.

"I believe it was." His tone implied that what it really was did not figure in the balance sheet, except as enhancing the credit of the decorations, "but it isn't the facts. It's the way they're handled-treated."

"I see." She sat silent a moment. "But if nothing happens, what does one do to get out of the rut? I should love newspaper work," she finished, in a tone of fervor that was positively alarming-to an editor.

Warner decided to go all out on the scoop theory of advancement. He did not want a young female besieging him with postal packets of manuscript which would probably have no return stamps. He decided to be more wary.

"A scoop is really the only way," he repeated dogmatically. "Something mysterious happens, or something that can be made to look so."

"Here in Bispham?" Her tone was raillery itself, but she waved to him to proceed.

"If you're the first in the field you can offer your stuff to almost any newspaper and, later, you can possibly work into a post on it. Now what about finishing the round?"

She played so badly that he knew her mind was wandering. It is a curious fact, he reflected, that your mind may be on something else, and you can do your work quite decently, but let your mind wander ever so slightly at a game, and the game is ruined. Which looks as if games were harder than work...a little third article might be made out of the idea, treated humorously...

He thanked her when they were back at the clubhouse again, and suggested cocktails. She declined. Her father expected her to be home to pour out tea, but she spoke as though half dreaming. He watched her long stride making for the gate with some misgiving.

"I hope she won't murder the verger so as to qualify for a post with me," he thought. "She looks capable-of a good deal."

At the rectory, Alfreda came to a sudden halt in the shabby old hall. Surely she knew that hat, that voice, and stepping through on to the veranda there rose up before her the man whom she had never expected to see again-Lawrence Gilmour. The sun glinted on his brown hair and seemed to shine in his brown eyes. Suddenly a wave of hatred passed over Alfreda such as she had never dreamed that she could feel. He to stand there smiling, after leaving her to the tender mercies of the village gossips! For the first time she dared to realize how much she had suffered. In pride, in dismay, in hopes lost, in the pity and the scarcely veiled amusement of the countryside, and which of those two last had been the harder to bear she could not tell. It all welled up inside her now. Usually pale, there was a flush like a soft rose in her thin cheeks, her lips were a vivid bow of color unhelped by any cosmetics. Alfreda did not use cosmetics. They were expensive, and what was the use-at Bispham? Her eyes were sparkling as she looked into his.

"Alfreda!" he said, coming forward and taking her hand. "I find that I can't get on without you. Have you missed me, too?"

She could not speak. She dared not. Words were thronging behind her clenched teeth which it would have been madness to utter. She seemed to be standing outside herself, and she was amazed at what she was watching. A shiver passed over her. Alfreda closed her eyes, and as he put his arms about her, felt as though she could have struck the face bending down to kiss her, and struck it again and again. Hard.

"Why did you leave me?" she asked in a low whisper. "Because I wanted to be sure. And to give you time to be sure too," he replied gravely. "I am sure now. Will you marry me, darling?"

"No!" she said with a sort of shout, and then saw her mother come into the room. Mrs. Longstaff jumped. "Alfreda! Mr. Gilmour!"

"Mrs. Longstaff, I've come back to marry the dearest girl in the world."

Mrs. Longstaff could not conceive of Alfreda in quite that light.

"Indeed?" was all she could say for the moment, then came the knowledge of all that this would mean. Only last week the charwoman had ventured to speak pityingly of "Miss Freda" for being so lonely. Her daughter well married...Gilmour was in the Civil Service, and had ample pay...there would be no pension for his wife, but he would, of course, carry a handsome life insurance...

"My dear children," said Mrs. Longstaff and gave a hand to each. Alfreda took it, and committed herself. After all, anything was better than the life she had been leading-the life with no outlook. Yet she felt for Gilmour only burning resentment. He could have spared her all this, these wounds to her pride, and yet he had not. She would never forgive him. But she would use him. He should be her stepping-stone to something different-larger. She told herself that she did not even believe in his supposed affection for her. It had suited him to play with her and leave her. It now suited him to come back to her...what was he saying? He wanted her to come and spend a fortnight in town at a big house in Chelsea which he and some friends had taken furnished for a few weeks. There was a lady staying there, a Mrs. Pratt, who would chaperone her. Perhaps Mrs. Longstaff would ring her up on the 'phone, the number was Flaxman 0000, and perhaps Alfreda would come back with him now, his car could wait. He had really gone into the friendly syndicate because he thought how heavenly it would be to have Alfreda up in town, staying in what would be, for a week, his house. He explained the idea to the two women, and Mrs. Longstaff went to the telephone and was soon in talk with Mrs. Pratt.

Mrs. Pratt was charming. She had taken such a liking to young Lawrence Gilmour, "a really delightful young man," and would be very pleased to chaperone Miss Longstaff during her stay at The Tall House. She hoped she could come soon. Her own daughter was there too. In fact, another engagement was expected...the two women chatted most pleasantly.

In the veranda Gilmour pleaded his cause.

"I thought, I hoped, I believed you felt as I did," he stammered.

"And you shall suffer as I did!" was her unspoken addition. Aloud she said, "I'll come to The Tall House for a fortnight since you ask me, but I don't promise to marry you, you know. At the end of the time I'll give you my answer."

"Oh, no, no!" he begged. "Surely I've left you time enough to know your own heart. Why, I brought you down this!" He opened a small case and something inside it flashed. Alfreda, for the first time, felt one of the bands of ice around her heart break with a little splintering sound, like the girl in the fairy tale...he must really love her to have bought her this...it was a charming half-hoop of diamonds. For a second she wavered. A month ago how she would have rejoiced. But four weeks of suffering leave a scar...she closed the case with a snap, and returned it to him.

"I'll give you my answer at the end of the fortnight," she said quietly, "and meanwhile I'm to be quite free. I promise nothing, except to come to town." Let him, too, feel the pleasure of uncertainty. "Is that agreed?"

It was not in the least what he hoped and wanted. But something in her tone warned him not to press her, unless he wanted to lose her. As for Alfreda, suddenly she knew what she wanted. She would go to town for the two weeks, and by hook or by crook at the end of them land a job on a newspaper. As for marriage-she had only wanted it as a key to open the world outside Bispham. Perhaps she could open it for herself by herself.

She refused to go back in his car with Gilmour, and her mother upheld her in this. After all, tomorrow would do quite nicely and one evening would give the two women and a seamstress time enough to alter that frightful evening frock that Alfreda had ordered from the sales because it was so cheap...So Gilmour went off alone, but with the promise that Alfreda would come to town on the following day in time for lunch. He had no doubt as to her ultimate answer, and decided that it was only her girlish way of paying him out for his delay in proposing, little dreaming how exactly he had hit the nail on the head, and yet how he had given it a slant quite off the true. He wanted to tell all the house-party about her, and burst out with the news to Moy that evening after dinner. They were playing billiards together.

"I can't keep it to myself!" Gilmour was playing wildly. "I've as good as got engaged to the dearest girl in the world, and she's coming here on a fortnight's visit. It's still Haliburton's week, but he's an awfully understanding chap...I'm not worthy to tie Alfreda's shoe-strings, but-well" —he gave a choked little laugh, "she'll be here in time for lunch tomorrow."

Moy was intensely interested. How would this Alfreda and the lovely Winnie get on together? He hoped there would be no unpleasantness. So far, things had been such a success. Even Frederick Ingram's presence now and then had done no harm. He was dropping in more frequently with papers for Charles, and would sometimes stay and have a chat or even a bite with the house-party...yes, he repeated to himself, everything was going on splendidly. As for Haliburton's kindness in letting Gilmour ask this girl up, Moy liked Haliburton, but in this instance he saw no reason to fall over backwards because of his altruism. Ingram too must be charmed with the notion, he thought. Just then the door opened, and Ingram, looking anything but charmed, stepped in.

"I heard voices, and thought my brother-in-law was here," he explained. "Why do one's relations always want to see one?" he asked in what might be assumed discomfort as he closed the door on himself.

"I'm afraid, if rumor is correct in the case of this particular brother-in-law, it's because he hopes to touch Ingram for a fiver," Gilmour suggested with a grin. Moy nodded agreement. "What between Frederick and his brother-in-law Edward Appleton, Ingram must have plenty of use for his spare cash."

"Yet he was once a first-class actor, I've been told," he said.

"He's a first-class gambler now." Gilmour bent over the table again. "The two don't see much of each other. I don't think Appleton has been to the flat more than twice this year. Now, as to Frederick, he'd live on Ingram's doorstep if he could. After all, poor Appleton's no one's enemy but his own. Whereas Frederick is a regular out-and-out wrong un."

"It was you who stopped Ingram from putting his money into that silver-fox ranch, wasn't it?" Moy asked. "Ingram consulted us, and, of course, we advised against it. But I rather thought he would do it, until he mentioned next time that you'd shown him regular proofs that it was all a clever swindle."

Gilmour's teeth flashed out of his tanned face for a second. "I showed Frederick up proper, as the Tommies say, and enjoyed it. Mind you, on paper the scheme was beautifully worked out..."

"It was." Moy remembered it. "We only advised caution on principle and Ingram refused to hear a word against it at first. Frederick had pleaded with him for a chance to earn an honest living, and Ingram thought if he could settle him in the wilds of Scotland it would be cheap at any price."

"I hated to destroy his dreams of a future home without any Frederick around the corner," Gilmour said sadly, "but I had to do it."

"Did Frederick thank you for it?" Moy asked, grinning in his turn.

"At any rate, he's not the kind to bear malice," Gilmour said easily.

Moy raised his eyebrows. "Think so? For a couple of years, I wouldn't go strolling along the edge of a volcano with him if I were you. Nor play at who can stay down longest under water." But he too was only chaffing and after a few more words about Miss Longstaff, Gilmour went in search of Mrs. Pratt.

Meanwhile Ingram had found his brother-in-law. He shook hands, with the look of a man steeling himself against something-himself, or his visitor.

Appleton looked at him very sharply as their fingers touched. Appleton had been a handsome man once, in a rather flamboyant way, and he still carried himself well. But everything about him twitched these days. His face was never still, and when for a moment his features seemed to rest, he would fall to pinching his ear or rubbing his nose with his thin, curved fingers. The hands were those of a fever patient, one would say, so hollow were the backs, so ridged and dry the nails.

He stood looking at the other, as though longing to plunge into some all-absorbing subject of his own, and yet not quite daring to do so. Ingram caught the glance and shook his head with an almost apologetic smile.

"Don't let's talk of it, Edward, there's a good fellow. It's far too dangerous a gift. My sister would never forgive me for one thing. And now, what about cocktails? Will you have them in here or in the garden?"

Appleton did not speak for a moment; he was standing with his face turned to the fireplace, his back to Ingram. After a short pause he said that he would rather stay where they were and, so saying, he began to examine some of the prints on the walls. From them he passed to the furniture. He seemed so appreciative of both that Ingram, apparently anxious to make up for his very definite refusal of something much wanted by the other, took him upstairs, and showed him the floor on which his own bedroom was.

Appleton seemed greatly interested. "I wonder if the chap who owns these would be willing to sell anything," he murmured. Ingram knew that Appleton often acted as intermediary in such transactions. The one-time actor had long ago run through the fortune left him and, except for his wife's steady income, his household would have been in straights long ago. Ingram had helped Appleton many a time, and would do so many a time more, but not to any large amount. He had learned that that was folly.

He did not feel at liberty to show him the inside of any of the rooms except his own and Gilmour's, who, he knew, would not mind all the world tramping through his quarters. As it was, the two rooms and the corridor kept them quite a while, for Appleton seemed to have a passion for trying to date furniture. He suggested once or twice that his brother-in-law should leave him, but Ingram assured him that at the moment he had the time to spare. But at last he grew restive and frankly glanced at the clock on the landing below them. Appleton caught the glance. Ingram apologized. "I had no idea the time had flown so," he said then. "As a matter of fact I am rather rushing some work to its end-and to the printers. So if you really won't stop and have a drink?..."

Appleton said that he too was rather in a hurry, and took himself off, after insisting that Ingram should not come down with him.

Moy happened to be coming down the stairs as Appleton was shown out. In the shadowy recess of the landing sat Tark, his head bent over his note-book. He seemed to have as much love for figures as had Ingram. Whenever Moy ran across him, if he was by himself, Tark would be writing in his rather large note-book what looked like sets of figures. He would do this in the oddest places, perched on the side of a tub, squatting on the stairs or astride the window ledge. Wherever an idea struck him, if idea it was, Tark would bring out his note-book and well-sharpened pencil, and seem to lose the world for some few minutes. He never appeared to be afraid of being overlooked, though, as far as Moy knew, he never talked of what he was entering with such care.

As Appleton took his hat from the butler he turned and faced the landing. At the same second Tark looked down to the front door. The two men looked at one another. It was an odd look, Moy thought, to pass between a couple of strangers, or mere acquaintances. It was so straight and so long and so utterly blank. Then the door closed behind Appleton and Tark, putting his note-book away, ran lightly down the stairs into a little room on the left of the front door. As it happened, Moy was on his way to the room on the right, and there, thinking of Appleton and Tark and that silent look, he glanced through the window netting. Appleton was lighting a cigarette on the pavement. He was just outside the window of the room where Tark was and, as he threw away the match, he looked at it and shook his head with a quick but decided shake, then he walked on. Moy told himself that writing plays, or trying to write them, was bad for one's brain. Appleton was always shaking his head or twitching his forehead or whisking something invisible off his cheek. And as for Tark, his indifference towards his fellow-men was quite real, Moy felt certain, and went to the bone. It was no acquired armor. True, he had seemed at first desirous of talking to Ingram, but that desire was so patently not shared by the mathematician that Tark seemed to have quite given up all attempts to have a word alone with him, and now to include Ingram in his cold lack of interest.

CHAPTER 4

EVEN Tark looked quite alert, for him, next day when he came to lunch. Gilmour and his fiancée-for so the household called her-had not yet come in. Mrs. Pratt was radiant and chatting gaily to everyone. Winnie was silent, but her cheeks glowed with so vivid a rose and the color faded so noticeably as the minutes passed that Moy wondered whether Mrs. Pratt had just slapped them. A slanderous thought. They were due to firm applications of a sponge and hot water. When Winnie did talk it was to Ingram, ignoring Haliburton.

Then the door opened and there fell an absolute hush as Gilmour and a lithe, dark-haired, pale girl came in. Every eye was riveted on Alfreda. Even Ingram who had heard her name mentioned in connection with Gilmour some time ago, had never met her, managed to be looking at the door. He was curious to see the face that could eclipse the beauty of Winnie Pratt's. Miss Longstaff stood a second half-smiling at the interest that met her. It was an enigmatic smile, Moy thought. And a rather enigmatic face. Perhaps that was what had attracted Gilmour, who began to introduce her to Mrs. Pratt in a boyish way that was very taking.

As for Ingram, he could hardly believe his eyes. He had known beforehand that she would fall short of Winnie's standard, but that this elfish, peaky-faced chit could keep a man from realizing the loveliness of Winnie-why Gilmour must be blind! Haliburton thought the same. Moy too was disappointed. Yet he could see something, that, supposing it appealed to you, would be found in Alfreda's face but not in Winnie's. For one thing Miss Longstaff looked clever, he thought, also discontented-or was it merely dissatisfied? She talked well at lunch, with an air of doing so for her own amusement, not merely to brighten the lives of others. Mrs. Pratt alone had welcomed the newcomer warmly. As for her daughter, after one swift glance at the other girl, she ignored her. Gilmour did not seem even to remember Winnie's existence as he devoted himself to the girl now seated beside him. Once when Gilmour got up to lay her gloves aside for her, she followed his figure with a look that intrigued Moy. There was not a spark of affection in that glance, he would have said, only something coldly inquisitive. She caught his own meditative look full, and in return fixed her own dark, unfathomable stare on him. Neither seemed to wish to be the first to look away. Then she finally turned her head aside to Miss Pratt. Looking at the beautiful curve of the slightly averted fair head there came into Alfreda's face a smile that showed unexpectedly strong white teeth, and there was something else, something sardonic, Moy fancied for an instant, before the smile passed. Miss Pratt seemed to sense it too, for she looked around swiftly, came to life, and began to chat and laugh, and finally went off gaily with Alfreda for a trial on the tennis court. There was no question as to who was the better player. Miss Longstaff seemed to have tireless muscles. Moy, watching with the other men, decided that she was playing Miss Pratt as well as the game. She sent her merciless balls at merciless angles and made a pace with which Winnie could not possibly cope. But Winnie fought with unexpected pluck and grit. She did not let any game go without a struggle. At the end, hopeless though it was, she was playing better than at first, that mark of the good fighter. One advantage she had. She looked like a child of sixteen with her tumbled curls against her softly flushed little face. It was wet with exertion, but it only looked like the dew on a flower. Miss Longstaff showed no hint of color in her thin pale cheeks, but she shot a glance at the other when the set was over that looked vexed, Moy thought, and as though something had not turned out quite as she meant it to. Fortunately Winnie took it all with great dignity, Moy thought, until later when he went into the hall to consult an A.B.C. on a side table. From a room beside him a voice which he knew was Winnie's and yet which he hardly recognized as hers.

She was saying: "I won't let her have him! It's no use, mother. She shan't have him!"

"Haven't you got any pride?" came in withering tones from her mother. At least Moy called the tones withering, but Winnie survived. For she said still in that tense, desperate voice: "I won't give him up to her! She doesn't love him. Oh, mother, if it came to a test between us, he would see which of us really loved him! A real test would soon prove — —"

"I don't recognize you," Mrs. Pratt interrupted in a voice that suggested a genuine difficulty to do this. "He doesn't care for you. He loves this charming young girl."

"Young girl! She's old enough to be his m —well, she's over thirty." Winnie had evidently realized that by no stretch of dislike could Alfreda be Gilmour's mother.

"She's about three years older than you in years I fancy, my dear, but a lot in sense," her mother replied. "The trouble with you, Winnie, is that you're spoiled. You've always had what you wanted, so you're tired of what you can get, and are hankering after what you can't have. Let me tell you, my dear girl, there's nothing more fatal to happiness in man or woman." Mrs. Pratt spoke with real feeling. "The fox was wise who said the grapes he couldn't have were sour. A fool would have set his heart on them just because he couldn't have them. That's what you're doing."

"I'm not! Lawrence Gilmour would love me if I only could show him —"

"You've shown him sufficiently, and everyone else too. Come, Winnie, pull yourself together. Have some pride. Haliburton wants to marry you. But if you keep this sort of thing up he won't feel like that much longer. You ought to show Lawrence Gilmour that though he may not care for you, others do." Mrs. Pratt's tactics were too transparent to succeed, Moy feared. He himself at the moment was no more conscious of the impropriety of listening than if he had been at a theater.

"But I like Charles Ingram better." Miss Pratt sounded as though she was smiling again. "And he too wants to marry me."

Moy had taken a step sideways and could now see into the room. Mrs. Pratt's face startled him. She stood looking down on the bent head of Winnie as the girl fiddled with something on the mantel as though she could burst out into a perfect flame of violence-vituperation-despair-pleading&mdash ;but by an effort that was patently all but beyond her, she bit her lip in silence and led the way out through a farther door.

Two mornings later, Alfreda told Gilmour that she would not be able to go with him to a dog show as they had planned, or rather as he had planned for her.

"I've got so much fitting-out to do," she said with one of her unfriendly smiles, "and shan't be visible until one o'clock today." She seemed to have an early morning appointment, for it was only half-past eight when she left the house. She took some care to see that she was not followed, rather an odd idea one would have said, but she saw no one, and tests such as jumping on to a bus at the last moment and off when all but started, which reduced two conductors to close on apoplexy, assured her that no one had any interest in her movements. That ascertained, she made for a tube which landed her at Hammersmith Broadway. Here she turned into a street that was once lived in by city men who wanted the country. At a house with a black door and orange-painted pillars, she ran up the steps, inserted a latch-key with which she did not seem at all familiar, and finally let herself into a hall. A woman in a rather elaborate frock for the morning came forward with a mixture of graciousness and condescension.

"Miss Gray, isn't it? Your room's all ready for you. But wouldn't you like to write in the lounge? As I told you yesterday afternoon when you took the room, no one will disturb you there, only Mrs. Findlay ever uses it at this hour, and you'll find it warm and cosy. Better than being in the basement, don't you think?"

"Thanks awfully, I'll try it," Alfreda said brightly. And in a corner of a glassed-in lounge she ensconced herself, writing-pad on knee. But she did not write much. Her dark eyes flashed to and fro about the main corridor which showed through the side of the lounge. Presently the manageress entered with a big stout woman of middle age, who wore a sort of mantilla of black lace on her head fastened to her white hair in front with a large silver star and floating below her waist at the back. Two corkscrew ringlets dangled over each ear.

"This is Miss Gray." The manageress steered the older woman to the newcomer's corner. "She's interested in disarmament too, Mrs. Findlay, so I thought you and she would be congenial spirits." And the manageress left them.

"Oh, do you care too?" Alfreda asked eagerly, scanning the woman in front of her closely. "I didn't know anyone cared-really. Anyone but myself and the man I'm engaged to, Lawrence Gilmour."

"Lots of people care," Mrs. Findlay answered a trifle coldly. She had rather a forbidding eye and jaw. The woman was one of those people who are often pitied for being solitary, but who are that by choice. True, she had outlived all her family, and was practically alone in the world, but had she had a host of relations the result would have been the same. Now, after a few moments' silence, she made as if to go out again, but Alfreda sprang up.

"Don't go!" she said appealingly. "I'm so frightfully pleased to have met someone who can tell me about what we women can do. The idea of all these war preparations is awful. Surely, if we band together, we can be of some use."

Mrs. Findlay was conquered for the moment. This was her hobby, or rather it was more than that. It was the window through which her soul drew in a little air and light and so managed to exist in the desert that she had made of the rest of her life. At first reluctantly, then more freely, she let Alfreda draw her out on the subject. Alfreda, for her part listened as though to a Sibyl.

"Oh, I would like to join!" she breathed, when Mrs. Findlay mentioned the Women's Peace Movement, of which she was an honorary secretary. "So would Lawrence-Mr. Gilmour. I think you must have seen him at some of the meetings —" and she described Gilmour. Mrs. Findlay looked a trifle impatient. She said that she had not seen any young man at any of their meetings. Something quivered across Alfreda's face and was gone, but whether she wanted to hear an affirmative, or the negative that had been forthcoming, it was difficult to say.

At ten she put her papers together. "I write, you know," she murmured. "Just little things of no account. But I might be able to get in some article which would help."

This time it was Mrs. Findlay who looked eager and, on hearing that Alfreda expected to be in the lounge on the following morning at the same hour, said that she would like to continue their talk. Alfreda put her blank paper away in the little basement room that she had taken late yesterday afternoon and hurried to the door. But the manageress stopped her.

"I saw you having quite a nice chat," she said pleasantly, "and to no one else does Mrs. Findlay ever open her mouth. I told her it would be a change for her to meet someone who shared her interests. Generally she just sits there while her room is being aired, and we daren't talk to her."

Alfreda nodded and hurried off, her face a mixture of emotions; she jumped on a bus that would take her close to The Tall House, satisfaction and dissatisfaction were to be read in her quick, dark eyes. But at nine on the following day she was in the lounge again, and again she and Mrs. Findlay talked of peace, and of how to stop the preparations for war that were darkening all the world.

The next morning after that Mrs. Findlay referred to some books she had in her room, and Alfreda seemed so keen on seeing them that, after a second's hesitation, she asked the younger woman in to a large dreary bed-sitting-room as it is called. The books in question were stacked on a table, and Alfreda promptly took off the top one.

"May I take this home and read it?" she begged. "I'll bring it back tomorrow morning."

"Tomorrow a friend is coming to see me about this time," Mrs. Findlay quid in her stiff way. "As a matter of fact he too has just read that book."

"Can't I run in and hand it to you?" Alfreda asked, her face all innocence.

"I'm afraid my friend is elderly, and has so few minutes to spare, and counts too much on finding me alone," Mrs. Findlay said coldly, and she remained very cool for the rest of the time that Alfreda as usual spent with her, and when the girl left with the book, rather earlier than usual, Mrs. Findlay stopped for a word with the manageress in the hall.

"That Miss Gray who's just come seems rather a pushing young person," was her remark. "I'm afraid she'd be quite a nuisance if I weren't leaving next week. Please don't let her know I'm going; she's quite capable of asking herself down to my cottage in the country."

"I wouldn't breathe a word about your going," the manageress assured her. Mrs. Findlay had the largest room in the house, had taken it at a time when rents were at their highest, and, therefore, paid nearly double what it would now bring. Besides, she was leaving, she had just had an unexpected windfall, and the manageress hoped that some parting present might brighten her own none too gay lot.

"How did she come to speak to you about me in the first place?" Mrs. Findlay asked.

"She came in just after you the other afternoon. She was looking for a room, and after she had taken hers, we stood a moment chatting, and she said she thought she had seen you at Spiritualistic stances near here. I told her I didn't think that at all likely."

"Preposterous!" chimed in Mrs. Findlay.

"She said something about the star you wear, and I told her that was the Star of Peace, and that you were tremendously keen on there being no more wars, and disarmament and so on...She hardly let me finish, she was so eager to tell me that she and a gentleman friend, a Mr. Gil-something, I think that was the name, were both so keen on that too. She said she'd like ever so much to have a chance of talking to you. That you looked so clever she'd love to hear your views."

Mrs. Findlay's face relaxed.

"Well, of course, it was quite natural, under the circumstances I mean, for you to have introduced her that first morning...the truth is," Mrs. Findlay lowered her voice, "I wondered if she had got on the track of that little money I came into so unexpectedly the other day...it's to be paid me shortly and I she stopped herself.

"Oh, no! No one knows about that! You said it was strictly confidential!" the manageress assured her. "I do hope this Miss Gray hasn't been troublesome. She seemed quite the lady."

"Oh, I don't doubt it's all right, just youthful fervor" —Mrs. Findlay smiled a little at her — "but somehow, it seemed to me so sudden...and so very pronounced..." She half-stopped herself. "I felt doubtful of her sincerity," she finished, "but, as you say, it's probably just her way. But don't let her take to coming to my room. Should she ever speak to you about it, while I'm still here, please discourage her. I did ask her there just now in a moment of weakness, but she's such a stayer...and I'm so busy getting my things together...she spoke of coming in tomorrow morning, for instance, but I told her I should be engaged. Poor old Mr. Nevern would be quite swamped by her. It's his day to drop in for an hour..." and with a nod Mrs. Findlay swept on to her room and castle.

The manageress passed the conversation on to the head housemaid, her trusted assistant.

"Funny!" that young woman murmured. "I mean Miss Gray being so keen on Mrs. Findlay. She's not everybody's fancy, is she? I wonder if she has heard about that money and is making up to Mrs. Findlay because of it."

"She can't possibly know. And don't forget, you don't know anything about it, either!" the manageress warned her.

"Mrs. Findlay told me about it herself, just now. Said she had come in quite unexpectedly for some money and might easily come in for more. Said she was going round the world. I said I didn't wonder. I'd go round the world twice over if only someone would leave me a five-pound note for doing it. Wouldn't you?" and the talk drifted to what one would do if one came into wealth.

As the days passed, Winnie and Alfreda avoided each other, but when they met they were quite civil, especially Alfreda, who went out of her way to be nice to the other. She openly admired her beauty, and spoke of feeling as though Winnie were a lovely flower to be shielded from rough winds, something fragile that no tempest should touch. This much was gained by Alfreda's presence, that Miss Pratt spoke very little to Gilmour. She really retired into something resembling polite sulks, talking to Ingram, but hardly deigning to see Haliburton, and spending most of her time at other houses. As for Miss Longstaff, Moy thought her in her own way as aloof as Tark, but with something watchful added. She would fix that odd unreadable stare of hers now on one, now on another of the house party as though trying to understand something which puzzled her.

Frederick Ingram came more frequently to the house now. He avoided Gilmour as much as possible, but when the two met they seemed to be able to meet on a footing of indifferent civility. Miss Longstaff appeared rather to like Frederick, and as that young man was fond of an audience, he would often be found by her side if Miss Pratt were out of reach. He did not stay at The Tall House, but came and went, taking and bringing papers to his half-brother.

It was just a little over a week after Alfreda's arrival when all happened to be in the lounge around six. The cocktails had been handed about, and the talk turned on ghosts. No one afterwards seemed able to remember exactly how it started. Someone-Moy said he thought it was Tark, Tark said it was Haliburton, Haliburton maintained that it was Frederick, Frederick insisted that it was Gilmour, and Gilmour said that he felt sure it was Ingram-mentioned that a man whom he had met lately had spoken to him of what a splendid display Appleton used to give as a ghost in a Grand Guignol play. But all agreed that it was Frederick who said that The Tall House had a ghost, that one of its former owners had been found hanged. It was suspected though never proved that his valet did the hanging. The old man's ghost was said to walk.

Ingram said that a ghost was always part of the furniture of an old house, and asked Moy whether on the expiration of a tenancy it had to be handed back in the same condition as when taken over.

"Fair wear and tear excepted," Moy said at once, amid laughter.

"A safe provision," Haliburton pointed out, "as nothing could damage ghostly bones or clothes, not even bullets."

"The ghost had better not bank on that," Gilmour said with a most unaccustomed edge to his voice. "Personally, if I meet one, I shall fire at sight."

Something in his tone made the group fall silent.

"How will you let the ghost know of its danger beforehand?" Winnie asked with one of her tinkling laughs. "By a notice to the Psychical Society?"

"I think I have given notice by what I am saying." Gilmour's tone was still hard. "There aren't such things as real ghosts, there are only practical jokers. And, as I say, I warn any joker here that that particular piece of foolishness isn't a safe one to play on me."

"You seem rather warm about it," Ingram said dryly.

"Sorry!" Gilmour's tanned face looked apologetic. "I'm afraid I did rather get on my hind legs, but I was badly frightened by a so-called ghost as a kid, and the mere mention of them makes me see red ever since."

He looked round for Miss Longstaff. But that young lady had moved behind him to an open window. She was standing very rigid, her head and chin stuck out at an angle that was not at all pretty, but which suggested breathless excitement. One hand was fingering a string of beads she wore; it had an effect of being pressed against her heart. Moy remembered afterwards that not till the talk changed did she relax that absorbed pose of hers. Gilmour, still without seeing her, rose and left the lounge. Frederick Ingram followed him for a moment.

"He means it right enough," he said, coming back. "He's got it into his head that one of us is going to play that same prank on him again, and he wants everyone to know that he really intends 'to shoot at sight. I think he suspects me."

"Is he a good shot?" Tark asked in his creaky, expressionless voice. Everyone laughed.

"Very," Ingram spoke up now. "Very," he repeated, looking sharply at his brother. "But I don't think I'm giving anyone much of a surprise when I add that his revolver is loaded with blank."

"Blank or loaded, I have no intention of amusing Gilmour," Frederick said promptly. "But it's as well for the rest of you to know that you needn't drop on the floor when you hear a bang."

Ingram turned away and picked up a book near him. When he was not writing he was sure to be reading, Winnie had once told him. She crossed to his side now. "I can't imagine you without books." She smiled at him one of her softest, most radiant smiles.

"Let's take a turn in the fresh air," he said under his breath. "Somehow the air in here's a bit hot...electric...but as to being without books, there are other things I couldn't live without.

When this month is up, Winnie" —he had never called her by her first name before —"how are you going to choose?"

"My mother wants me to marry Basil Haliburton," she said evasively.

"Are you going to?" he asked, standing still and taking hold of a spray of Bokhara vine.

"You've spoiled matters," she said with one of her most flirtatious upward glances. "But for you, I shouldn't have hesitated. Until you came, I felt so sure I cared for him."

"What about Lawrence Gilmour?" The question came before he could check it. She cocked a supercilious chin at him.

"Lawrence Gilmour? Why, he's engaged. It isn't because of Mr. Gilmour that I'm not sure what I shall say to Basil Haliburton."

Even the adoring Ingram looked a bit doubtful, and the chin swept up still more.

"You alone complicate matters," she said softly and yet rather wearily. As she spoke they turned a corner and almost stepped on Haliburton himself. It was an awkward meeting. Even Winnie was nonplussed for a second, then she made some remark about the flowers, and the evening light, and the young man took it up pleasantly, but he avoided looking, or speaking, directly to Ingram.

CHAPTER 5

THAT night Moy was awakened by the last sound that the young solicitor ever expected to hear in a house-the sound of a shot. With it came a loud cry and then a thud.

Still rigid with bewilderment, he heard a sort of sobbing falsetto:

"Where's the light? God, where's the switch?" The voice seemed that of a stranger and yet there was something about it which reminded him of Gilmour.

Moy came to life and sprang out of bed. He rushed into the passage. Bright moonlight flooded it. Just in front of him was the big main passage leading down to Gilmour's room, the door of which faced him across the landing at the farther end. Halfway down the passage was Ingram's room and it was in front of that room that something bulky and white was lying.

Coming towards Moy and towards the heap on the ground, staggering as though he were drunk, and clawing at the wall with his left hand, was a man in pajamas. The right hand was outstretched and held something small that glittered in the cold, white light; glittered all the more because it wavered and swung to and fro, as though the arm were a broken signpost in a gale of wind. In the moonlight the man's face showed so blanched, so distorted with its protruding eyeballs and open mouth that Moy thought it was a stranger's for a moment. Then he saw it was Gilmour. Just by the white heap on the floor both almost collided with each other. Their hands met and closed on a switch. At the same instant other voices, men's voices, called out to know what was wrong, and lights blazed out in the cross passages.

Moy and Gilmour were both on their knees beside that motionless heap on the ground. It was heavy, and seemed to be wrapped in sheeting, but at last Moy got hold of a loose end of the stuff and flung it back-to show the dead face of Ingram, with a small red hole in the exact center of the forehead. He was still warm, still flexible. Moy stared down at him in horror. Yet there was nothing horrifying in the face itself. On the contrary it was beautiful in its own marble way, with a certain grand air of peace, profound and real.

"A doctor! A doctor!" Gilmour almost sobbed. "It's some awful mistake-it can't be! It was loaded with blank!"

Moy heard a sort of shocked cluck over his shoulder. It was Haliburton who was now bending down beside him.

"He can't be dead! The cartridges were blanks, I tell you. Where's a doctor? One hears of people being resuscitated after hours —" Gilmour was all but inarticulate, and was shaking violently. The revolver dropped from his grip as he spoke, and he pushed it to one side while he tried to raise Ingram's head and turn it to the light.

"A doctor will be fetched at once," Moy spoke in a whisper. This was a most dreadful affair. "But how did it happen? Where was Ingram? I mean, when you fired?"

The solicitor in Moy was seeking data, but Haliburton touched him on the shoulder.

"We must get a doctor here at once!"

They were in front of Ingram's own room. It had a telephone in it. Gilmour caught it up with shaking fingers. Then he turned his face to the others. He looked like a man living in a nightmare.

"I —I can't remember the name of any doctor. Quick! Who knows one? And what his number is?"

Moy reached for the directory. The shock had driven his own doctor's number out of his mind too, but Haliburton, with a sympathetic glance at Gilmour, took the receiver from him and in a steady firm tone gave the Mayfair number of his father's physician.

Moy laid down the directory. As he did so, he saw Tark just inside the door which he was holding open. But a Tark with all his usual air of sardonic detachment shed. This was Tark with the lid off, Moy decided, and the inside of the man seemed to be a seething cauldron. Neither then nor afterwards could Moy name the emotions that he saw frothing up together. In almost the same instant Tark stepped back, shutting the door noiselessly behind him, but not before Moy saw, on the stairs behind, hanging as it were like a moon in the darkness, a girl's white face and recognized it as Alfreda Longstaff.

"Look here," Moy said again while Haliburton was trying to rouse the household of the great man in Harley Street, "how did it happen, Gilmour?"

"I fired at a ghost, a blank cartridge, and then I heard it cry out, and —" Gilmour stopped and sank into a chair, covering his face with his hands.

"Where's the revolver?" Moy urged. It was partly kindness. He thought that anything was better than letting Gilmour live over in memory what had just happened. Gilmour did not lift his head. Moy, on the instant that he spoke, remembered the little glittering thing dropping beside Ingram's body, and, opening the door, now stepped into the passage again. He almost trod on Miss Longstaff, who, the revolver in her hands, was turning away from the body on the carpet. On her face was the last look that Moy expected to see, a look as unexpected as the shot had been, for it had in it a sort of vindictive satisfaction; a sort of excited gloating, he called it to himself afterwards.

"Hand me that revolver, please," he said sharply. "Is it yours?" she asked.

"I represent the absent owner of the house. And I represent Ingram's relatives. Hand me that weapon, please."

She let him have it, though reluctantly.

He broke it open. All five remaining cartridges seemed to be blank.

"How did it happen? Who shot him?" she asked, and again there was that suggestion of eagerness about her that was so ghoulish at such a moment.

"Do go back to your room," Moy urged. "This is no place for a girl. As you can see, there's been an awful accident, and Ingram's been shot." Suddenly he stopped. He noticed now that Ingram's body now lay covered by a sheet. He eyed Miss Longstaff inquiringly.

"He looked so dreadful staring up," she said, and for the first time there was a hint of confusion in her voice.

Ingram had not looked dreadful. This covered mound was much more horrible.

"No one should touch him," Moy said with the same sternness in his voice as when he had asked her for the revolver.

"Why? Was it murder?" She drew a deep breath and looked at him with that odd, unreadable stare of hers. "Who shot him?" she persisted.

"I did," came a dull voice from behind them. "I did, Freda." Gilmour had come out into the corridor again.

"Oh, please don't call me Freda, Mr. Gilmour," came the instant reply. "There's no question of any future engagement between us-after this. Of course, you realize that too."

Gilmour looked as though she had struck him. His white face went even whiter.

"You don't mean it! It's not possible! You can't —" he began in a strangled voice, taking an imploring step towards her. Her answer was to turn her back on him and walk away. As she did so there came the swift rush of feet down the stairs. Miss Pratt, looking a dream in a floating gown the color of sweet peas, ran towards Gilmour, her two hands outstretched.

"Mr. Tark tells me-oh Lawrence, I'm so sorry! So sorry! For you!" She thrust her little white hands into Gilmour's fists, who dropped the white fingers after the most perfunctory touch and took a step after the other slender figure, the one fully dressed, with the short straight dark hair brushed smoothly back like a boy's from the hard but vivid face.

"Alfreda! Miss Longstaff!" he began again. She turned, and standing still, bent on him again that inscrutable stare of hers, and something in it was so inimical that he stepped back and stood staring at her. As she turned a corner, he at last looked at Winnie.

"You shouldn't be here. Your mother wouldn't like it." He spoke as though his thoughts were quite elsewhere.

Alfreda had gone straight to Mrs. Pratt's rooms. She knocked at the bedroom door and called through the panels. "It's me, Mrs. Pratt, Alfreda Longstaff. Something has happened.

Your daughter needs you." There came a muffled sort of squeak from within, but the door was not opened for quite a long minute.

Then Mrs. Pratt stepped out. "What's that about Winnie? Where is she? What on earth has happened?" Her face looked oddly blotched as though some strapping or top dressing had been roughly pulled off.

"Mr. Gilmour has killed Mr. Ingram, and your daughter is telling him how sorry she is for him." The tone was dry.

There was nothing muffled about Mrs. Pratt's squeak this time. "Winnie, where are you? Wait for me! Wait!" And as though a performance were about to begin which she would not miss for worlds, she scurried in the direction of Alfreda's pointing hand. In front of Ingram's bedroom she stopped in horror. For once she had nothing to say for a full minute. Then she turned to Winnie.

"Come, dearest, we're only in the way here. We must get Yates up, and see to our packing. The kindest thing we can do for everyone is to get away as soon as possible. Come, Winnie!"

"I won't leave now-like this." Winnie spoke indignantly.

Mrs. Pratt turned to Moy. Her eyes asked her questions.

"Ingram played the part of a ghost and Gilmour fired at him a blank cartridge, as he thought-which must have been loaded. He's dead," he murmured, his eyes on the white mound to whom the "he" referred.

Mrs. Pratt turned to Gilmour with what looked like genuine emotion.

"Oh, you poor boy! You poor, poor boy! And, and-how awful!" She did not try to put the rest of her feelings into words.

Winnie let her mother lead her away. They found Alfreda pacing their little sitting-room.

"I suppose you're leaving, too?" she asked, as Winnie hurried on to her own room with her lips pressed together.

Mrs. Pratt closed the door. "I'm so sorry for you, my dear girl," she began gently, "and so shocked-so indescribably shocked for that poor boy!"

"We're not going to be engaged, if you refer to Lawrence Gilmour," Alfreda said composedly.

"What?" Mrs. Pratt fairly jumped. "But surely! But this is dreadfully sudden!" she finished lamely.

"His shooting of Mr. Ingram was dreadfully sudden," was the reply.

"But surely, for a time, you'll let things stand over!" Mrs. Pratt was almost pleading. "It will look so dreadfully heartless, to drop him the very instant it happened."

"I have no intention, now or ever, of getting engaged to Mr. Gilmour. I think you ought to know."

The door opened. Winnie came in. She could not stay in any one place for long.

"You're acting horribly!" she began.

"I'm not acting at all." There was meaning in the look the elder girl gave the younger. Winnie seemed to pay no attention to it.

"He needs you!" she protested instead.

Mrs. Pratt nodded her head emphatically. Alfreda shot the mother a glance openly mocking. But she said nothing.

"I'd go through anything with the man I loved!" came passionately from Winnie.

"Supposing he loved you," the other girl finished dryly. "Perhaps it's just as well for you that Mr. Gilmour doesn't seem to fill that condition."

Winnie's cheeks flamed.

"A girl would have to have a perfect passion for notoriety to marry him after this," Alfreda went on.

The door slammed behind Winnie. Mrs. Pratt looked half-gratefully, half-indignantly, at her visitor, who gave her one of her odd stares and went out to run lightly down into Ingram's study. She closed the door noiselessly behind her. For a second she stood sniffing the air. It smelled of...yes, of that odd tobacco Mr. Tark liked...but she had not come here to smell tobacco.

She slipped over to the bureau, found its top unlocked, stood obviously listening for any sound from outside and, hearing none, opened it and with swift, deft fingers looked through it. Every scrap of paper was glanced at. It was fairly empty. She turned over the drawers. Only blank paper was in them with the exception of the bottom drawer, which was locked. She was pulling at it when she heard steps coming down the back stairs close to the library door. Instantly she slipped out of the door by which she had entered, into the lounge and on up the stairs, along a passage, and up another flight of stairs. Here she let herself into an empty bedroom, and, closing its door to with the utmost caution, sat down at a little bookcase table on which stood a telephone extension. Very quietly she gave a number. It was that of the proprietor of the *Morning Wire*.

"Hello!" came a man's voice in answer to her ring. It was not the voice that she had heard on the golf links. "What is it?"

"I want to speak to Mr. Warner."

"Who are you? What do you want to speak to him about? I'm one of Mr. Warner's secretaries." The voice was not encouraging.

"Will you tell Mr. Warner that the Miss Longstaff who played a game of golf with him on the links at Bispham is staying in a house at Chelsea with a Mr. Ingram who has just been killed by his friend. The friend claims that it was an accident."

"Ingram...what is his first name, do you know?"

"Charles."

She heard a sound. The secretary had sprung out of bed. A couple of minutes more and Miss Longstaff heard Warner's voice saying sharply:

"What's this about Ingram's death? And who is speaking?"

Miss Longstaff reminded him of the game they had played together. "Now, Mr. Warner, I've really got hold of some interesting news. No other paper has it-yet. You told me that a scoop would get me a position —"

"What is this about Ingram's death? Where did he die? How was he killed?" Warner's tone was that of a man who would hang up unless answered immediately.

"He's been shot by the friend who shares his flat at Harrow, a man named Lawrence Gilmour. He claims it was an accident. He says he fired what he thought was a blank shot at someone pretending to be a ghost, and found that it was Mr. Ingram whom he had killed. The shot was not blank. That's Mr. Gilmour's story."

She heard another voice speaking, the voice of the man to whom her first telephone message had gone. "Yes, Gilmour. Of the Civil Service...That much is all right, sir. But as for the rest —"

"One moment," Warner's voice came again. "Now give me all the facts again, please. But only the ones you are sure of. First of all, where are you? And when exactly did this happen?"

Swiftly, she had that journalistic quality, and briefly, another great gift, and, all things considered, very objectively, she told of what had just happened.

"Now, Mr. Warner," she wound up, "suppose this could be shown to be not an accident...wouldn't it be the scoop which you said would give me a post on your paper?"

Warner had not said quite that. "She's probably just trying it on," was his murmured comment to Ryland, his secretary, "I mean, about its not being an accident...but if there's anything in it...she struck me as being a very resourceful young woman...and unscrupulous as they're made." Warner added this last thought as though it were an added point in her favor.

"Well?" she asked sharply, "have I the promise of a post on the paper if I can prove what I claim? That Mr. Gilmour's story can't be true?"

"If you can prove that, Miss Longstaff, we'll give you a trial."

"I want the offer in writing," came her answer.

Warner, with a faint smile, told Ryland to write a note which would do until the usual contract could be sent. The draft was read her and she graciously deigned to approve.

"It's not often a paper has such a chance offered it," she said.

"Nor an outsider either, Miss Longstaff," Warner barked back.

"Oh, of course. These things have always to be mutual," she murmured as cynically as an old company promoter. "My name mustn't come out, of course. That's to be absolutely guaranteed."

"I'll send one of my men down at once. Name of Courtfield. Give him all the information you can. He'll know how to put it into shape. Be on the look-out for him and let him in yourself, if possible. He's a small man-dark-turned-up nose-cleft in his chin. He'll be wearing a big yellow buttonhole and will loiter about on the pavement opposite The Tall House. You'll have to prove all your assertions."

"I don't know about all," came Miss Longstaff's voice, "but I shall be able to prove the one that matters most."

"You'll have to prove, or be prepared to prove, any we print," Warner said authoritatively. He thought this young woman needed firmness.

"Personally, I shouldn't be surprised if she killed him herself in order to get a chance with us." Warner's hand was over the transmitter. "But Courtfield will soon find out..." He uncovered the instrument. "Who else is staying in the house, Miss Longstaff?"

She told him. He passed it on, again with the transmitter covered.

"Miss Winifred Pratt?" Ryland spelled it with one "t" in his interest, "the Beauty? We have her picture taken the night she was presented..."

"Ah," Warner murmured, "possibly she's the explanation. Well, if so, Courtfield will find out. If the beautiful Miss Pratt is roped in to the affair, so much the more stir. I don't need to tell Courtfield to keep his eye open for libel actions. Though I don't think Miss Longstaff will cross the line. Too clever by half."

CHAPTER 6

MEANWHILE a hitch had occurred. The doctor to whom Haliburton had telephoned was just getting into his car, when an urgent summons reached him from a patient who was hovering between life and death. He dashed off to her bedside, and left his secretary to suggest over the 'phone to Haliburton that, since death had already occurred, and from an accident, Haliburton had perhaps better send for the police. This would have been suggested in the first place, had it not been that important young man himself who had spoken over the wire.

Haliburton jerked his lower lip sideways and set his teeth together as he did when anything happened which he greatly disliked. He glanced at Moy and repeated what had just been said.

"Of course!" Moy said impatiently, "obviously we need the police, and at once. It's like a ship with plague on board. You must get the officials in before the passengers can get off. We're in quarantine until the regulations are complied with."

"The police..." Haliburton hesitated. "It's most unpleasant for-the women. There's no mystery here."

"No, but there's been a death by misadventure. Of course we must have the police."

Haliburton looked up the name of the nearest police station. Moy went out into the corridor. He felt as though unless he moved so as to keep pace with his surging thoughts, they would leave him behind-an idiot-and rush on whirling and spinning of their own volition. As a matter of fact, he was not thinking at all. He was feeling, and feeling to the exclusion of everything else. Horror. Regret for Ingram, that fine mathematician and charming personality; sympathy with Gilmour; amazement at Alfreda Longstaff...There she was, by the way, scanning the carpet as though intent on mending it...He caught up with her.

"I wonder if you realize," he began, "how greatly your breaking off of your engagement will bias the police against Gilmour." He spoke temperately, but he felt warm. She looked at him with a smile that increased his dislike of the girl. Oh, she was deep...unfathomable. Quite unlike lovely warm-hearted Winnie Pratt.

"I wonder," she murmured, and stood a moment quite still with downcast lids.

"Perhaps I've been too hasty," she said now with a singularly unconvincing accent of regret. "I really know nothing of what's happened, except what Mr. Gilmour has said, and, of course, he is so upset. Did he really fire at Mr. Ingram?" she asked in a tone of intense interest which he found hard to answer civilly.

"As you heard. He did. With a cartridge which he thought was blank and which by some horrible mistake was loaded. And which killed Ingram."

Again she looked him straight in the face with that unreadable stare of hers.

"What a good shot he must be!" was her quite unexpected comment.

Moy almost jumped. "Look here, if you say a thing like that, you render yourself open to a libel action." He spoke severely.

"But why? If he thought he was firing blank?" She met his scrutiny with bland nonchalance. "I think he and Mr. Ingram practised revolver shooting a good deal," she went on.

"I don't know," he muttered.

"The first time I met Mr. Gilmour he said something about it." She was standing in the window now playing with the tassel of the curtain.

"Where did you first meet him?" he asked and, on that, he had the satisfaction of seeing a look cross her face that said quite plainly that she wished the words unsaid. Then her gaze returned to the street. She saw a small man walking briskly along the opposite pavement. In his coat was an enormous yellow buttonhole.

"Oh, down in the country," she replied, as she began to walk towards the stairs and descend them with an air of doing so almost mechanically. The front door was out of sight of where Moy was standing. With cautious care she opened the door. It was not bolted, she saw. Instantly the man with the yellow buttonhole came in. He dropped the decoration into his pocket as he did so.

"Thank heaven it was early. The only yellow flowers I could find were some paper daffodils from my diggings and two men already have asked me if I was doing it for a bet. Now, Miss Longstaff, will you give me your news, please. My name is Courtfield. Here's my card."

He was studying her as he spoke with a pair of eyes that took her in from head to heel. Everything for his paper would depend on this young woman's trustworthiness. Could she be relied on? That was the paramount question. But behind it was another that interested the crime expert almost as much. Why had she volunteered to give the information in the first place? Was it vengeance for the dead, or against the living? He had met Ingram, and he had met Gilmour. He knew of the friendship between the two men. Why did this girl believe, or pretend to believe, that the latter had killed the other? Civil Servants are not, as a rule, a bloodthirsty lot. Gilmour had seemed quite the average pleasant-tempered chap one meets at every turn. Ingram had not shown any irritating peculiarities...then why had this young woman 'phoned as she had done? Meeting that stare of her black eyes he felt a personality here, a will of steel...Was it merely because of the offer of a permanent post on the paper that she had come forward or was there some other sharper spur? The presence in the house of the lovely Miss Pratt, did that stand for anything?

But Miss Longstaff was now speaking to him. She led him into a small room rarely used by any of the present household. It was chiefly given over to some defunct owner's butterfly collection, and there she said a few swift sentences to which Courtfield listened as though they were directions concerning the finding of hidden treasure. Then he slipped out again. He did not want to meet the police. No paper would care deliberately to flout them, and he would be at once asked how he got into the house, and what he intended to print. His name, for once, would not appear below his article. It was to be strictly anonymous and to remain so.

Upstairs Moy paced the corridor back and forth, that strange look on Alfreda's mobile face haunted him. And the look that she had fastened on Gilmour's bowed head as she came into the room where Haliburton stood telephoning. A suggestion of a future triumph, of a "you wait!" vindictiveness about it...What was she going to do? For Moy felt sure that she meant to take some active hand in matters...or could it be that she had already taken it, and was now waiting for the harvest to appear? He believed that she was glad of the awful position in which Gilmour stood...But surely no one could even pretend that this was anything but a genuine accident? Or a terrible blunder. Though Gilmour was an unusually careful and neat-fingered young man. Was it possible that this was a crime on Gilmour's part? But Moy, putting aside all preconceived idea as to Gilmour's character, could not see the likelihood of that. The two lived together. If Gilmour, for some as yet absolutely hidden reason, wished to murder Ingram, he could have done so in a dozen better ways without ruining his own life. For no matter how sympathetic the jury or the coroner might be-supposing him, or them, to be in a kindly mood-the fact remained that Gilmour's whole life was ruined. He could never forget, and the world would never forget, that he had killed Ingram. There was only one chance for Gilmour that Moy could see, and that was that, supposing a crime to be here and not an accident, Gilmour could discover its author. But even if he succeeded in doing this, or even if the police succeeded, could it be proved? Say that someone who hated Gilmour, had secretly substituted a loaded cartridge for the first blank one, the deed was done. Could the past give up its secrets in anything so difficult to prove, so swiftly accomplished? Moy did not see how Gilmour could ever be set free from suspicion, or rather from the pillory of being a marked man all his life unless the crime could be brought home to the real criminal-if a crime, and a criminal, existed behind this death of Ingram. Assuming it not to be due to accident, the murderer, Moy reasoned, must be someone with a motive for killing Ingram, and also someone who knew where the revolver and the cartridges of Gilmour were kept. Suddenly his face blanched a little. He saw that he must go further-much-than this, and he realized that if a crime lay here, then the criminal must have overheard or been told of, that talk only this evening in the lounge, when Gilmour had warned the company that if anyone tried to frighten him by playing a ghost he would fire at it. A sound came from behind him. It was the butler, looking quite gay in pajamas of rainbow hue and a green dressing-gown.

"Is anything wrong, sir?" he asked, looking about him and quickly taking in all that there was to be seen. Hobbs had served in the War and his gaze dwelt on the white mound farther down the passage.

"It's Mr. Ingram," Moy said. "I rang for you for nearly five minutes on end."

"We sleep on the top floor now, sir, and the bells don't reach us. But I heard doors closing, and came along to reconnoiter, and nearly ran into Mr. Tark who was coming to wake us up...He told me what had happened. I've told the housekeeper to let the others know. Have the police been notified, sir?"

As he asked the question, came the sound of a car drawing up with a swish, and a quiet press of the electric bell. Quiet and yet insistent.

Hobbs ran down, and Moy bent over the landing balustrade. He did not intend to leave the corridor to itself again. Through the big front door slipped a short, stout man, a doctor, Moy rightly guessed. Then came a figure that filled it well. Chief Inspector Pointer was a tall, soldierly-looking man with a tanned, pleasant face and a pair of very steady, tranquil, dark gray eyes, the gray of the thinker, without any blue in them. He was followed in his turn by three other men.

"It's Mr. Moy, sir," the butler said as he looked up at the young solicitor.

Moy thought that such an introduction was open to misconstruction seeing what had just happened, but he only leaned over and asked if they would all come up to him as he did not want to leave the corridor.

"The body is here," he added.

The chief inspector said a word to the butler, who remained behind with one of his men, then he took the stairs three at a time, noiselessly as a cat.

Moy introduced himself. "I represent the dead man, Mr. Ingram's relatives, as well as the owner of the house. Both are-were, in the case of Ingram-clients of mine." He stared hard at the young man facing him. Much would depend on the officer in charge of this case.

From Gilmour's point of view one could almost say that everything would depend on the inquiry being conducted with absolute open-mindedness and fairness. Let him fall into the hands of a stupid man and he might find himself in a position which Moy did not care to contemplate. The longer Moy looked into the face of the chief inspector, the more reassured he grew. Here, he felt, were better brains than his own, brains of no common order, and there was, besides, that indefinable something that makes a man stand out above his fellows as a leader, as an organizer.

Chief Inspector Pointer, too, was giving the young man in front of him a far more searching scrutiny than his apparently casual glance would have suggested. He, too, liked what he saw. Moy was tremendously upset, and not at his best, but the shrewd observer facing him knew that he was not trying to be at his best. Here was a young man frankly rattled, not in the least endeavoring to pull himself together, not seeking to make any definite, arranged impression. Also Moy's face was his fortune all his life long, little though he guessed it. For something warm, and impulsive, and unselfish, looked out of his ugly features and spoke in his voice.

"Just what has happened?" Pointer asked, as Moy led him and the doctor to the white heap at the farther end.

Moy explained very briefly what he himself had seen and heard, and what he had been told by Gilmour.

"Who drew the sheet out from under the body?" Pointer asked as, after giving it a look, he lifted it off and began to fold it up. So his one glance had told him that the sheet's position had been altered. Moy, on that instant, realized a little of the quick perceptions behind the chief inspector's quiet, steady, gaze.

"One of the ladies. She thought his face should be covered," he said slowly. Time enough to name Miss Longstaff later on.

Pointer and the doctor now bent over the stiff form.

"Bullet still inside the head," the doctor said. "Well, there's nothing further for me to do here." He had an urgent call to an ambulance case. In a few words he and Pointer arranged for the fetching of the body and for the post-mortem. The doctor hurried off. Pointer turned to Moy again.

"How do you know this is the same sheet as the one which you saw draped about him. Were you here when it was drawn out from underneath?"

Moy had not been, but he identified it by the bullet hole close to the hem. Pointer asked him to initial in pencil one of the corners and then locked it away in his case. He had Moy show him where he was standing when he first caught sight of Ingram and Gilmour. Where Gilmour's room was, where Ingram's.

Then Pointer went over the floor of the passage inch by inch. He picked up from a cream-colored flower in the carpet a piece of what looked to Moy like a torn scrap of cream wrapping paper roughly the size of his hand, and near it a spent cartridge case. He sniffed at the latter. When he had made quite sure that there was nothing else to be found on the ground, he examined the walls and the few articles of furniture standing against them. Last of all, he stopped for a moment at one blind, whose cord was tied into a sort of bunched knot.

"I saw that done," Moy explained, "one of the girls staying in the house did it absent-mindedly, while talking to me only a few minutes ago."

"Then the blind was up?"

Moy, for a second, did not see how this simple fact was so patent. Then he nodded. "Yes, she pulled it up while talking."

"And pulled it down again?" Pointer asked.

Moy nodded.

"Did she open the window?"

"Yes, it was for that reason that she had drawn up the blind," Moy said. "Then after a moment's gulp of fresh air, she closed it, drew down the blind, and went off."

Pointer looked out of each of the others in turn and saw that this window was the only one in the corridor that showed the opposite pavement. The view from the other windows was blocked by a ledge above the first floor.

"Was it the same young lady who drew the sheet out from under the body?" he asked when leaving the window as he found it.

Moy assented, saying that he supposed the signs of hauling on the sheet had made the chief inspector guess what had been done.

This time it was Pointer who nodded and then asked if the position of the body had been much altered. Moy said that as far as one could judge by looking at it, the body lay exactly where it had been before and in the same attitude, Pointer next asked where Gilmour was, as he would now like to hear his account of what had happened.

"I suppose he still has the weapon with which he claims that he fired the shot?"

Moy said no, that he himself now had it, and could vouch for its being the identical weapon. He handed it over. Pointer looked at the little nickel-plated thing, examined it carefully, smelled it, broke it open and counted the cartridges still in it-all of which were blank-and put it, too, away in his attaché case after requesting Moy to make quite sure that he could identify it again in court.

"Now who exactly are the people in the house?" was the next question. "And where is the host or hostess?" Moy explained briefly, but sufficiently, what the position was. Then Pointer, leaving one of his men to watch the body unostentatiously, followed Moy to Gilmour's room at the end of the corridor where Winnie Pratt hurried up to him. She had been lurking on the landing above, apparently.

"You're the police, aren't you? Or from Scotland Yard?"

Moy introduced the chief inspector.

"Oh, please don't arrest him! Please don't believe it was anything but a dreadful accident!" she begged in tragic accents. "Why, Mr. Ingram was his great friend! Besides-Mr. Gilmour's engaged to someone else."

Pointer said nothing. She was very cryptic. Was this really just a silly girl defending a man in peril? There is no more charming sight if sincere than that reversal of the usual roles between the sexes, but it must be sincere.

He asked her why she thought that he would look on the death as anything else but an accident.

She wrung her exquisitely kept hands with their tangerine-enameled nails.

"Because the police always do doubt things. And suspect people! But in this case that's absurd. It's not in Mr. Gilmour's nature to do such a dreadful thing!"

Pointer asked her a few questions about herself, about Gilmour, about Ingram. But she would hardly give an answer to any set question.

"Mr. Ingram wanted to marry me, you'll hear all about that side of the story, and I— I—well, I wasn't sure...and I liked Mr. Gilmour-just as a friend. And I showed that I did. And...well...some people will say, so my mother says, that it was all my fault. That I oughtn't to've talked so much with Mr. Gilmour...but that's such nonsense. He's in love with Alfreda. Longstaff. And besides, it was only friendship-ever. And besides, even if it hadn't been, he wouldn't have shot Mr. Ingram. It's a ridiculous and horrible idea."

Again Mrs. Pratt appeared looking for Winnie. Moy did not wonder. Really, what the girl needed this morning was an attendant from a Home for the Feeble-minded, he thought savagely. Of course it was all Mrs. Pratt's fault, trying to make Winnie see the error of her past ways and overdoing it. But what a perfect simpleton the girl was...though a dream of loveliness...

Pointer looked after the dream with a thoughtful frown.

CHAPTER 7

MOY took Pointer into the room where Gilmour sat with his head hidden in his hands. He looked up with a start as the two came in. Moy, after a word of introduction, would have left them alone together, but Gilmour asked him to stay.

"My memory seems to've gone spotty. You may be able to prompt me."

An assenting glance from the chief inspector said that the young solicitor's presence would be quite welcome, then he turned to Gilmour and asked for an account of what had happened.

Gilmour said that he was awakened by someone opening his bedroom door with a snap and giving a hollow moan or groan. As he sat up in bed, the door was left open, the corridor outside was flooded with moonlight, and he saw a sheeted figure walking down it away from his room. He stepped to a chest of drawers by the door and took out his revolver which he had loaded with blank for just such an occasion. In answer to another question he said that owing to some talk about ghosts in the evening, he had rather thought that someone might play that old joke on him. He had never thought of Charles Ingram, but of Moy, or possibly Frederick. Taking his revolver, he went into the passage, where the ghost was now half-way down. At his call of "I'm going to shoot, you'd better disappear!" the "ghost" turned round and faced him with another moan. He fired full at it, and, to his horror, heard it give a cry, and then sag to the floor. After that awful second Gilmour said he could not be sure of what happened. He tried for a switch on the wall but could not seem to find one. The next thing he remembered clearly was lifting the head of the ghost and finding that it was Ingram, and that he was quite dead.

Pointer then began his questions. Gilmour said that he was a good shot, but that on this occasion he had not troubled to take aim, though it was possible that, as the head would be thrown into relief against the oak paneled door, it would have offered a target at which he had fired without consciously selecting it.

Pointer asked for a very careful account of the ghost's appearance. Gilmour, looking very white, shut his eyes, and described minutely a figure draped in a sheet, with the end drawn over the head and covering the whole face to below the chin, walking with head thrust forward and a shuffling gait.

Moy noticed that Pointer took Gilmour over this part very carefully, harking back and repeating several of his questions, though in different forms.

Next he produced the revolver just handed him by the solicitor. Gilmour identified it as his, and again went over how he had loaded it, where the box of blank cartridges were in the drawer, and where the loaded ones. He said that he and Ingram shared a flat in an old house in Harrow which stood quite isolated, and for that cause both of them kept a revolver and some cartridges handy. He went into details about where he had purchased his, and finally handed the chief inspector his license.

Pointer next wanted to know whether anyone had been in the room with him when he had loaded with blank. Yes, Gilmour said, Ingram had been. He had done it on coming up from the lounge only this evening, or rather, since it was now early morning, only last evening, after the talk in the lounge.

He gave a brief outline of that talk.

"So that Mr. 'Ingram would have expected you to fire blank shots?" Pointer said thoughtfully, "and would not be concerned when you pointed the revolver at him?"

Moy was sorry for Gilmour. Gilmour looked appalled at the question, but he answered it with a brief acquiescent gesture.

"Was the dead man fond of playing practical jokes?" was the next question.

Gilmour said that that would be the last thing anyone could say of Charles Ingram. "But," he went on, "he had a theory, which I now think he must have been testing last night. He said that, given any sudden emergency, or waked from sleep-as I was —a man would only do what he was accustomed to doing. That is to say that, however much I, or any other ordinary

Londoner, laid his revolver ready, given an emergency, he would never think of using it, but would dash out empty-handed. Unfortunately he was wrong," Gilmour added.

Pointer asked next on what footing he and the dead man had been. Gilmour said very simply that he and Ingram had always got on well, and that no subject of discord had ever come between them.

"Has he any close relations?" Pointer asked next, turning to Moy, so as to give Gilmour a little time to recover. He looked as though he needed it.

Moy said that Ingram had a sister married to a man called Appleton, and a half-brother, Frederick Ingram. Mrs. Appleton had two children and she and they were, according to Ingram's will left with Moy's firm, Ingram's sole legatees. As to how much he had to leave, Moy said that he had no exact idea. But he fancied that the dead man's income was around five hundred pounds a year. Gilmour, appealed to for corroboration, said that figure would be fairly accurate, though, as Ingram lived at the rate of four hundred, there were possibly some savings to be divided up. Ingram, Pointer was told, as he knew already from Who's Who, had taken high honors in mathematics at Cambridge, where he also held a Fellowship for a few years, only relinquishing it to become examiner and lecturer in his especial field. He wrote on many other subjects as well, though they were all more or less kindred ones, such as ciphers and odd numerical puzzles.

Pointer now asked something which was exceedingly painful to both men. He wanted Moy and he wanted Gilmour again to go over the incidents of the shooting. That is to say, Gilmour was to act as far as possible as he said that he had when he was first awakened, and Moy to do as nearly as possible what he said that he had done when he heard the shot, the cry, the thud.

It was an ordeal for both, but they each of them bore out what they had said as to their different stations at the different times of the tragedy.

Pointer thanked them and went on by himself into Ingram's room. It was the bedroom of a very orderly man. The only untidy thing in the room was the bed, which showed that the sheet had been hauled off without any regard as to what other bedclothes were dragged on the carpet with it. Rather oddly so, Pointer thought, considering that the man who was supposed to have dragged it off would be supposed to want to sleep in that same bed again. But it had been the top sheet, so, though the foot of the bed was undone, the bolster and pillow end were apparently untouched. Slipping his careful hands under the bolster, Pointer found some shreds of tobacco; Player's Navy Cut. Yet Ingram's waistcoat hung over the back of a chair by the armholes, and he had no pipe in the room. Examining the waistcoat, Pointer found some shreds of tobacco in the pocket where the tobacco pouch was kept. He also found a very unusual long inner pocket on the left hand side running down nearly to the bottom and closed at the top by a zip fastener. It came well below the top of the waistcoat so that it would not show, whether open or closed. Pointer examined it very carefully. There was nothing in it now. The size was four inches wide by nine long. It would hold quite a long envelope. He put the waistcoat away in his attaché case. The dust of that peculiar pocket might tell what it usually held. Ingram's other pockets held a handkerchief, a fountain pen, a book of stamps and a small pencil stub. A letter case with letters of no importance, a key ring with keys on it fastened by a chain, and some money-under three pounds.

He rang for the butler. Since there was no sign of any books or writing materials in the room, the chief inspector rightly guessed that Ingram used some other room in the house as well. But first Pointer wanted to see the footman who usually woke Mr. Ingram and probably valeted him. Pointer had learned from Moy that the staff consisted of two men and four women. Windover, a fresh-faced young countryman, was summoned by the butler. He waked Mr. Ingram at half-past seven every morning, he said, took away his shoes and anything that needed brushing, and turned on his bath.

Where did Mr. Ingram usually keep his waistcoat? Pointer asked next. Windover fancied that it was under Mr. Ingram's pillow or bolster, as it was never in sight of a morning. In the evenings, Mr. Ingram would often leave it out. Now Pointer had noticed just such another pocket down the back of Ingram's only pair of evening trousers. He asked the two men whether either of them had ever seen Mr. Ingram use it, or the inner one in his waistcoat. Neither had. Nor had the footman ever found anything in those particular pockets when he brushed either article of clothing. Windover, however, closely questioned, seemed to be concealing nothing and really to have nothing more to tell, so Pointer followed the butler to the ground floor and into the library, which he was told was given over to Mr. Ingram's sole use. Mr. Ingram had last been seen by Hobbs sitting writing at the bureau in the window when he brought him in, as usual, a decanter of whisky and a siphon. Mr. Ingram was a very moderate drinker, the butler added, generally asking for a small bottle of beer in preference to anything stronger but occasionally, as last night, whisky would be brought him. Mr. Ingram had told him to take it away again and had seemed unwilling to be disturbed by even the briefest of questions as to what he would prefer instead.

"He had that small clock over there down beside him on the writing-table, sir, and motioned me when I came in not to come closer," Hobbs went on. "Stopped me just by the door, and told me he wouldn't want the whisky."

Was it usual for Mr. Ingram not to let him come up to him? Pointer asked. The man said it was Ingram's invariable rule.

Questioned further, the butler could only say that Mr. Ingram had no visitors last night as far as he knew, but in a household of five young men who brought their friends in with them at all hours, it was impossible for him to be sure on this point. As to Mr. Ingram himself, the butler evidently had liked him immensely. The same seemed to be true of all of the five temporary owners of the house except of Tark. Of him the butler could only say that he had a nasty silent way, which the maids much resented, of showing when he did not like things. However, bar that trifle, he had never served easier gentlemen than the five. Yes, they all seemed to get on very pleasantly together. Mr. Ingram and Mr. Gilmour too? Oh, certainly. The butler was quite sure that up till last night, at any rate, there was no slightest hint of ill-feeling between them.

The butler seemed to have been squeezed dry and Pointer let him go, and began to go over the room inch by inch. Three pipes lay neatly on the mantel, pipes that had smoked Navy Cut recently. The top part of the writing bureau yielded nothing of interest. Ingram apparently did not use the blotter except as an underlay for his hand. On a copy of yesterday's late evening paper was a candlestick with some drops of sealing wax on it. The wax itself lay on another corner. So something had been sealed since that paper came into the house. In the bottom drawer of the bureau was a locked attaché case. The lock was a most peculiar one. Unpickable, Pointer fancied. Unlocking it with one of the keys on Ingram's bunch, he found it chiefly filled with books neatly strapped together and three piles of manuscripts.

The first was on *Baphomet of the Templars*. The second consisted of the first seven chapters of a book on *The Law of Rationality of Indices*. The third was the first volume, finished apparently, of a work on cryptography. It dealt exclusively with ciphers. Ingram seemed to be just finishing an exposition of Dr. Blair's clever three dot system with sidelights on an adaptation of the A.B.C. system in use during the war.

He stood awhile looking down at the pages. They seemed to have been proof-read by some other hand, a sprawling, rather smudged hand. Apparently the bundle was just about to be sent off to the publishers...He examined the books. They were works on ciphers, such as that of Andrew Langie Katscher, there was one on Lord Bacon's famous two-letter cipher, a copy of Bacon's *De Augmentis*...and many others, mostly on the same subject, or on some mathematical point. He also found, last of all, two dictionaries, one a Chambers, one a Nuttall's. Opening them he found beside many words a dot or a collection of dots. The compiler of a cryptogram might well have made them. That was all, barring some notes on *The Theoretical Measurements of Angles*.

Pointer stood a moment deep in thought. Was the motive for Ingram's death, if it were, as he thought it might be, a murder, to be found in this attaché case which had been so carefully locked? Was it possible that he had been killed for the sake of a clever cipher? Had he by chance stumbled on one like, or sufficiently like, one in use by some foreign power, or great business interest, to make it necessary to remove him? It seemed rather a melodramatic idea for the present day, but so was the notion of murder.

Ingram's despatch case was laid beside the one which Pointer had brought to the house with him. He passed on to the fireplace. In the open grate was the remains of a wood fire. On the tiles inside the fender were some burned matches evidently pitched there by a smoker. Three were like the ones on the mantel, two were of a different kind taken from a match booklet. There was no such booklet among Ingram's belongings. The carved oak fender was moveable and, lifting it out, he found underneath it, as though blown there by the draught, some little scraps of paper with words or parts of words printed in Ingram's writing. They were quite fresh. The paper had been torn so small that none of them held more than four letters on it. Each scrap was carefully collected and put away in an envelope.

He next turned to the waste-paper basket. It had a lot of odds and ends of paper in it but someone had knocked the dottle of his pipe over all, presumably Ingram, since it was still the same tobacco. He stood looking at it thoughtfully. Then his eyes went back to the bureau. Its was odd. The bureau had been searched, of that he was quite sure by many a little sign, things laid where there was dust beneath them, dustless vacant places...the outline of a rubber in one place and the rubber itself in another...the very way the papers were put together told the experienced eye of a good searcher that all these had been gone through. But not the basket...Whoever had been hunting here was looking for something which they were sure would not be thrown away; something of value. The basket stood where it was impossible to be overlooked. Pointer added its contents, too, to his collection, and continued on around the room.

In the seat of an armchair beside the bureau he found a bus ticket. It was for a Fulham-Sloane Street stretch. It was rolled into a tight squill. That too he took. Then he left the room. The door remained unlocked, but one of his men was placed in an inconspicuous position in another room through whose wide open door he could watch the library. Pointer wanted to know if anyone in the household had been interrupted in their hunt for anything, and would resume it if they thought that the coast was clear.

He asked for a word with Moy again. They went into the dining-room, a huge and spacious place where, in a corner by the fire, no one could overhear them.

"It's about Miss Pratt," Pointer said, "and Mr. Gilmour."

Moy broke in. "I've been wanting to tell you about her, chief inspector. It would be so easy, even for you, to get quite a mistaken idea of how things are. Ingram, poor chap, was in love with her, so is Haliburton, but as for Gilmour, as Miss Pratt said, he's all but engaged to another girl who is also staying here, a girl called Alfreda Longstaff. Just at present she's angry at the idea of getting into the newspapers and, of course, Gilmour will be in the spot-light for a while. That can't be helped. But though Miss Pratt is evidently kinder-hearted than discreet, I can assure you that all of Gilmour's heart and attentions were devoted to his own girl."

Pointer said that he had got that, and then asked how the household now at The Tall House had got itself together. By which, he explained, that he meant who had proposed the plan in the first place.

"Frederick Ingram," Moy said promptly. "Because he knew his brother Charles wanted to please Miss Pratt who had said she'd like immensely to stop in a really fine old London house for a few weeks, not just for a few days."

"And Frederick Ingram is by profession?" Pointer asked.

Moy hesitated for the fraction of a second. But there was no use trying to make Frederick out a man of substance held in high esteem in the best clubs. He acknowledged that he was a bookmaker's partner for a season. By original profession he was an architect who did very badly and tried to turn his hand to many things since he left Oxford. His mother died when he was a lad and left him originally a much larger fortune than eventually came to his elder half-brother from their father.

"Where did he live?"

"All over the place," Moy said. He went on to explain that most of the time Frederick lived with his half-sister, Mrs. Appleton, or had lived with the Appletons, paying his share of their little house in Markham Square, but that he, Moy, understood him to say that he had left there some months ago and taken rooms in Hampstead. Since Charles had come to The Tall House for five weeks, Moy believed that Frederick had gone back to Markham Square in order to be nearer his brother.

Markham Square, Pointer reflected, was off Fulham Road. Anyone living there and wanting to take a bus to The Tall House would use just such a ticket as he had found. As for Appleton, Pointer learned that Edward Appleton had once been a well-known actor, that Miss Ingram had married him-he was a distant connection of the Ingrams-just before he came into quite a little fortune, on which he had left the stage and appeared to have gone the pace a bit. Certainly very little of the fortune seemed to be left. There were two children of the marriage. Appleton had been raising, or trying to raise, money lately on his life insurance, Ingram had learned, but that was securely tied up.

"Look here, chief inspector," Moy broke out, "you don't think there's anything wrong about this shooting, do you? Some of your questions seem to me a bit wide sweeping."

"In case it should turn out different from what you think, it's always just as well to have all preliminary questions over and cleared up," Pointer said evasively. "And now, I'd like to see Miss Longstaff."

Moy looked worried. "She's not herself at all this morning," he repeated and left it at that.

Pointer rather expected to see a case of wrecked nerves, but the girl who came in almost immediately did not look as though she knew the meaning of the word. She explained at once that, though she had come to the house as Mr. Gilmour's guest, there was no question of any closer relationship growing up between them.

"Mr. Moy told me that it would prejudice you against Mr. Gilmour to be told that," she wound up. "I don't see why." She fixed that baffling stare of hers on the chief inspector.

He had a feeling that he was seeing her in some moment of triumph, and yet her face struck him as fierce and starved and repressed all at once. Three dangerous ingredients to mix together. As far as words went, she was very controlled. Of course she did not disbelieve Mr. Gilmour's account of what had happened, she said, it was corroborated by Mr. Moy, but she had no intention whatever of marrying the man to whom such a misfortune had happened.

"Once unlucky, always unlucky, I think," she said with a curious little smile. "I really couldn't marry an unlucky man."

"Am I to understand that you and Mr. Gilmour were engaged then, until the death of Mr. Ingram this morning?" Pointer asked stolidly.

"Not at all," she replied at once. "We weren't engaged at all. He asked me to stay here for a fortnight, while Mrs. Pratt would be here, and I don't deny that the idea on his part was-that after my visit, I might perhaps agree to marry him. I think Miss Pratt's stay in the house here suggested the scheme to him. The agreement was that I should have a little time in which to make up my mind. It's quite made up now."

"When did you first meet Mr. Gilmour?" Pointer asked. And she explained, a trifle hastily, that they had met at her father's rectory. Questioned as to what she herself had heard of the tragedy, she said that she was awakened by a shot and a cry, and rushed downstairs as soon as she had collected her startled wits.

Pointer was rather surprised that she, or any woman, would have known that it was a shot that she had heard, for Gilmour's automatic would make but a comparatively small pop, not anything like as loud in the front of the house on an upper story as a car backfiring, and her bedroom was at the other end of a side wing.

"Why did you draw the sheet out from around and under Mr. Ingram?" Pointer asked next in his most official voice.

Miss Longstaff shot him an odd look from those impenetrable eyes of hers.

"Oh, just the natural impulse to cover up a dead body," she said, still eyeing him with that blank but by no means meaningless stare of hers. Had she picked anything up in the corridor, he asked her next. She said that she had looked at the automatic before handing it to Moy. She had seen no spent cartridge case. Pointer asked her to describe exactly how the sheet had been wrapped about the body, and the position of the body itself. Her account tallied with Moy's but was much more detailed. She had a most unusually accurate eye for details, Pointer saw. He left the question of the sheet and asked her about the dead man, but she seemed to have no knowledge of him except from her stay here at The Tall House, and nothing helpful to say about him. Yet he was certain that something was stirring in her connected with the death. If so, she refused to let him catch hold of it. Whenever he thought that he was getting close, she would dive from sight with it down into deep water again. Finally he thanked her, and, with an ironic little acknowledgment of his thanks, she left him.

A dangerous young woman to a detective just now, he thought, for she was keen on some purpose of her own, and quite capable, he believed, of putting a false clue down, or taking a real one away, as suited her own plans. She was mentally agile too, for Pointer had been clever with his questions. Both by nature and by training he knew how to ask the one slight query which, added to one previous little question, would make a quite unexpectedly complete answer.

He stood staring down at his shoe-tips after she had gone, rocking himself backwards and forwards deep in thought. Was she in the crime itself, if a crime had been committed here? Even Pointer could not yet say, but if this was a crime, it might very possibly be one into which malice entered, and certainly Alfreda Longstaff could not be set on one side in that case.

CHAPTER 8

POINTER saw Mrs. Pratt next. She struck him as a woman of great force of character. Also of unusual energy. She seemed to have some difficulty in knowing, or at least in saying, just what she did think of the dreadful event. Pointer got the impression that, provided her daughter took it sensibly, it would rank as a wise decree of Providence, though very sad and dreadfully pathetic, of course. But if her daughter lost her head still further, then Mrs. Pratt would look on Ingram's death as an act of God ranking with plague, pestilence and earthquakes. She struck Pointer as being more on edge, tenser, than he would have expected. Where her daughter was concerned he could understand it, but that would only be connected with Gilmour, one would think, whereas she seemed, to the astute and penetrating brain studying her, to be most in tension where Ingram was concerned. More than that he could not gather from his brief talk. Mrs. Pratt was an experienced wielder of shields, and turned his cleverest points aside with nimbleness. She had hardly left him when the door was opened and in darted the lovely girl he had seen before, but now in something jade green and white which made her look more like an exquisite flower than ever. She was still all exclamations, all protests.

"Oh, he's not guilty! He never did it! He never meant it!"

"Who says he's guilty?" he asked quietly. She checked herself and stared at him.

"Why, my mother says that everyone says —I thought he acknowledges that he shot Mr. Ingram —"

"By accident, yes," he finished.

"And of course it was an accident," she protested again, with that air of defying the world to say it was not, that seemed so utterly uncalled for. She made a bad impression. It might be but the result of some nerve-storm, but she certainly protested too much. Was it love defending, or its opposite suggesting? She fled out again as swiftly as she had entered. Pointer looked after her. If her looks covered a criminal, there was nothing in them to suggest a pioneer, a high flyer. Pointer would expect always to find Winnie Pratt on the beaten path whether that path were the right one or the wrong one.

Tark came next. His face would have arrested any detective's interest at once, it was so intentionally impenetrable, his eyes so studiously blank, his mouth suggested so rigid a curb. He gave his answers as briefly as possible. He was a mining engineer by profession, he said, but he had been at a loose end for some years, owing to the closing down of some mines in Russia. He was born in Beausoleil, aged thirty-seven, the son of the Curator of the Duke of Monaco's Deep Sea Museum. He remained docketed in Pointer's mind as the man with the coldest eyes and the tightest lips that he had met for some time. It was a very determined face, nevertheless, with its hint of utter callousness to human emotions. It was the face of a man of no nerves, who would hardly know the meaning of the word fear. He claimed to know nothing of the dead man and never even to have seen him until his visit here, except for a chance meeting at Haliburton's flat.

Haliburton came next. He explained about himself and Tark with his usual air of quiet frankness. Tark was at The Tall House simply and solely as his friend, he said. Like Tark, Haliburton seemed to take it for granted that Ingram's death was, as Gilmour said, the result of a terrible accident. A taxi drew up as he was talking. Pointer had expected the dead man's sister or brother-in-law before this. He knew that Moy had notified them of the accident as soon as the police had been telephoned for.

Now he saw a neatly-dressed woman get out and glance up at the house with dark eyes full of horror. It was Mrs. Appleton. Pointer went to the door to meet her. She came in with a look of almost unbearable anxiety, and hardly listened to the chief inspector's brief introduction of himself and his few words of grave sympathy.

"How did it happen?" she asked breathlessly.

He told her.

A look of relief swept over her face. "I see," she said, drawing a deep breath. "Poor Charles! Poor Charles!"

Moy came down the stairs murmuring in his turn some expressions of sincere sympathy.

"Were you there-when it happened?" she asked, catching at some word of his that seemed to bear that meaning.

"I was."

"Do you mind telling me again just how it happened?" she asked, and resting her hands on a little occasional table in the hall beside her, she listened very intently. When he had done she asked:

"Where is Mr. Gilmour? I want to see him."

Moy was afraid of a scene. Something in the woman's face suggested nerves that had been, if they were not now, strung up very tensely. He temporized.

"He feels it terribly-naturally. He's not fit to be questioned much and give coherent replies, I'm afraid, Mrs. Appleton."

"Of course I want to hear what he has to say! You didn't really see how it happened! Of course I must know! Charles was my only brother."

She did not seem to rank Frederick as even half a brother. On her face the look of terrified anxiety that had been there when she hurried into The Tall House was returning in part.

"Shall I ask him to come down here?" Moy turned to Pointer, who nodded. While they were alone he did not speak to Mrs. Appleton, who stood staring down at the table as though some map were spread out on it, and she were trying to find her way by it.

When Gilmour came in, he stood for a moment in the doorway, an expression in his brown eyes that was at once dumbly pleading and heartbroken.

Mrs. Appleton came to what seemed like natural life for the first time since Pointer had seen her. She took Gilmour's hand very warmly.

"Poor Mr. Gilmour! How terrible for you! But please tell me exactly what happened. Forgive my asking you to speak of it so soon, but I must know. I *must!*" For a second her voice shook, and Pointer saw her bite her lip hard.

Gilmour drew a deep breath. "I fired what I thought was a blank shot full at him, Mrs. Appleton," he began brokenly, "and-and I killed him. There was some mistake. The cartridge was loaded-not blank."

"But what was he doing?" she asked, as though groping in a mist.

He explained about the dressing up as a ghost. "Charles?" she said in a tone of utter bewilderment. "Dress up and play a joke of that kind!"

He repeated the explanation that he had given the chief inspector, and a little of her amazed look passed off. "Yes, that's quite a possible reason..." she murmured. "Testing a theory...? Poor Mr. Gilmour!" she repeated gently, and her face looked as though some terrible weight had slipped from shoulders that could hardly bear it. "Thank you for telling me everything. There are still lots of questions that I want to ask. Naturally. But I don't think there's anything more I must know immediately." She held out her hand, and Gilmour, taking it, thanked her with a twisted sickly smile for her kindness and walked up the stairs as though he could hardly lift his feet.

Mrs. Appleton turned to Moy.

"Can I see him? Is he-is he-much disfigured?"

Moy told her that the body was not in the house. He explained about the necessity for an autopsy. "And there's another little matter," he went on. "Have you any objection to my opening your brother's will? It's still in my possession. It leaves everything to you, as you know. Do you mind if I let the chief inspector here see it at once?"

"The chief inspector? Oh, I took you for someone staying in the house-for a friend of my brother's." A taut line showed for an instant around Mrs. Appleton's well-cut, decisive mouth. Pointer saw that she could be quite formidable on occasions, and also that she had not heard one word of his own self-introduction.

"Of course the police have to look into it, Mrs. Appleton," Moy said soothingly, "and with a man of your brother's position, since it is within the Metropolitan area, the Yard takes charge of the investigation. Just as a precaution."

"Fortunately my brother's death is so evidently due only to a terrible accident," she said, and immediately looked as though she wished the words unsaid. Pointer took her to be a very truthful and not particularly diplomatic woman. The relief in her voice was the most interesting part of her remark.

"I'd like to sit a while and pull myself together," she said now. "The room my brother used as a study is on this floor, isn't it?" She turned to Moy who, after an assenting glance from the chief inspector, opened the door of the study and closed it after her.

"Well, really," he said in a low tone, coming back to the chief inspector, "if I didn't know Mrs. Appleton, I should fancy she was trying to get points as to how to shoot a person by mistake. She seemed positively insatiable-couldn't seem to have the account of how it happened told her often enough."

Pointer waited for three minutes by the clock while Moy talked on, then:

"I want another word with her," he said in an equally low tone, and walking lightly across the hall's thick runner, he opened the door of the library and stepped in. Moy followed.

Mrs. Appleton was leaning far out of the window. She turned her head over her shoulder and with no sign of emotion, drew back into the room.

"I was smelling the heliotrope in the window boxes," she said. "I love flowers. Well, I feel better now. I think I'll go home. My husband wanted to come, but as he had a most important engagement, I wouldn't let him put it off. The children will be wondering what has become of me. How they will miss their uncle!" With a little bow, she went on out and they heard the front door close behind her before Moy could get to it.

"She was very attached to Ingram, I know," Moy said. "She's a domestic sort of person anyway. Devoted to her home and her family, whether brother, or husband and children."

"Devoted to flowers, too," Pointer murmured dryly, and Moy looked at him inquiringly.

Pointer had decided to take the young solicitor into his confidence to a certain extent. As far as Moy could help him, that was to say. Even if guilty, there were certain facts which the criminal could not now alter. Supposing there was a crime here, and even supposing Moy was connected with it, which Pointer did not suppose, knowledge of how the inquiry progresses is often of no use whatever to the criminal, who cannot change the past nor alter the traces left by it.

"I wonder if she thinks cigarette ash helps flowers to grow," Pointer indicated a Majolica saucer which he had last seen full of cigarette ash. "I have quite a lot of the ash that was there done up in an envelope. The rest is now on the window-box. She's shifted that blotting pad, too. But the paper basket hasn't been touched..."

"Those books, too." Moy followed the other's keen eyes. "Yes, they've been shifted. Every one of them. Ingram always kept the line forward, so that the backs projected over the shelves. They're all back now against the wall behind them."

They had been pushed back when Pointer had seen them before. It only confirmed his belief that the room had been searched before he got to The Tall House. But he had a test of his own as to whether Mrs. Appleton had also gone through them.

"I put slips of paper in at page twenty in six of these books, beginning with the first and taking every tenth on this row. I wonder if they're still there."

Two of the slips were in the paper basket. The others had either not yet been touched, he thought, or had been put back at random.

What was she looking for? Both men speculated. A later will cutting her out? But some of the books were too short to take a sheet of paper the length of the usual will. Whatever she had been looking for, again in her case, it seemed to be something which she felt sure would not be in the paper basket; it was odd-taken in conjunction with her manner of seeming relieved-immensely-by the account of how her brother had been killed.

Pointer believed Ingram might have sent some letter or parcel off by late registered post from the sealing-wax and candle on the late evening paper. But he had not yet found any registration slip. Was this what was being hunted for? And hunted for by several people?

Pointer next interviewed the servants. He learned that the front door had been left unbolted last night. The butler never bolted it, but the last in of the five usually saw to it, though it had been forgotten once before-by Mr. Haliburton, who had assured the butler that he would be more careful in future. The fact, therefore, did not amount to much, for supposing there were a crime here, a murderer with any sense, if a member of the household, would have taken the elementary precaution of undoing the door so as to suggest an outsider. But there was also the fact that Ingram had sat on working in the library last night after the others had gone to bed.

It would have been quite easy for him to have stepped out, and drawn the bolts back and admitted anyone. Did his sister think, or know, that he had, and was that why she had tipped the cigarette ash out into the window box so that it could not be identified?

Apart from the fact of the door being found unbolted this morning, there was one other interesting piece of information that came to the chief inspector. The second housemaid told him that last night, while crossing the landing, she saw Mr. Ingram and Mrs. Pratt meet, on their way out to the car with the others for a dinner to which all were going. Mrs. Pratt had said something very low and very quickly to Ingram as thought not wanting to be overheard. But the maid's sharp ears had caught the final sentence. "Please be Sure and burn it." Mr. Ingram had nodded and said what looked like words of reassurance and agreement. He looked very grave and very disturbed, the housemaid thought. Where exactly had this meeting taken place? Just outside Miss Longstaff's door, the maid said. Miss Longstaff was still in her room, she thought, but she could not be sure. As for the bus ticket, the housemaids had found similar ones several times before and all during this last week. And always in the morning, when there had been no known visitor to account for it in the evening. The butler added one more time during the day when a similar ticket had been left on a wine tray after Mr. Frederick Ingram had been in.

Pointer asked for another word with Mrs. Pratt when he had finished with the servants.

"What exactly did you ask Mr. Ingram last night to burn?" He put the question without any preamble, as soon as he had closed the door behind himself.

"I beg your pardon?" she asked as though hard of hearing. Pointer repeated his question.

"Oh, a ridiculous doggerel I had written about some theory of his, to do with circles and squaring them," she explained lightly. "It really was such silly stuff that I didn't want it lying around and read by everyone who might think that I fancied such rhyme poetry!" She smiled pleasantly at Pointer.

"When had you written it?" he asked, as though chatting.

"A few days ago," was the airy reply. Mrs. Pratt evidently did not intend to be pinned down to hours.

"By the way, have you seen Mrs. Appleton this morning?" Pointer asked next.

She opened her eyes. "Who's Mrs. Appleton, pray?"

"Mr. Ingram's sister. I had an idea —" Pointer's tone expressed surprise that the two did not know each other, but either Mrs. Pratt was a splendid actress or she really had not even heard the name before, and thanking her, Pointer opened the door for her.

Those burned papers in the library fireplace, were they the result of this talk? Was it for them that someone had searched the room this morning before the police arrived and was it for them that Mrs. Appleton was looking? It was because of the similarity in the double search that Pointer had asked Mrs. Pratt whether she knew the sister of the dead man.

There was a ring at the front door. Pointer went on out. A short, rather round-shouldered, slender, young man was stepping in with the air of one of the family. Moy hurried past with outstretched hand. This was no moment to stay on personal likes or dislikes. After a few words of horror and regret he turned and introduced the chief inspector to Frederick Ingram. Had he been a horse, or a dog, the chief inspector would not have bought him. Frederick Ingram had a treacherous eye.

Frederick listened now with an appearance of deep grief to Moy's account of how his brother had met his end. Then he moved towards the library.

"As his literary executor, I take possession of all his papers, of course. I think I'll have them removed *en bloc* to my rooms at Hampstead."

"All of them?" Pointer asked.

"Well, perhaps I needn't burden myself with all," Frederick said promptly, with the air of a man conferring a favor. "I'll make a selection." He walked on into the room. Pointer and Moy followed.

"The work I was correcting of his was locked in a case in the bottom drawer. If you'll hand me over his keys I'll take it along for one thing-and his letter case and so on...I'd better have those too..." He spoke carelessly, but his small eyes darted round the room in a very searching look as he bent over the pigeon-holes. For a second he ran through their contents then he turned. "The keys?" he said pleasantly.

"They're at the Yard," Pointer said as pleasantly and as carelessly. "Just for the moment, of course. They and the attaché case."

Frederick's smile turned into a mere show of teeth. But he said nothing.

"You were here last night," Pointer went on, remembering the bus ticket. "Did Mr. Ingram seem just as usual?"

Frederick Ingram said nothing for a moment, merely went on turning over some papers in his hand.

"Just," he said, laying them down and turning round. He had pleasant manners as a rule. The trouble with Frederick was that when they were not pleasant they were so very much the other way.

Now if ever a loosely hung mouth spoke of garrulity, this young man's did, but not even Tark's tight lips could have answered the chief inspector's question more briefly. There was a short silence.

"I take it that my brother's papers-and keys-will be handed to me as soon as all the usual formalities have been complied with?" he asked the chief inspector, who said that he should have them back as soon as possible. "I think I ought to go through them to see if there's anything missing. Among his papers, that is..." Frederick went on.

Pointer said that if Mr. Ingram would use his, the chief inspector's car, he would be taken to Scotland Yard and shown all the papers belonging to Mr. Ingram.

"I can soon tell you if anything is missing," Frederick promised.

"Do, and we'll send them, as soon as we've done with them, to Markham Square." Pointer seemed to be finishing the interview on a note of meeting the other's wishes as far as possible.

"Oh-eh-Hampstead, please. I only stopped with my sister while running in and out of here, as I had to do several times a week. After this terrible tragedy, I shall go back to my own digs."

"But Mrs. Appleton is her brother's chief legatee, and also an executrix. I think it might be as well if you and she worked through them together with Mr. Moy," Pointer persisted.

"But surely I'm his literary executor," spluttered Frederick, turning indignantly to Moy who shook his head.

"He's left a bequest to the Author's Society and asks the secretary to appoint a regular literary agent to act in that 'capacity-we to settle the remuneration," Moy murmured.

"Still-even so," Frederick went on as though in anger, "even so, there will be all sorts of family papers and so on that my sister won't be competent to deal with. I'll just look through what you've taken, chief inspector, let you know if any are missing, and then we can talk over what had better be done with what's left."

He was clearly in a hurry to see the papers.

"Mrs. Appleton seemed to miss nothing," Pointer threw in casually.

Instantly the little dark eyes fairly snapped as they looked at him.

"Oh, indeed? My sister has been here, has she? Gone through his papers?"

"She probably did when she was here in the library," the chief inspector seemed to think that of no importance.

"She was in here? When?" There was something very attentive in Frederick's voice and face.

Pointer explained how Mrs. Appleton had gone into the room to recover after coming to the house. Frederick's eyes had a gleam in them as he said good-by rather abruptly.

At the Yard he went through everything very carefully after asking to be left to himself-he put it that he need not detain anyone as he would ring when he had finished, he knew how busy the Yard always were, etc. They seemed charmed with his thoughtfulness, and one pair of eyes was on him throughout his careful but most painstaking search. When every paper had been unfolded and shaken out, every envelope searched, he had locked the case again and laid the keys on top of it. Then he sat a moment smoking a cigarette with what looked like a frown of concentration on his face.

He took quite a brisk walk along the embankment until he made his way by tube to Chelsea, and to Markham Square. Here, in a little two-story house that looked on to one of the melancholy cats' gardens of town, he rang a bell. The outside of the house might be dingy, but inside everything glittered, and it was a very efficient-looking elderly woman who greeted him with a smile of acquaintance.

"Mr. Appleton's in, Mr. Fred. He's been 'phoning you, so I think he expects you."

He walked on past her into a neat but cold room.

"Please excuse there being no fire. It's gone out and I haven't had time to lay it again yet. We're upset with Mr. Ingram's dreadful death. Dreadful to think of! His own friend to've done it! And him being all dressed-up as a ghost makes it seem worse, somehow." She was shedding her prim "official" manner as she spoke. Fred stared at her for a second as though he wondered impatiently of what she was talking, his narrow little head, the head of a man who would always prefer to gain his ends by scheming, rather than by force, a little aslant, as he murmured some brief acknowledgment. The next moment the door was swung open with a certain deliberate regal air and there stood Appleton. And he stood a full minute framed in the cream painted doorway staring at his brother-in-law with his head thrown back, an eyeglass fixed in one rather wrinkled eye, before, with an effect of some spiritual meaning in the physical act, he took a step into the room and, still staring at Fred, closed the door behind him without shifting his steady gaze.

CHAPTER 9

POINTER had got from Moy-to that young man's bewildered curiosity-the name of the painters and decorators who had last done up The Tall House. At the shop in question, he produced the piece of torn paper which he had picked up from the carpet where Ingram's dead body had lain. The cream-colored scrap was a torn fragment of wall paper printed in tones of dun, blue and heliotrope. It had lain in the passage with its reverse side uppermost.

The firm stocked no such papers, he was told. The foreman, who had worked at The Tall House, could further assure the chief inspector that nowhere there-not in any cupboard, nor on any wall, had paper been hung. All throughout was paint, or distemper, or paneling; and had been so for the last twenty years.

The scrap shown him was, he thought, about ten years old. Very cheap in quality, and put on with cheap paste. It must have dried away from its wall-some chimney breast he would suggest, and have been loose some considerable time. A couple of months wouldn't be too long. As to its makers, he could only shake his head. A cheap old pattern that would not be found anywhere in stock today. Of that he felt sure.

The two detective officers went on to the Yard together, and there Pointer decked his subordinate in a sheet which was the exact duplicate of the one which, with a hole shot through it, he had at the moment in his locked attaché case. The hole on this, the experimental one, was marked with red ink.

The chief inspector worked hard draping the linen on the mystified Watts now in this way, now in that. He had him lie down, he had him sit up, he had him walk about, or stand at ease. Finally he took the sheet off and handed it to the other.

"Suppose you try it by yourself. You're about Ingram's height. How would you put that sheet around yourself if you wanted to dress up as a ghost. Remember Gilmour says that it more or less covered the body and came down over the head to below the chin."

Watts flung it around himself in a quick swirl, and drew one end over his face, hanging loose at the lower edge. Pointer nodded.

"Just so. That's how I've been trying to do it. Now don't duck, this is the fatal shot!" and he flung something light and sticky at the other. Watts could feel it strike fair and square in the center of his forehead.

"Do I give a screech here and topple over, sir?" he asked. He could not see the other's face, only the floor in front of his feet.

Pointer's hand raised the loose end.

"No good. You've done no better than I. The point is this: I want you to see if your ingenuity can devise some way of wearing that thing that will bring it fairly round your body, over your head and over your face below your chin, and yet let a shot which hits you bang in the forehead make a hole only four inches in from the edge. Personally I don't, and didn't, think it could be done. But have another try. Or you might drape it on me."

"Might as well drape it on the Cenotaph, sir." For Pointer was well over six feet, though he did not look his height. "But this really is a teaser! I don't often feel as certain that a chap is telling the truth as I do with Gilmour...let me have another go at it this way..." and again and again Watts turned himself into a mannequin and pulled and twisted while Pointer flung the fatal shot of dyed putty. All to no good, the putty would not mark within a foot of the red outlined shot hole.

"I didn't think of that at the time," Watts said finally, "but it can't be done, that's plain."

It had been plain to Pointer from the first, and he believed that it had been plain to Miss Longstaff too. Or so he read her manner when he had spoken to her about the sheet.

"You see, sir," he said a little later to the assistant commissioner when finishing his account of what he had found at The Tall House, "the trouble is that the body was left in the passage for five or ten minutes with no one watching it. Mr. Gilmour, Mr. Haliburton and Mr. Moy were all concerned with telephoning for a doctor or the police. The result is that the sheet found lying on the body when I arrived may not be the original sheet worn by Mr. Ingram as a 'ghost' at all."

"What makes you doubt it?" Major Pelham asked.

"The hole doesn't fit his story, sir." Pointer went into details. "What it fits is an idea that Mr. Ingram was shot in his bed, lying down with the sheet drawn up to just cover his face. The hole fits that perfectly, given the marks of the tuck-in at the end, and Ingram's height."

"No scorch marks on it?" Pelham was interested.

"If he was shot in his bed, we may possibly find that a piece of asbestos was put over the linen sheet. There is some in the housemaid's pantry, used for an ironing stand. But it's a very small revolver, sir. Even without any asbestos there would have been very little scorching if anyone had fired from even the foot of the bed."

"You think Gilmour's lying, then?"

"He speaks and looks like an honest young fellow, but his story doesn't fit the hole. It may not be the same sheet. Someone may have purposely substituted one that won't hang together with his explanation. It would have been a simple matter to burn a hole of the right size in another sheet, and then change them. It could even have been done in the time that the door of Ingram's room was shut with Ingram's body lying just outside. In fact, if any substitution has taken place it was probably done then."

"And the sheet Ingram really wore?"

"May have been disposed of in some way. Packed with articles of clothing. We have no power to search for it, of course. Or handed to someone outside the house. The one person known to have laid a sheet over Ingram, the sheet in my attaché case, is also the same person who stood watching from the one window that shows the opposite pavement." He explained about the blind and Miss Longstaff.

"She knew about that hole, of that I've no doubt," Pointer went on, "though whether merely from sharp powers of observation or not, I can't say."

"She's the girl Gilmour is in love with, isn't she?" Pelham glanced at the notes.

"She is, sir. But she's by no means the girl who's in love with Mr. Gilmour," Pointer said dryly and again explained about Miss Pratt.

"Odd," Pelham thought, "now if the girls were reversed one could understand some act of revenge...that sort of thing...but apparently that doesn't fit."

"Apparently not, sir," Pointer agreed.

"And what about the cartridge being loaded when he thought it was blank, what about that?"

"Anyone could have substituted a live cartridge, sir. Mr. Gilmour placed the automatic, after loading it, in an unlocked bureau drawer in his bedroom late yesterday evening, before he went on to a theater with the ladies of the house party."

"How about alibis? Anything possible in that line?"

There was not. Everyone in the house claimed to have been in his own bedroom and in bed long before the time that they were all disturbed by Gilmour's shot and the subsequent cry. The whereabouts of the trio of the dead man's sister, half-brother and brother-in-law was not yet established.

"Has all the look of a pretty nasty little plot," Pelham murmured with a grimace, "and perhaps directed as much against Gilmour as against Ingram. Unless it's really entirely aimed at Gilmour, and the author of it didn't care a hang who was fired at with that first shot, so long as it would place Gilmour in the dock on a charge of murder. He's in an appalling position-if innocent. And he certainly could have hit on some quieter, simpler, method of making away with Ingram than in this public way. He and Ingram were climbing in the Peak country only last month, I've learned."

"Plenty of openings there for an enterprising young man," Pointer agreed with a smile-he himself was a fine rock climber.

"Anything to make you suspect a crime besides the hole in the sheet which is too near the hem?" Pelham asked after a little pause.

"Several curious odds and ends, sir."

Pointer explained that the dead man's bureau had quite evidently-to Pointer-been searched, though not the paper basket. That it looked as though Mr. Ingram had sent off a sealed letter or package, unless it had been taken. Finally Pointer came to the specks of pipe tobacco under Ingram's bolster, though his pouch and pipe were in the ground floor library.

"And that means?" Pelham started a fresh cigar.

"It looks as though the someone who had searched, or stolen from, the waistcoat, did not know of his habit of placing it under his pillow. Or rather, didn't know that we would at once learn of it, and so had hung the waistcoat over the back of a chair to prevent us from guessing that it had held anything of importance." Pointer went on to speak of the curious long inner pocket in it, and in the dead man's evening trousers.

"Couldn't Ingram have placed it under his pillow the night before with whatever he sent off last night, by post or by hand...the something he sealed, you think? Isn't it possible the maid was slovenly, and didn't make the bed properly?"

"The housekeeper told me the sheets in the house were only changed once a week, but yesterday was the day for changing them, and the sheets themselves bore out her words. They were quite fresh from the laundry."

"Ingram would hardly have undressed and gone to bed, placing his waistcoat in security, and then decided-for some reason, some spasm of distrust or fear-to send off what was in the pocket, have got up, removed the waistcoat, taken out the contents, disposed of it-or them-and then gone back to bed hanging his waistcoat on his chair now that it was no longer of importance?" Pelham asked.

Pointer had thought of this, but it seemed to him, as he said, that for Ingram to have again got up and played the ghost-supposing Gilmour to be telling the truth-seemed rather erratic behavior on the part of a young man of very quiet, very routine habits. If Gilmour was not telling the truth, and Ingram had not played the ghost, still this idea meant that Ingram had gone to bed, then got up again and dealt with the mysterious valuable thing in his possession, and then returned to bed and had time to fall soundly asleep before he was shot. All that left rather too little time, Pointer thought. Unless something else suggested it, he thought it simpler to assume that someone else, rather than Ingram, had hung that waistcoat on the chair. He went on next to speak of the scraps of paper beneath the moveable oak curb. "I handed the lot to Mr. Twyford-Brees just now," the chief inspector named one of the cipher experts of the Foreign Office Intelligence Department, "as Mr. Ingram was so good at ciphers—"

"A perfect genius at them," Pelham said.

"Mr. Twyford-Brees promptly got together two little groups of three words each, which he thinks might mean that they are part of some tri-lingual cipher," Pointer went on.

"Ingram specialized in foreign ciphers," came from Pelham as he stretched his hand out for two sheets of glass fastened together around their edges with adhesive tape. Between the glass were gummed two groups of three words each. They were:

VON and HELL OF   LIGHT DE   CLAIRE

"All the words were printed in characters, sir. And there are some more bits which Mr. Twyford-Brees thinks he may make something of."

Pelham looked musingly at the paper. "Ciphers...humph...Anyone in the house whom you suspect of having been the searcher or searchers of the library?"

"Before I got there? Well, Miss Longstaff doesn't strike me as the sort of person to be prevented from any feeling of delicacy, had she felt curious. And curious about that whole affair, she certainly is. Then there's this Mr. Tark. He seems to've been floating around rather freely. The butler ran into him on the stairs that lead up past the library to the top of the house. Miss Pratt says he was passing her door-which would be one way down to the library-altogether, I shouldn't be surprised if either, or both of them, had been there. Then there's Mrs. Appleton —" he described her visit. "She was thankful, I think, to learn that there seemed nothing odd about her brother's death. She was tremendously keen on tilting out that rather peculiar cigarette ash...find out the smoker of that kind of cigarette, and I fancy one would have a lead as to whom she suspected of having been with Ingram last night and of having murdered him. In other words, sir, Mrs. Appleton, I think, knows of a reason why her brother might have been murdered, and is thankful that his death seems to be from misadventure."

"Umph...like the two girls, that's odd,"-Pelham said thoughtfully, "for as far as we can find out, there's nothing linking Mrs. Appleton with ciphers. Whereas Mrs. Pratt! Know anything about her? I've just had my mind refreshed for me."

Pointer had expected to get from Major Pelham the particulars of the people at The Tall House which he had not been able to obtain on the spot. He murmured that he would like to hear all that the other had learned.

"There was a frightful scandal at Geneva," the assistant commissioner said, "where, as you know, her husband was one of the British secretaries. Her maid was found to be an international spy. Name of Aage Roth. One of those convenient people who work for any paymaster and bring in everything they find to one of the big international bureaus there who sell to the highest bidder. She went rather too far and got caught. Sent to an Italian prison. Mrs. Pratt was much pitied for the awkward position, but still...well, it didn't do her husband any good. Accidents like those shouldn't happen in well regulated households. He resigned a year later and he and his wife went for a sea voyage. He fell overboard one dark night. Tragic story." But there was more, something else than pity in the Major's bright blue eye. "Oh, I'm not hinting at anything," he went on virtuously, "I'm merely giving you the facts. They may be of use, they may not. But taken together with those two little groups of torn words it does rather make one wonder...Mrs. Pratt at The Tall House...Ingram, the cipher expert, asked by her to burn something...anyone in the house who strikes you as possibly being a foreigner?"

"Tark has certainly other than English blood, by the look of him, but I rather thought Hungarian, or that sort of thing." Pointer was putting his papers together as he spoke.

"It boils down to this, so far, then," Pelham was ticking the items on the table with his pencil point.

"Ingram seems to have been in possession of something which others knew that he owned, and which they seemed to think worth hunting for, and which they felt sure would not be in the paper basket. He may have posted it late last night by registered post or otherwise. If the former, the registration slip is missing. This idea that Ingram owned something of value holds good for your two alternative solutions. First, that Gilmour is consciously lying as to how Ingram's death took place. Secondly, that he is telling the truth, but that the cartridge was changed, and so was the sheet through which the shot went which he fired and which killed Ingram; the changed sheet to look like the original one, and yet to have been faked so as to throw doubt on his story, by the position of the hole. That it, in a nutshell?"

In a cocoanut shell, Pointer thought, but he only said that it was.

Pelham watched him with the absent-minded gaze of one whose thoughts are elsewhere.

"I said just now that this might be a crime aimed at Gilmour and the exact victim be almost immaterial to the author, but it's also possible, isn't it, that he was used as a convenient way of getting rid of Ingram without its being suspected that a crime was being committed."

Pointer agreed that this explanation was possible.

"There's one thing, sir. If it's been aimed at Mr. Gilmour our attention will be called to the hole in that sheet. So far, no one has tried to make me think it anything but an accident. Personally I'm wondering if the newspapers will give the suggestion...Miss Longstaff may be in touch with a reporter..."

"You seem to think anything's possible with her," chaffed the A. C.

"Pretty well, sir," Pointer agreed as he left the room. Within half an hour the chief inspector knew that his guess was right, and that it was to be by way of the papers that doubt was to be cast on Gilmour's account of what had happened. Or rather by way of the *Morning Wire*. Its front pages were black with capitals and snapshots of The Tall House and portraits of Charles Ingram.

Diagrams of the sheet, too, were spread across pretty well the whole page with a cross for the hole and another for where it ought to be. Diagrams of ghosts and ghostly wrappings...Pointer felt that he knew the writer of the article, no matter what the name was printed below it.

At the house itself it was Gilmour who first secured a copy of the paper from a passing newsboy who was shouting "The Tall House Puzzle" as he ran down the street.

A few minutes later he stepped in to where Moy was busy writing. His face startled the young solicitor. Had some fresh tragedy occurred?

"Anything else wrong?" he asked. Gilmour sank heavily on to the arm of a chair.

"This is just out! Read it!" He thrust the early edition into Moy's eager hands and stared straight ahead of him.

Moy read the article, and dropped the paper with an exclamation.

"Just so! If that's true, I was lying. But I didn't lie. So it's not true." Gilmour spoke doggedly. "The hole can't have been where they mark it in that diagram, for everything took place exactly as I described it. Am I ever likely to forget one item of what happened? I've just been in my room and in the passage and tried to live it all through once more. I haven't been out in the tiniest detail, I'll swear."

"Yet the hole was like that, near the hem," Moy murmured. "There's no use in getting rattled. I wonder if you've been mistaken in the whole thing. I mean if Ingram wasn't shot by you at all, but that in some devilishly clever way you were just made to think you did it?"

Gilmour stared at him. Then' he shook his head.

"Impossible! I fired. I heard him scream. I heard him fall. I turned up the switch-at last-to see him lying dead with my bullet hole in his forehead. Ingram, who never hurt anyone in all his quiet life!" His voice shook. There was something bewildered in his face since he had read the paper. He took a turn up and down the room.

"This article!" he went on passionately. "Someone's not content with what I shall suffer all my life. Someone wants me to be publicly branded as what I'm not, and that's a murderer. Should the worst come, as it may, after that article, will you act as my solicitor?"

Moy held out his hand and gave the other's a warm clasp.

"Depend on me. But it won't come to that-probably." The last word was brought out reluctantly. "Though there's no use denying that the situation is serious. Something's going on...something underhand...but there's one thing for you-the lack of all motive. But about this article in the paper," Moy was thinking hard, "who on earth could have written it?"

"Some reporter, of course, or some press agent got it all from the police." Gilmour did not show much interest in the authorship. Whereas Moy was keenly interested. He did not believe that the chief inspector would have been so guarded just now if he had meant to speak to the press. But supposing someone wanted to harm Gilmour, that piece of print had given him a terrible chance. He pulled himself together.

"The inquest is this afternoon. We must be prepared, of course. Fully prepared. Now suppose I go through the questions the coroner's sure to ask you. Among them will be when did you meet Ingram, how did you come to share a fiat with him, and so on."

Gilmour answered truthfully but baldly. His answers told nothing new. His best defense, as Moy had just said, was lack of motive and plenty of better opportunities, as the solicitor had not said, but contented himself with thinking. He looked again at the printed diagram of the sheet and the hole.

"Whoever did that is trying to fasten a murder on you," he agreed.

Gilmour looked at him a long minute.

"There's only one person here who hates me," he said finally.

"Frederick Ingram?" Moy asked promptly. He had thought of him at once.

Gilmour looked surprised. "Fred? Bless me, no! He wouldn't have the grit to hate any one. Besides, all that old story is forgotten between us. We're quite good friends now. No, I mean Miss Pratt."

Moy almost gasped. Gilmour smiled a trifle crookedly.

"You've wondered at my standing out against the fair Winnie. Apart from being in love, deeply and truly in love, with another girl, her display of interest in me strikes me as so-so," he seemed to be groping for words, "so artificial. I can't express it in words, but she doesn't care a hang for me really, Moy. Whatever the reason for her apparent preference for me, it was only apparent. Miles away from the real thing."

Moy stared at him. He was certain that Gilmour was mistaken. He felt sure that he himself had got Winnie Pratt well taped, all her measurements taken, and they were those of a silly young woman who had hitherto always had what she wanted presented to her on a silver salver, and so from sheer mischief had decided to ask for the moon. Now, had Gilmour said that Miss Longstaff didn't care a hang for him, Moy would have quite agreed with him. Suddenly Gilmour leaned forward. He had decided to say more, go further than he had intended to a minute ago.

"You said just now there was no motive that could be drummed up against me. I'm not so sure. Ingram was madly in love with Winnie. It might be twisted to look as though I, too, had been, and had shot him to get him out of the way."

"Come, come!" Moy could scotch this idea at once. "We all know to the contrary, and could show that you avoided her whenever and wherever you could. Besides, she herself——" He stopped. It would be a very unpleasant avowal for Winnie Pratt to be asked to make.

"Just so!" Gilmour said meaningly. There were tense lines about his young mouth. "What about Winnie Pratt herself! Supposing she chose to say-swear that my manner was only a pose."

Moy was genuinely worried. "But I say! Good Heavens! Why should she?"

Gilmour did not reply.

"You mean, that you think she will?" Moy asked in horror, for if Miss Pratt did any such thing Gilmour might indeed be in a tight place.

Gilmour was silent quite a long minute, fingering the newspaper. Then he said with a sigh:

"Being in danger alters one's point of view. I should have said yesterday that nothing would make me give a girl away, but after that article there," he flicked at the front page, "this may be a hanging matter. You've said you'll act for me, so, well, I wouldn't bank on her not taking that line."

Remembering whom he had seen adjusting the all-important sheet over Ingram's body, Moy felt sure that Gilmour was exactly reversing the feelings of the two girls, and that time would yet show that Winnie really loved him, whereas it was Miss Longstaff who, for some reason of her own, had chosen to pretend, very casually and carelessly, that in time she might be willing to marry him.

"She's got at Alfreda in some way," Gilmour went on, lowering his voice. "Alfreda wasn't like that down at Bispham. I know as well as I know my own name that the other has made her think there have been tender passages between us, and that it's only because of my not wanting to stand in Ingram's way that I wouldn't openly join her train of worshipers."

A short silence fell. Moy was re-reading bits of the article before them. Then he turned a quick, excited face to the other's hopeless one.

"Look here, I begin to wonder if the sheet was changed. While we were in here. If so...where could the real one have been put...any place near by?" He was talking to himself, and stepped out into the corridor as he spoke. Suddenly he pounced on a door close to Ingram's room. "That's the linen cupboard! It's just possible! I wonder! You wait here. It's better that I should look by myself!" Moy was almost incoherent, but Gilmour waited quietly enough. Two minutes later Moy reappeared. "Andy! Andy! Puss, puss!" he called, and in answer to his voice along stalked a black Persian which had adopted Moy as his particular friend. After another two minutes or so Moy came out again. His eyes were alight, but he said nothing until he had drawn Gilmour into a room and shut the door.

"Got it! The sheet is there! The real one, for it's got the hole in the right place!" he said in an exultant whisper. "Oh, no, I didn't take it away. I had a brain-wave instead. I got hold of the cat, took off his collar with its bell, teased a corner of the sheet through the hamper where it had been tossed with other soiled linen, worked the cat's bell into the bit that hung out. The basket stands in a corner, the bell doesn't show, but should anyone try to get hold of that sheet, it'll ring. Now, stay here, and keep your ears open for a tinkle-tinkle, while I go and tell the policeman on the landing all about it."

He was gone, and for the first time since he had fired the shot Gilmour's face showed a slight relaxation of its lines.

The detective listened carefully to Moy while the cat sat by and washed a paw.

"You've found another sheet? Also with a bullet hole through it?" He looked keenly at the young solicitor. "I see. And you've fastened a bell —" He stopped. Tinkle-tinkle-tink! came a light, clear sound.

Andy, the cat, listened with a bewildered look upon his intelligent face. Surely that was his bell...he scampered down the passage straight for the linen room and only just dodged out of the way as someone slipped out of the door. The someone was Miss Longstaff. Behind her came Frederick Ingram. "The maids seem quite demoralized," she said promptly, "I've been ringing for hours for a towel for Mr. Ingram. Do you know where they're kept?" She had nerve, Moy thought, as he replied stiffly that he had no idea where the linen at The Tall House was stowed, but that a pile of hand-towels was usually to be found in the locker of the downstairs lavatory.

"Were you ringing for her in there?" he asked blandly, "it sounded for all the world like a cat's bell."

Miss Longstaff murmured a word that did not sound like any bell, and went on downstairs with Fred. The detective sat on the basket which Moy had pointed out to him, from which a little round bell still dangled, fastened into a corner of a sheet.

"I wasn't present when you found this?" the detective, a young Oxford man, said with a faint grin, eyeing Moy very closely.

"You weren't present either when Ingram was shot," Moy countered. "Yet you don't deny that fact."

"Oh, no, it's no use denying facts!" the young man gave another grin.

"Why this attitude then?" Moy held out his cigarette case.

"Because this hamper and the two others were searched when we arrived this morning. You don't suppose Chief Inspector Pointer overlooks any mouse-hole, do you? No sheet with a bullet hole was in this room then."

Moy stared at him. "I found it at the very bottom..." he said slowly.

Bosanquet shook his head. "Not there this morning. However, that's between ourselves. At any rate, this has got the hole in the right place." He was spreading out the sheet and looking at the little round scorched hole which was a good foot and a half in from the edge.

Moy initialed it carefully with an indelible pencil. Then they put it back in the basket and the detective announced his intention of sitting on guard on the hamper until the chief inspector could see it.

————————————————

CHAPTER 10

FREDERICK INGRAM touched Moy on the arm.

"Look here, that was just Miss Longstaff's idea-that towel excuse-the fact is, I think as my brother's representative, he was your client, that you oughtn't to take sides with Gilmour, as you do."

"Take sides?" Moy repeated, ruffled. "I don't understand. What do you mean? I'm in the house when a terrible accident happens; I see it happen-practically. Naturally, I form my own conclusions. Who's more able to than the man on the spot? I do believe Gilmour's story. Why shouldn't I?"

"Because Charles was your client," Fred said slowly and weightily. "Gilmour shot to kill, Moy. You should consider that view of my brother's death and see if it leads you to-Gilmour's side."

"It's just as well there are no witnesses," Moy said to that. "You must have some reason for your words."

"Oh, it's so obvious," Fred Ingram said loftily, "so obvious that you're all overlooking it. Of course my sister, Mrs. Appleton, swears that it's an accident, but then" —a very nasty sneer crossed his face —"what's easier? Shoot a man openly, and then claim you thought you were shooting blank...Perfectly safe to get away with that."

"And the motive?"

Frederick hunched his shoulders. "Some private feud, of course. They shared a flat together. A dozen motives may have arisen of which no outsider would know anything."

"The chief inspector is coming over at once," Moy said after a moment's thought. "Why don't you speak to him of your suspicions?"

"I'm going to," was the reply, and Fred swung on down the passage.

Pointer was on his way to The Tall House when the message from his man was received for him at the Yard. He heard the news with his usual impassive gravity. Then he went up and inspected the place where the second sheet had been found. The detective who had taken charge of it had already made his inquiries. The room was naturally never locked, the sheets had all been changed yesterday morning in readiness for the laundry which would call for them some time during the afternoon.

"We looked them all over, sir," Bosanquet murmured. "Wasn't here then. But unfortunately all the sheets in the house are exactly alike, except those used by the servants."

"So we shan't know off whose bed it came," Pointer finished.

Up till now it had not been possible to examine any bedrooms, let alone beds, except those of the dead man and of Gilmour. Pointer went there now. The sheet was still missing from Ingram's bed. It was quite impossible to say which of the two claimants to be the original top one was genuine. Even the housekeeper could not tell any of the linen apart.

"Quite useless trying to find out," Pointer said to his man. "Evidently it was in, or on, a bed when we first came early this morning." He examined the hole. If not caused by such a shot as would come from Gilmour's little automatic, then it had been burned with the pointed end of something of a size so exactly right, that whoever did it must have known exactly what size was wanted, even though the other sheet had been taken away by Pointer.

A tap came on the door. Fred Ingram would like to speak to the chief inspector when he should be at liberty, said one of the plain-clothes men.

Pointer had finished here. He took the second sheet and laid it away in the despatch case which always accompanied him while an inquiry was on. Pointer saw Frederick in one of the downstairs rooms. Frederick informed him that he felt sure that Gilmour had intended to kill Ingram. That all this "stuff" about thinking it was loaded with blank was "tosh." Of course the cartridges now in it are, but the first one was a genuine affair, and known to be by Gilmour..

"And what did your half-brother own, Mr. Ingram, that would make Mr. Gilmour-or any-one else for that matter-want to murder him?" was the query, and the gray eyes just swept the other's by no means ingenuous face.

Frederick clenched his teeth together until his cheek muscles bunched. "That's a very police way of looking at things," he sneered. "His purse or a five pound note, you mean? I don't know what the motive is, but I can guess." He shot his rather underhung jaw forward. "When there's a lovely girl staying in the house with two men keen on marrying her, it wouldn't be difficult to add a third."

"But Mr. Gilmour claims to care for another lady."

"Oh, that! Have you seen them both?" Frederick demanded rudely. "Well, where are your eyes, chief inspector? They'll tell you how much truth there could be in that tale. But whether she was the reason or not, the fact is all that matters here. And the fact is that Gilmour has very simply, but quite successfully, drawn the wool over all your eyes. All except Miss Longstaff's. Look here, if Gilmour were innocent wouldn't she be the first to feel it? She doesn't. She's so sure he's guilty that she's having nothing more to do with him."

"Well," Pointer said with carefully obvious patience, "as I understand it, Mr. Ingram, you have only suspicions, nothing definite, to go on? No past quarrels, for instance, overheard by you?"

"Nothing but my common sense," Fred said shortly.

"And what about your own little disagreement with Gilmour?" Pointer asked pleasantly. His shot at a venture went home. Fred's face flushed.

"That has nothing whatever to do with my certainty that the man's lying, and is gulling you all." And with that he left the room rather hurriedly.

Pointer was entering a note or two when Moy came in search of him.

"Has Frederick Ingram spoken to you yet?" he asked.

"On several occasions," was the reply, with a twinkle. "About Gilmour, I mean. Just now?" Pointer said that he had.

"Then please listen to Haliburton, too. Here, Haliburton, you promised to be kind enough to tell the chief inspector the tale of the foxes that weren't clever enough to fool Gilmour. I must be off to the office."

Haliburton, in his slow, pleasant way, rather jibbed a bit at first, but finally told Pointer all about that old affair. He added that Fred claimed to have been as much taken in as was his half-brother, and Ingram apparently believed him, since it was after it that he offered him the post of his reader, but Fred had never let an opportunity pass, since then, of jumping on Gilmour behind his back. Before his brother he was forced to show a certain neutrality for fear of arousing even Ingram's unsuspicious mind to make a few connections.

"You're confident that Mr. Frederick Ingram knew the real state of things?" Pointer asked.

"I don't see how he could help it. And any other business man would tell you the same. Charles Ingram wasn't a business man. And one didn't like to call his half-brother a swindler, so one had to let it pass. As, thanks to Gilmour, he hadn't lost anything, one could let the matter rest and hope that Fred Ingram would be more cautious in future."

"Did Mr. Gilmour show any especial skill in detecting the-weakness-of the proposal?" Pointer asked. He wanted to know if the dislike of Fred for Gilmour was reciprocated.

"None. Just used his brains, read what was written between the lines as well as what was in them. Ingram was the sort of fine chap who never would dream that anything could exist between lines."

"Yet I thought he was rather an authority on ciphers," Pointer said.

Haliburton said that he too had heard as much, but he seemed to feel no interest in that subject and referred back to the silver fox farm without telling anything fresh.

"Did Mr. Frederick Ingram ever threaten to make it unpleasant for Gilmour?" Pointer asked.

Haliburton drew in his rather long upper lip. He shot the detective officer a speculative look.

"He did. Told him he'd teach him to mind his own business. But I don't think Fred Ingram the sort of chap who would keep his word-even to himself-if it were at all troublesome."

"What terms were he and his brother on?"

"Excellent. As far as any one could judge Charles and Frederick were united by a really strong family tie."

Pointer drove on to the Yard turning Frederick Ingram over in his mind. Where lay the key to the motive for this murder-if it had been one?

He informed the assistant commissioner of the discovery of a sheet, whose hole would fit Gilmour's statement, tucked away where it would have been sent to the wash with the other sheets and where the hole, even if noticed, would have been taken for a burn from a cigarette end.

"And it may be just that-or something hot-which did it," he wound up. "Mr. Gilmour even might have recollected its position before the paper came out, and tried to put a blunder on his part right before it should be too late. He could have done that, of course, and just waited for someone to make the discovery."

"Yes, like his story, it's inconclusive," Pelham agreed. "Can't you clinch the matter by the sheets themselves? Or do they all match each other?"

He was told that they did.

"And again it was Miss Longstaff who is connected with this, sheet as with the other. Amusing notion of the cat's bell. And you say Fred Ingram was with her? Odd..."

Pointer went on to speak of the fox farming idea and Gilmour's part in preventing Ingram dropping quite a nice little sum over it.

"Aha!" Pelham cocked an ear like a hunter who hears a crackling out in the bushes. "So Frederick Ingram told you he suspected Gilmour of murder, did he?" The assistant commissioner passed a paper over to Pointer. "Here are the brief outlines of Fred Ingram's career, as far as we know them," he said. "Not at all the sort of saint who wouldn't try to do his half-brother out of a few shekels. Trouble with him seems to be that he once made a really good win at Cannes, baccarat it was, that most fascinating of naughty little games, and since then he flutters around any casino candle like the proverbial moth, and to very similar effect. However, this last couple of years, as Haliburton says, he seems to be a reformed character. Though he still knows some shady people...I wonder if it was he who sold the story of the sheet to the paper, and not Miss Longstaff...somehow she really seems so incomprehensible...if she did it, I mean. Gilmour apparently so in love with her while she sells him to the press..."

"Yet it is Miss Pratt, sir, who by her words throws the greatest suspicion on Gilmour, the suspicion of a possible motive. As far as I can learn there is no foundation whatever for her idea that Gilmour cares for her. But she seems to think he does. Must."

"Perhaps more may come out at the inquest. What's your position going to be at it?"

"Knowing nothing, suspecting nothing, and believing everything," Pointer assured his chief, and the other let him go with a smile.

Back in his own room, Pointer looked through the Yard's news-sheet of crimes that had happened last night. It was part of every officer's routine. There was one item on it at which he stopped, an attempted robbery of a small post office off Leicester Square. That office had happened to have rather a large sum of money in its safe last night, a fact that seemed to have leaked out; but not so the other fact that the authorities had taken precautions accordingly.

A masked man had entered the office only to find himself confronted by a group of resolute postal officials-all armed. He had decamped on the spot. He had rushed down a side street, and it was this fact that interested the chief inspector. For, supposing Ingram to have posted a letter late last night, then he would have done so from either the Leicester Square or the Fleet Street post office, as being the two nearest to him which' were open all night. And coming from Chelsea, there was a short cut from Piccadilly Circus by way of Lisle Street which was the identical street used by the masked man in running away. Lisle Street had just been freshly laid down, and on a pair of shoes, neatly placed under the foot of Ingram's bed, were the marks of having recently been walked over some newly tarred road surface. Pointer already had sent a man to that office asking whether Ingram-to be identified by his portrait in the paper which had printed the diagram of the sheet with the hole in the wrong place-had registered a letter or parcel there last night. A message on the 'phone while he was still studying the map, told him that a clerk on late duty had recognized Mr. Ingram as the sender of a late fee letter or package by letter post, some time shortly after one o'clock last night. There had been some question of making exact change and Ingram had offered a half-crown which was bad. He had handed in another, and had stood chatting about his first piece and how to identify such a one in future. Unfortunately the clerk could not remember the name to which he had posted the package or letter, and knew that by no effort could he do so, but he was certain of Ingram's identity, and his description of the rather hesitant, pleasant voice tallied exactly with the dead man's, who, the post office clerk said, had been alone. He had glanced at the clock at the same moment that Ingram had pulled out his watch and compared the two, and he was willing to swear that the hour was shortly after midnight. Five or six minutes past twelve.

Now that was just a little before the time that the masked man would be running down Lisle Street, which would probably be otherwise quite deserted at that hour.

Pointer was making a note about the bad half-crown when Chief Inspector Franklin came in. He was looking for a ledger on Pointer's shelves. Franklin was an older man than the other, a cheery soul, with a liking for a joke which found little scope in his profession. He was in charge of this attempted robbery. Pointer looked up quickly.

"I was just wanting a word with you about this post office robbery of yours," he began. To judge by their talk, all the men at the Yard might have been criminals, there were such constant references to 'this forgery of yours,' 'this attempted larceny of yours,' this blackmail of yours that didn't come off.'...Pointer explained to Franklin now how Ingram might well have met the running man.

"Of course the man would have had his mask off...Ingram may have recognized him...had no idea what he was hurrying away from...the man would see to it that he slowed down to a quick walk...if he knew Ingram, he would have snatched at the chance of walking on with him, supposing Ingram to have been hurrying home, which would give the man an excuse for running-he could claim to be running after Ingram..."

"And what about bad half-crowns?" Pointer went on.

"Ah!" Franklin nodded again with a grin this time. "I told Blackwell that we hadn't heard the last of that coining den of his, but he would have it that it was all cleaned up. You never clean up forgers or coiners."

"I wonder if that bad coin had anything to do with Ingram's death," Pointer mused, "...or did he meet this running man of yours and recognize him?...I've been rather inclined to the idea that he had some important document, cipher or cipher-reading, which was wanted by the murderer. But a false half-crown...and a man desperately trying to escape detection..." Pointer's voice died away into thought.

Franklin was greatly interested. "Of course, supposing my man was known to Ingram, he might have told him some cock and bull story about always running at night in full evening rig so as to slim, but he would know that when Ingram got the morning papers with their account of the attempted robbery in them, his tale would be torn. I think you've struck a good line there, Pointer."

Pointer did not look delighted. "It's a pleasant mixture," he said. "As a rule, in a shooting case, if a man wasn't on the scene of the crime, then he's presumably innocent. But here, the members of the house party who were out of the house last night will be the most suspected, and heaven only knows where anybody was. I've only their word for it...No way of checking it..."

"Well, if your murder is the result of my raid," Franklin said, quite unconscious of anything humorous in the phrasing of his sentence, "then it looks to me as though a bigger and better raid was being planned. You think he was someone staying in the house?"

"Whoever murdered Ingram was either stopping at The Tall House, or knew the house well." Pointer explained about the sheet and the blank cartridge and Franklin agreed that that seemed certain. Pointer ran over the people in the house to him, describing them.

Franklin was not interested in Haliburton or in Gilmour, one wealthy, the other with a good pay and a good pension. Both men he did not consider as probable post office robbers, but

Tark seemed another matter. He, too, however, seemed to have means of his own, apart from his profession of a mining engineer.

"He's the one we know least about," Pointer finished. "But so far what he says should be easily verified. Born at Beausoleil, studied at Bologna, studied mathematics...got his doctorate there in Letters...claims to have a moderate but sufficient income from his father who was an English biologist worker for the Duke of Monaco on some of his deep-sea expeditions. Hence the house in Beausoleil which the father bought."

"Beausoleil, not Monaco, I notice," Franklin said meaningly.

Pointer had noticed that too. It might mean little. But anyone living in Beausoleil can spend as much time as he wishes at the Monte Carlo Casino, which is not the case should he live within the walls of the little principality itself. On the other hand, Beausoleil has its admirers, quite apart from any question of gaming, and it was understandable that a man working for the Duke when not required to be in residence might prefer to be outside his jurisdiction, and yet almost as near as though living in Monaco itself.

"I suppose it's out of the question for Ingram himself to have had a hand in anything shady," mused Franklin; "been the directing spirit, say? Come out to watch how his little plans were getting along? That bad half-crown was very casually 'planted.'..."

Pointer could only say that few things were impossible, which was what made life, and especially the life of a detective, interesting, but that it seemed a strange idea. Not borne out by anything yet found.

"It's much more in Fred Ingram's line, one would say, but even with him —" he proceeded to pass on his information about the younger Ingram.

"Do you want this robbery of yours mentioned at the inquest?" Pointer asked. He was folding up the *Yard News*.

Franklin emphatically did not. And said so. He watched the other mark some papers and tie them together.

"What do you call this case-The Tall House puzzle?" he asked.

"Personally I think of it as the 'Either-Or' case," Pointer replied.

"Either Gilmour is telling the truth, and is innocent, or he's lying and is the murderer." Franklin laughed a little. "Nothing peculiar about that I should say. This suggestion as to a possible motive in my robbery for Ingram's death seems rather to suggest that he's telling the truth."

Pointer nodded in his turn. "But here again, taking Ingram's death as a murder, either the motive was to escape detection when Ingram read the morning papers or it is something quite different. And I don't see what part the posting of the package or letter would play in the plot if Ingram was merely killed to avoid recognition, or to prevent his handing over someone to the police next morning."

"And why should the posting of the letter play any part in the crime?" Franklin paused in the act of lighting a cigar to ask.

"Well, the murderer knew about the ghost talk, and the threat of Gilmour's to shoot at sight, he would certainly know about Ingram's going out to post or register a letter. The odd thing is that he was allowed to send that package...and that no attempt was made on his life beforehand..."

"Well?" Franklin was forgetting to light up.

"Yet one would think that the murderer must have foreseen its posting. He was so well up in all the other details of life at The Tall House. Ingram was working hard at something all afternoon, and more or less all evening...the murderer must have been expecting that it would be sent off. It looks, so far, as though he wanted it posted."

"Waited for it, you think?"

Pointer said that it looked like it so far. "If so, it cuts the ground out from under my idea of Ingram's chance encounter with the man who took part in your robbery."

"Unless," Franklin's blue eyes darkened, "that package contained something to do with counterfeit coining? Say Ingram was suspicious...had got on the track of some coiners, tested a piece of silver and found it bad, and...but he had posted the package first."

They discussed the further possibilities for a brief moment. Then Pointer was ready to go.

"I always think of you as soaring far above facts in your deduction flights." Franklin chaffed him.

"When I'm in a fog, my dear chap, facts are like palings to which I cling, groping for a fresh one before I let go of the last. You've laid my hand on some fine fat fellows with this robbery of yours, and I'm much obliged, though a bit lost yet as to where they're going to lead me."

Franklin burst into one of his big laughs. "Are you in a fog here?"

"Either-or," was Pointer's only reply.

"I don't envy you this murder of yours," Franklin said as they parted. "Which of the people up at The Tall House strikes the oddest note? Fred Ingram or this Tark?"

"Neither. Miss Longstaff," Pointer said promptly, and was gone.

CHAPTER 11

POINTER turned over very carefully the new idea as to why Ingram might have been murdered, as he drove back to The Tall House.

It was rather suggestive, the notion of a man escaping from a balked robbery, running slap into someone whom he knew, fobbing him off for the moment with some sketchy excuse, and having to kill him before the papers should give the details, unless he was prepared for arrest and penal servitude. Someone who knew The Tall House, who had heard or had been told of this talk about ghosts...seeing the lateness of the hour the probabilities were strongly in favor of it being someone who had himself heard that threat of Gilmour's. In fact, the only certainty that Pointer had, so far, was that the murderer knew of that talk.

He let himself quietly into the big house with its raking sky line of five floors and a battlemented coping. The room next to the library was locked. Why, no one seemed to know. Inside it sat a plain clothes man watching the unlocked library. The man had a careful list of all who had gone into the room, and through the keyhole, by means of a tiny ended periscope, had been able to watch what each person did. Pointer had "salted" the library a little while ago with papers tucked in books or odd corners. Some of the papers were quite blank, some of them were written on in what looked like Ingram's peculiar, and, therefore, easily copied, writing in what purported to be either mathematical formulas or ciphers. Green of the Yard could dash off a forgery in a couple of seconds which would defy any but his own eyes to detect. His formulas and his ciphers were the merest conglomeration of figures or letters, but they looked quite impressive. Tark had been in that room for nearly ten minutes now.

"Mrs. Pratt has been in twice just to have a look-see," the man finished. "She's as good a watcher as one of us. Hangs round one of the rooms opposite, seems to give everybody three minutes, and then slips in and is quite surprised to find anyone there, offers to help and is politely thanked, and then whoever it is goes off and, after a second, she looks about her and goes off too."

Pointer was now watching Tark pounce on a slip of paper, studying it with the look of a ravenous animal on his usually impassive face. Then he stood a moment the picture of indecision. As the door opened he tossed the paper behind the couch.

It was Mrs. Pratt in a smart black and white frock which only made her look gray and lined.

"Back again?" she murmured with a faint contemptuous smile. "Perhaps I can save you trouble, Mr. Tark," she said with that sparkle in her eye that Pointer generally found meant hasty impulse in man or woman. "The letter isn't here. It was burned."

"I don't understand you," Tark said stolidly.

"Oh, I think you do," she replied, still with heightened color. "I saw you looking up at us when I handed it to Mr. Ingram. Well, it's burned and you won't be able to use it-as you would like!"

"I don't know what you mean," Tark repeated. "I saw you hand a paper to Ingram, yes, but papers you hand your friends don't interest me, Mrs. Pratt." His cold eyes flickered contemptuously over her.

Mrs. Pratt only gave the equivalent of a toss of her head. "As though I don't know how much you would like to find it-and use it!" and with that she was gone again.

Tark stood looking after her, and seemed to think that this was no time to continue his hunt, for he too went on out, leaving the door ostentatiously wide open. After a second Mrs. Pratt came back, closed the door, stood a second listening, and then scrambled at full length under the sofa for whatever it was that Tark had tossed there on her entry.

Pointer decided on a few words. He stepped in so swiftly and so noiselessly that until he shut the door she had no idea anyone had entered. Then she tried to wriggle back from her undignified position and Pointer gravely assisted her, moving the sofa to let her get up. She looked anything but grateful to him as she did so.

"Look here, Mrs. Pratt," he said on that, "I have an idea you want something back that you lent Mr. Ingram. Something besides that poem you asked him to burn. Now we've taken quite a lot of papers away with us. Unless it concerns the murder we don't want to keep any of them. Yours may be among those that we have. Suppose you tell me what is in it."

She stared hard at him, pursed her lips and straightened her dress, flicking the dust off it here and there. "Mr. Ingram burned those silly verses, as I just told Mr. Tark, who would like to get hold of them and tease me about them."

"A playful nature, evidently," Pointer murmured.

She shot him a cold and haughty glance, but he did not seem to see it as she made for the door. He held it open without another word. Mrs. Pratt was not going to talk. She did not return to the opposite room but went on up the stairs too. Pointer had his man join him in the little room which he used as a sort of temporary police station. There he looked through the man's list of names and times spent in hunting in the library. First had come Miss Longstaff; she had spent a quarter of an hour when Mrs. Pratt had dropped in. The detective thought that Mrs. Pratt was distinctly suspicious of the younger woman's motives for being there at all. Miss Longstaff had said that she had mislaid a return ticket and a letter from her mother while in there earlier in the day, and "must have them back." Mrs. Pratt, as had been said, showed a certain skepticism of this reason.

"Your letter in here? How very odd! Did you bring it down here, or do you think one of the maids carried it downstairs from your bedroom?" she had asked sweetly. Miss Longstaff said she had no thoughts on the matter but that she had been reading it when the dreadful shock of this morning had made her come running down with it, and possibly the ticket too, in her hand. Since then both had disappeared. Like everyone else (here the detective said she had given Mrs. Pratt a certain lingering look) she had wanted to see the room where Mr. Ingram had worked...she might have dropped it then...but did Mrs. Pratt want anything in particular?

Mrs. Pratt said that she had handed Mr. Ingram a very silly set of verses about angles and angels, and so on, and only hoped it had not fallen into the hands of the police; she would feel so very silly if any eye but her own and Ingram's ever saw the lines. And then it had been Miss Longstaff's turn to be surprised. "You wrote poetry on Mr. Ingram? Now do you know that is the last thing I should connect with you, Mrs. Pratt," and so it had gone on for a few more sentences. Then Mrs. Pratt had sat down and said she wanted to write a letter, would Miss Longstaff mind letting her have the room to herself for a few minutes? She had always found that she could write best in the library. "Poetry?" Miss Longstaff had asked with one of her stares but she had left the other woman alone. After a minute or two Mrs. Pratt had gone out. Her aim had evidently been to see the girl off the premises. Then had come Frederick Ingram. He had gone over every scrap of paper, and the description of his face while doing so tallied remarkably with the look on Tark's face, with the effect of half-savage desire, half-indecision which the chief inspector had watched on the man to whom Mrs. Pratt had spoken her odd words. Then again Mrs. Pratt had drifted in, and again had asked the seeker what he was looking for. Frederick said that he had left some very valuable notes here, which Ingram particularly wanted him to rush through for his next book.

That he had laid them down while talking with Ingram and did not remember where...Mrs. Pratt seemed to have two strokes to most people's one, and she saw Frederick Ingram safely out of the room, having another look when he had gone. What was the woman after? Pointer could only guess that she was not so satisfied as she seemed that Ingram really had burned whatever she had handed him. What could that be? The field was too wide and rested too entirely on speculation for the chief inspector to waste any time over it. Certainly the two men examined any scrap of paper no matter how tiny, whereas Mrs. Pratt only looked at sheets of note-paper that resembled that stocked in the writing-tables of the house, and used by Ingram himself in the library, a gray paper with black heading.

That much bore out her statement about the silly rhyme, but only that much. At all events, she and the two men did not seem to be in each other's confidence.

As for Tark and Frederick Ingram, they seemed to be strangers to each other, at any rate neither had been seen talking to the other at The Tall House since Ingram's death.

The inquest was fixed for the afternoon. For a while the coroner seemed inclined to dally with the idea of the unbolted front door, but as a coroner's court has only to decide the cause of death, and in this case it was most clearly and undisputably death from a bullet, he could not waste much time on that.

Frederick Ingram ventilated his doubts of Gilmour's story as to a blunder having been made. But all the other witnesses who knew the two men, including his sister, spoke so warmly of the years of uninterrupted friendliness between them that he did not make the impression which he obviously hoped to do.

And, very fortunately for Gilmour, a very eminent Cambridge don, a friend of the dead man's, told of an incident which had happened only this last Easter on Scawfell. Ingram and Gilmour had tried a rather hazardous cross cut, Ingram had slipped to a narrow ledge and lay unconscious. Gilmour had reached him with some difficulty, and sat between him and the precipice, signaling and calling for help. The Cambridge master had been out, too, with some friends, and had heard the cries.

Ingram had been rescued, and after a day in bed was none the worse for an adventure which, but for Gilmour, might have turned into a tragedy. This piece of evidence flattened out any effect made by Frederick.

As for Winnie Pratt, she gave Gilmour an impassioned testimonial which secretly roused him to feelings little short of homicidal, and even Moy bit his lips nervously. But Winnie was only questioned for a moment, she could give no evidence of any fresh kind. Miss Longstaff was not called.

The weapon was produced, the man who sold the blank cartridges showed how next to impossible it would have been for the suppliers to have made a mistake in a box labeled "Blank Cartridges." The police put in the two sheets each with a hole in it, one near the hem, one a good fifteen inches from the edge. Gilmour gave his version of what had happened and explained the substitution of a faked sheet for the real one as an idea of some member of the house party fond of a dramatic incident, who wanted to see how the police would come at the truth. Here his glance fell on Winnie Pratt, who smiled gently and encouragingly back at him.

The police themselves offered no objection to this theory. The coroner summed up in a way certainly not hostile to Gilmour, the jury went further, and brought in a verdict of death by misadventure, expressing their sympathy with the sister of the dead man, and with his friend, the unfortunate firer of the fatal shot. They put in a rider as to the danger of practical jokes, and the likelihood of them having unforeseen consequences.

"I congratulate you," Moy said warmly to Gilmour as they left the coroner's court together. Gilmour looked at him.

"Would you like to have to sit down under a verdict of Not Proven?" he asked quietly. "Would you let the woman you love think you a murderer?"

"How can she think it! What motive ——" Moy said again, almost impatiently.

"Miss Pratt has represented me as being secretly devoted to her own fair self, and only faithful to Alfreda because I thought I owed it to her." Gilmour spoke bitterly. "I knew something had poisoned her mind when she came up to town-it's all that wretched girl's doing. Alfreda loved me sincerely, down at Bispham. I gave her, as well as myself, time to be sure of our feelings and went down there and got her to come and stay with us. I noticed a slight change then...a coldness, a sort of indifference...I thought she was vexed that I had gone away, but I think now that she had heard something about the beautiful Winnie being here. At any rate, the girl who turned up next day for lunch was no more my bright, amusing Alfreda, best of companions, cheeriest of comrades, than it was a Dutchman. She had been 'got at.' In other words, she thinks she has reason to be jealous, and a jealous girl is never at her best." Gilmour finished with a sigh. "She'll come round of course," he added, "but when-how ——" and he fell silent.

Moy said nothing. He had told the police, but not Gilmour, of the meeting in the linen room this morning. What was Frederick Ingram doing in there with Alfreda Longstaff?

The assistant commissioner had been present too-unofficially-at the inquest. He was discussing it with Pointer as they drove away.

"I rather hoped to find out who was Gilmour's and Ingram's enemy," Pelham said, lighting up, "for if the man's telling the truth, and he made a truthful impression, he has an enemy and a bitter one! Personally, apart from the impression made on me, his absence of any sort of a good yarn to account for that first sheet sounds like an honest man. You've been delving deep into Ingram's past. Have you found out any peculiarities? Moy speaks as though it were the plain and level high road."

"There's one odd thing," Pointer said. "Moy doesn't seem to know about it. How did Ingram manage to change the eight thousand odd his father left him, after death duties were paid, into thirty thousand odd? For that's the sum he has left behind him. Allowing for the rise in the securities his father left him, and the ones he himself has put his money into-and he seems to have chosen well-that still leaves the fact of eight thousand pounds turned into thirty."

"Fact? Call it a miracle these days," Pelham said wistfully.

"He went in chiefly for gold shares," Pointer said.

"Well, that does explain the miracle a little. Still, even so, I wish I had taken him as my financial adviser!" Pelham spoke enviously now. "Or is this where the counterfeit half-crowns come in? Blackwell will be still more on his toes when he hears this. He's still hoping to be able to find in Ingram the devilish schemer, the secret head of all coiners who, according to him, really exists somewhere in Europe or America." Pointer was silent for a moment, then he said, half to himself:

"Faces mislead, of course, as I'm the first to acknowledge, but generally because they're only looked at as features, as it were, two-dimensionally —breadth and height-but depth is in Ingram's face too. If ever a dead face looked like that of an upright, honorable man it is the face of the 'ghost' at The Tall House. Fastidiously honorable, I should say, unbendably upright."

"That's his reputation," Pelham said. "Everyone seems to agree on that. But how he turned that eight into thirty..." Pelham lost himself in financial speculation.

"He regularly, every quarter, these last five years has had his stockbrokers send in to his bank securities to the total of roughly a thousand pounds. He has spent for some six years exactly four hundred a year on himself-one hundred every quarter. His scholastic books seem to've brought him that and a bit more. His father's capital constantly turned over very much to its increase, and this strange thousand pounds every quarter of the last five years, also well invested and frequently changed, makes up the rest."

"What do his stockbrokers say? Who are they?"

"Cash and Weirdale."

"I know them. Good but old-fashioned. Nothing dubious would pass them, I think. What do they say about the thousand pounds a quarter? Was it sent them by check in the usual way on Settling Day-or paid in by half-crowns?" Pelham finished with a smile.

"Neither, sir. Mr. Ingram would personally drop in every quarter day, quite irrespective of whether it was End Account or Buying for New Time, and hand over personally ten packets of one-hundred pound notes."

"'Forgeries?' asks Chief Inspector Blackwell at that point in the story," Pelham said with interest.

"No, sir. Not as far as we know. The firm had had dealings with Mr. Ingram for years or they would have refused such a way of dealing, but in his case, of course, they accepted it as a quaint bit of oddity."

"Very quaint, and most uncommonly odd!" agreed Pelham. "A thousand pounds every quarter day...is it possible we have here that never-yet-seen-in-the-flesh character, the gambler with a certain System which consistently wins?"

"I thought of that, sir," Pointer said.

"You would!" Pelham spoke in a resigned tone. "Well?"

Pointer laughed. "Well, sir, we sent his picture to all the big gambling resorts and he's definitely not known there. Nor has he ever been away for long from his flat or house. But there is a roulette table, old and dusty, in his rooms in a cupboard, snowed under, and not been used for at least a year. But there it is. For what it's worth."

"Do you think it's worth anything?" Pelham asked, cocking an eye at him.

"It may be some legacy of Fred Ingram's, sir. But I confess it's odd...Yet against the gambling idea, apart from no hint of it ever having been whispered about him, as far as we know, is the fact that he only paid in, never out from, his account any largish sums."

"Looks like the half-crowns," Pelham murmured in jest.

"It's a case with many possibilities," Pointer agreed. "That possible encounter with the masked man after the post-office robbery —"

"Mrs. Appleton looks twenty years older," Pelham said suddenly, "yet she and her brother didn't see much of each other these latter years, and if Gilmour's story is true, she would consider that he died as the result of a sheer accident. You said she looked vastly relieved when Gilmour told her exactly what happened."

"She did. But as you say, sir, she didn't look relieved today at the inquest."

"Has she been searching the library too?"

"Not since her one search. But I told her that we wondered whether any visitor had been in Mr. Ingram's bedroom last night, and she promptly made an excuse and slipped in there-unobserved, as she fancied. Again she emptied all the cigarette ash out of the window."

"Was there any? I thought Ingram didn't smoke cigarettes."

"There was some left in a couple of ash trays," Pointer said with a faint smile, "just to test Mrs. Appleton."

"You think she's afraid someone was there last night? Appleton or Fred Ingram?"

"Her relations with her half-brother seem very cool, sir. Nor can I think she would have looked so immensely relieved if he had been in her mind —I mean when she first heard of how her brother was actually killed. It looked to me, and still does, as though she feared that someone very near to her had had a hand in that killing."

"Which means her husband?" Pelham asked.

"Yes, sir."

"And you think she thought he might have left something compromising, identifying, behind him?"

"I think so, sirs. But the curious thing is she didn't know what to look for, nor where. Odd, if her husband really had spent the night at Markham Square as she says. Anyway, it looks as though she knew of the existence of a motive...and knows that her husband was not where she says he was, at home and in bed at one o'clock last night."

"All four women then stand for larger or smaller mysteries in this case. The two elder women as well as the two girls."

"Mrs. Appleton seemed oddly disturbed when Moy told her just now —I was present-of the amount of her brother's fortune. I couldn't say it was alarm, but it certainly was not pleasure, when she heard the unexpectedly large sum he has left behind him." Pointer was looking at his shoe-tips, deep in thought.

"Well, that is odd!" Pelham said frankly.

"Moy has told me something that rather alters things," Pointer went on. "By their marriage settlements she and Appleton agreed to go halves in any legacy left them. There was a wealthy great uncle of both who was expected to leave one or other his money. He did, to Appleton, who quietly wriggled out of paying over the half to his wife until he had spent it all. But the settlement wasn't changed. So Appleton is really a co-heir with his wife, though it's only a question of the interest on the money, which goes intact to the children."

Pelham smoked thoughtfully without making any comment. They were back at the Yard by this time, in the assistant commissioner's room. He reached for a book behind him and opened it at a page which he had marked with a slip.

"I bought this at an auction last week. It's an old work on crime by Luigi Pinna, translated by some contemporary. There's a delightful passage which puts the case beautifully, and in words of one syllable. Listen: 'In numerous cases the sole difference between success and failure in the detection of crime is a sort of osmotic mental reluctance to seep through the cilia of what seems to be and reach the vital stream of what actually is.' How do you propose to seep through the cilia, Pointer?"

"Well, sir, it sounds rather odd. But I want to have all disappearances during the last three months to six months in, or near, London looked up. I'm only interested in solitary people-men or women-preferably odd looking. No dwarfs wanted, nor giants, nor very thin people..."

"What in the name of Minerva are you up to?" the A. C. asked. "Disappearances and Ingram's death? How are they linked?"

"I hope you won't press that question, sir. I would be very grateful if I needn't answer it at this stage. I may be quite wrong. It's just a possibility..."

"The classic answer of the gifted sleuth," Pelham murmured good humoredly. "The dark curtains being drawn before they part with a bang and the lights go up, while the audience cheers, eh?"

"I wish I could feel certain of that last part, sir. What if the lights refuse to go up, and the audience laughs instead? But seriously, there is just a possibility which has been in my mind from the beginning...if I can find what I'm feeling for, it would lead straight to the solution of the puzzle."

"And to the motive at the same time?" Pelham asked. Pointer shook his head.

"Not necessarily, sir, but it would lead to the criminal-if it leads anywhere."

"Humph...well, I'll let you answer my questions at your own convenience then. But as to motive...no ideas at all?"

"I can't think of anything that will fit the case, sir. And I assure you, it's not due to osmotic mental reluctance."

Pointer laughed. "I've been trying to find out if Mr. Ingram went in for crossword competitions. It would be odd to win so regularly, but he has brains that would lend themselves to that sort of thing, one would think.

"It seems, however, that he particularly disliked them. Mrs. Appleton told me that if the children started asking 'what word of four letters means feeble,' or 'one of seven means dashed hopes,' and so on...he would fly, and everyone else tells me the same thing."

"Looks like ciphers," Pelham said, serious again. "Big business firms will pay anything you like for unreadable ciphers, or for help in solving those stolen or intercepted from rival firms. And of course there still remains government ciphers and Mrs. Pratt's one-time maid, you know..."

"And her husband who fell overboard..." Pointer finished. "I've looked up the record of that. Apparently Mr. Pratt was really out on deck by himself when he fell over."

"It's a subtle crime," Pelham said after a moment's silence. "This of Ingram's death. And clever. To get another man to do your shooting for you is really good. The curious thing was that change in the sheets..."

"Very," Pointer agreed. "It paid us such a compliment. Most of the people one meets seem to think a detective can't see things unless he stumbles over them."

"I never heard anyone who ever met you, let alone saw you at work, speak of that as one of your failings," Pelham murmured.

"Still, sir, it was a compliment to us to feel so sure that we would notice the wrong placing of that hole, if done purposely..."

CHAPTER 12

ABOUT an hour after the inquest, Moy got a message that Mrs. Appleton would like to speak to him on the telephone.

"Do come round to see me as soon as you can," she begged. "I'm thinking about Mr. Gilmour. It's a dreadful position for him. I'm staying at my brother's flat at Harrow for the present, as you know, but I shall be at Markham Square all the afternoon."

When Moy went round, as he did at once, he found to his surprise that Tark was in the little drawing-room talking to a rather distrait-looking hostess. As Moy was shown in, Tark said that he would wait until Moy had finished, and go back with him, if he might, as there was something that he wanted to talk to the solicitor about.

Mrs. Appleton gave a nod that suggested inattention more than agreement, and Tark stepped out into the little passage, and Moy heard him opening and then closing a door farther down on the same side. The door of Appleton's den. So he could find his way about the house...Moy had thought that he did not know Ingram's sister or brother-in-law...but Moy dropped Tark, and what he might have to say to him, and devoted himself to Mrs. Appleton.

She had been deeply moved, she said, by the look of suffering in Gilmour's face and she had just heard that Miss Longstaff had broken with him.

"I don't know that there's anything one can do, Mrs. Appleton," Moy said rather hopelessly. "I quite agree with you, it's awful for him, but how to help him is another matter."

"I can't bear the situation!" she said suddenly to that. "It's an intolerable one for me, Charles's sister!"

So it was not for Gilmour that she wanted to see him after all, Moy thought.

"You know, I've been wondering whether some one couldn't have shot Charles over Lawrence Gilmour's shoulder, just as he fired the blank cartridge..." She looked very white and very tense as she said this. "I mean, Mr. Gilmour may be right in thinking he fired a blank shot, and yet Charles may have been shot dead-but by someone else."

"I've thought of the same possibility myself," Moy said, "but it seems so far-fetched. Besides, it would mean that someone was in Gilmour's room, unknown to him, who fired through the open door at the exact second that Gilmour did."

"Well? He would lift his arm to fire. There would be plenty of time to know when he was going to pull the trigger." Her voice sounded harsh, as though her throat were dry. "Mind you," she went on hastily, "I wouldn't say this to the police for worlds. Nor have them know I ever thought it." Her vehemence told Moy that her nerves must be frightfully on edge. "But as you're our friend-friend to all three of us, Charles, Edward, Gilmour and to me —I know I can talk things over with you without fear of consequences."

Moy assured her that she could. But he looked at her a trifle oddly.

"As Gilmour thinks that he was alone," he went on, "your idea would mean that some one hid in his room and stepped out just as he himself stood in the doorway with the door open, and while your brother was walking away down the passage."

"Well," she said, "there is a built-in cupboard just by the fireplace exactly opposite to the door. It's not used. The room is carpeted from wall to wall."

"True," Moy said slowly, "he wouldn't have had even to step out, just swing the cupboard door wide open...counting on the fact that when Charles fell Gilmour would rush forward and leave the bedroom door open...but I think I should have seen him..."

"You too rushed to Charles's side. And were trying to find a switch that would work," she said under her breath, her eyes wide and dark.

It was true. He had paid no attention to the rest of the passage except to the white mound on the floor outside Ingram's room half-way down.

"That would mean that your supposed murderer was a good deal taller than Gilmour-which might easily be, for he's short-or have stood on a hassock."

"There is a hassock in that room, a huge leather one." She twisted her fingers tightly together on her knee.

"He'd have to be a crack shot, as well as a particularly callous brute," Moy finished hotly. Mrs. Appleton kept her eyes fastened on her tightly clenched hands. "Yes," she said so low that he barely caught it. "Or have been mad."

"Mad! No madness in such a plan!" he retorted almost reprovingly.

"But madness is wanting a fortune at any cost-at any price!" she finished still under her breath.

"But how would Ingram's death have given —" Moy stopped, and suddenly he saw what all this meant. The woman's white face, the horror in her dilated eyes...So Appleton had not been at home last night. The alibi that she had given was false. She suspected her husband of having murdered her brother...a horrible position. But she had nothing to go on, surely...Of course Appleton was a splendid shot. He got many an invitation on that account in the autumn, and he was just the right height to have fired over Gilmour's shoulder, or even over his head, at Ingram...But he wouldn't know about that cupboard. Appleton had never been upstairs in The Tall House. Besides, he couldn't be sure that his wife would still inherit under her brother's will, though it wouldn't be like Ingram to change his will without letting Mrs. Appleton know...Where was Appleton, by the way? He had not seen him except for a few minutes at the inquest. Moy remembered now that he had come in after his wife and sat down some distance away. Near the door.

"You didn't see anything that bears out my fantastic idea?" she said, looking at him with tragic eyes. "I mean, now, thinking back?"

He assured her that as he had just said, he thought the idea not easily credible, but was not prepared to say it was quite impossible.

"Then-then" —he saw her pass her tongue across her lips —"if not impossible, it must be looked into. I mean it's our duty to do so. For Charles's sake, and above all for Lawrence Gilmour's sake! I can't imagine anything more horrible to Charles than to have his friend suffer for something that he never did."

"One has to think these things over very carefully, Mrs. Appleton," Moy began. She flashed him an almost scathing look.

"Do you suppose I've thought of much else since-it first occurred to me as a possibility," she said. "I hoped, I thought that Mr. Gilmour might quite clear himself—I mean..." She stopped and then went on with another sentence. "Friends talking on the way home showed me that because of that article about the sheet with the hole in the wrong place he's by no means cleared. Who could have written it? It seems so motiveless. Just to throw a wicked suspicion on him and not to carry it any further. It couldn't be just a newspaper idea, could it? To help their sales?"

Now Moy himself was rather thinking along those lines. Had he known of any person belonging to that particular paper being at The Tall House he would have thought of it much sooner. But this smaller mystery sank into insignificance besides the one concerning her husband...He must ask after him in common decency...He rose and murmured something about her having given him a great deal to think over, and the necessity of great care in such matters. He supposed Appleton was out? And hoped she, the children were well. Moy ran it all together in a sort of vague mist of good hopes. She did not reply to his words.

"I'm going away for a long voyage with the children." She seemed to be already far away. "That's why I had this talk with you. You will know just what to do about everything."

Moy did not in the least share her confidence in his universal knowledge. He could imagine few more perplexing positions. Any careless move on his part, one incautious word, and the two Appleton children would or might, be in the position of the children of a suspected murderer. How could he help Gilmour without harming them-Ingram's little nephews? He left the house feeling as though a weight too heavy for him had been suddenly thrust on him. He had completely forgotten Tark and any talk with him. But that gentleman did not seem to mind being forgotten. He had drawn up an easy chair to the window and sat looking through the lace curtains, smoking a cigar, and now and then entering figures in his note-book as Moy had so often seen him doing. He put it in his pocket as Appleton passed the window. A minute later the master of the house came in. Tark waited until he had closed the door of the little room, before he rose from his deep easy-chair. Appleton swung round with an exclamation as he saw his guest.

"How did you get in? I had no idea —"

"You have been out each time that I asked for you before. Now then, Appleton, what's your best offer?"

The two faced each other in silence. A long silence. Appleton's forehead and lips began to twitch.

"I don't understand you," he said at length.

"I think you do. Which is why you've refused to be in whenever I've 'phoned. Now then, what's your best offer?"

"I don't understand you," Appleton repeated. He tried to speak defiantly, but his voice suggested a bleat.

"Try a little harder," suggested Tark with a sardonic smile, "for I don't want to go into details. I don't want to know them. I'm quite willing that you should enjoy what you've run such risks to get."

"I haven't run any risks. I haven't got hold of anything!" came from Appleton fiercely. Tark waved him away with his hand as though he were a smoke ring.

"I'm quite willing, as I say, not to start any unpleasant inquiries, provided you give me a written understanding that we go shares in your-we'll call it 'purchase.' Fifty-fifty, Appleton. Come now!"

"You're mad!" came angrily from Appleton, whose eyebrows were going up and down like some sign in a window. "Mad! Fifty-fifty? For what?"

Tark came quite close. "For your neck, Appleton. Fifty per cent is none too high for that, and I mean to have that promise. Or hand you over to the police. I know you've got the-information —I want. And I know how you got it. And if the police knew the first fact, they too would know the second. At present, they're hunting for a motive. One word from me, Appleton, one word as to what I expected them to find among Ingram's papers, and what becomes of you? You with your double motive, that paper, and Ingram's will?"

"You're all wrong! All wrong!" Appleton said hotly. "He gave me the paper. Handed it to me as a free gift."

Tark's short, low, sneering laugh was his answer to that last assertion.

"Your wife feels as sure of that as I do," he said. "It's true!" flamed out Appleton suddenly. "Damn you, it's true! She's been talking to you, has she!"

Tark eyed him with the intent, unmoved, watching gaze of a man accustomed to use his fellow-men, to make the most of any opportunity that came his way.

"No matter how I learned about it," he said briefly, "I do know, that's enough. Now then, what about the offer in writing for which I'm here, to be left behind when we set off for foreign parts? Just in case history should repeat itself, eh? Just you and me on a trip together-Fred Ingram is still hunting."

Chief Inspector Pointer had taken the bus ticket to the head office. There they told him that it had been punched late on the evening on which Ingram had been shot, and was for the distance from before Markham Square to a little beyond the street in which was The Tall House. He was now for the first time able to see the ticket collector who had been on duty at the time. Pointer reminded him that it was the night of the heat wave, one of the hottest nights in England for the last fifty years. The man remembered it perfectly. He had only had one passenger inside. A tall chap with a twitchy face. He remembered him, because he had jumped off the bus so hastily on catching sight of a friend on the pavement that he had all but fallen headlong in the road. The conductor had steadied him.

"Did you see his friend? The man on the pavement?"

"He was just turning a corner. Couldn't catch sight of his face."

So that Appleton, for the description fitted him, must have known the man quite well to have recognized him from that glimpse.

"Was your fare any of these?" Pointer laid some photographs before the man.

"That's him!" The collector touched Appleton's picture. "He's often up and down our way. Lives along there."

He had not seen him in company with any of the other faces shown him. Did he see the actual meeting between the passenger and the man on the pavement? "A bit of it." His fare had hurried after the other man, overtaken him, and caught hold of his elbow. They seemed quite friendly. At least the other had not snatched his arm away. Pointer further learned that the pedestrian might well have been Ingram, though this was purely negative, inasmuch as the man had not been old, nor big, nor fat...

Pointer next went on to see Appleton, and that was how he came to send in his name just as Tark was putting a folded paper away in his letter-case while Appleton stood watching him with a face of fury. Tark shot a swift glance around as the maid entered with "a gentleman to see you, sir," and held out Pointer's card.

"I'll go out that way," Tark breathed in the other's ear, and made for the double door leading into some other room. Appleton detained the maid.

"When you've shown, the gentleman in, show this other out. Be sure he goes at once."

Pointer looked very grave and very stiff.

"Mr. Appleton, why have you not told us that you walked back to The Tall House with Mr. Ingram the night on which he was shot? That you had a talk with him in the library there." This was guess work, due to the ticket, and Mrs. Appleton's interest in cigarette ash. Appleton was smoking a very peculiar Greek brand of cigarette.

"For the very good reason that I did none of these things," Appleton said sharply. His twitchy face was absolutely still as he turned it to the other. Pointer felt as though it were held so rigid that a finger pressed against the cheek would not even make a dent.

"You were recognized," he said warningly.

"I couldn't have been, since I wasn't there," Appleton tossed back in as firm a voice. "What you mean, chief inspector, is that someone thought he recognized me. He made a mistake. I often did drop in for a chat with my brother-in-law, but not as it happens on that evening." He drummed on the table. His fidgets began to come back, now that the strain for which he had pulled himself together had gone, or lessened.

"Pity," Pointer said thoughtfully. "You might have been able to help us. Supposing Mr. Ingram's death was not accident, can't you suggest anything, Mr. Appleton, which might have been a motive for his murder?"

Again the face stiffened, grew still and set.

"His work, for instance," Pointer went on, not apparently glancing at the other man, "or something connected with his writing."

Appleton was quite pale, but he shook his head. He sat down in a chair so hastily that it looked as though he fell into it.

"The inquest has just decided that it was death by misadventure," he said in a curiously halting voice. "I don't pretend, chief inspector, that I think things don't look odd...anyone could have tampered with that revolver, as I've said from the beginning." He shot an odd, sly look at the chief inspector, sly and yet determined. "I don't pretend to agree with the finding of the inquest," he said again. "I'm glad you're looking into the matter." He did not look glad, but he did look oddly persistent and haunted.

"Yes, I have a horrid sort of fear that perhaps it wasn't an accident," he went on. "I had intended to say nothing about such a possibility, but-well-somehow I feel it would be letting

Ingram down. I have an idea he had some cipher or other of great potential value, and that he was murdered for that..." Appleton threw out his chest and pulled himself in until he looked like a majestic pouter pigeon. His dark, large, flat eyes fastened themselves on the chief inspector's face. "Don't you think yourself, chief inspector, that there's something odd about the affair?" he asked.

"It's quite an idea," Pointer replied evasively, and as though much struck by its novelty. "But can't you suggest what sort of a cipher...where we ought to look for the criminal if there is one?"

No. Appleton assured him that he had only a vague uneasiness that things were not right, but that he had no idea as to who could possibly want to murder his brother-in-law.

"Of course if it was a cipher," Pointer murmured, as though confiding in his cigarette-one of Ingram's —"one wonders whether his proof-reader wouldn't know something about it..."

Appleton drew in a quick breath, his eyes bulged for a moment but he said nothing, only tapped the knuckle of his first finger reflectively against his teeth, which gave him an odd appearance of uneasiness.

"Possible," he muttered. "That's really what I wondered. Whether...it's a ghastly idea, suspecting this person and that, but if it was anything to do with his papers, why of course Frederick Ingram would be by way of knowing about it..."

Appleton leaned forward, one hand on the table, a white, well-kept hand but thin and hollow-sinewed; the hand of a man who was really very ill.

"It's ghastly for everyone," he went on in a tired voice, "I mean anyone who also feels uneasy, not to know who did it. But in confidence, chief inspector, I think you ought to keep an eye on him-and on Tark," he added vindictively and suddenly.

"I thought you were doing that," Pointer said innocently.

Appleton turned very gray. "Tark? I, or no, he...I...no, I hardly know him," he murmured.

"Yet you correspond..." Pointer seemed puzzled. "I may as well tell you that I saw a letter from you to him —" So Pointer had, but in Tark's letter-case. Appleton had a very odd writing, rather beflourished and with exaggerated capitals.

"Oh, merely a reply to a question that came up once at The Tall House," Appleton said swiftly. "We were discussing some question of engine power of the new little B.S.A. cars, you know the ones with the fluid Daimler drive, and I stated definitely some figure which surprised Tark. When I got home I found that I had misread a statement of the B.S.A. Co. chairman's, and wrote putting right my mistake." His fiat eyes flitted nervously across the other's impassive face. Pointer could not tell him he was a liar. It was a possible explanation but Tark hardly looked the kind of man to carry such a letter around with him. And the envelope that Pointer had seen in his case was quite well worn.

When Pointer left, together with Appleton's cigarette, he knew that Appleton had been to The Tall House for some reason-after some object-that he could not, or would not, avow. That search of Mrs. Appleton's for some paper or papers...it looked to Pointer as though her husband had got it, or them, since he himself made no effort to rummage among Ingram's belongings. But Tark had done so, and Tark had been followed to this house, and had been heard several times asking for Appleton over the 'phone. He knew that he was in the house when he himself had arrived. Pointer's watcher had told the chief inspector that Tark had come quite openly. Was that because he had to? Because Appleton would not meet him outside? Pointer would learn with interest whether Tark now discontinued his search or not. From the look of purple fury on Appleton's face, he, Pointer, would not be surprised if Tark had got the better of the other in some battle of wits or wills or threats. The question was-even supposing that Appleton had got some document for which the other, and possibly his wife too, had been looking-did it stand for anything in Ingram's death? Mrs. Appleton had shown plainly enough, Pointer thought, that she suspected something of the kind She had left Markham Square at once after the tragedy and gone, with her two little boys, to her dead brother's flat at Harrow, merely notifying Gilmour of the fact after she had installed herself, saying that the children needed fresher air than they were having in Chelsea and that she would see to it that they did not overflow into his rooms. Gilmour had assured her that the entire flat was at her disposal for as long as she would like to stay there.

Mrs. Appleton's face and manner quite negatived-to Pointer-the idea that she had come on some clue pointing to her husband which she had suppressed, and that her husband felt himself safe for that reason. Appleton did not look as though he felt himself safe. Quite the contrary. Appleton looked a man living in the shadow of some fear, but Pointer thought that the fear was a definite, not a vague one. There were parts of his path in which he felt himself quite safe, and parts where he inwardly trembled, so the chief inspector, an unusually astute and penetrating observer, read the man. Tark disclaimed all knowledge of Appleton, as Appleton did of him. Appleton had traveled a good deal...gambled a good deal...Tark lived near Monte Carlo...Mrs. Pratt came from Geneva...VON OF DE which the expert still claimed was part of a cipher...Mrs. Pratt had once had a maid who was an international spy...HELL LIGHT CLAIRE...The tobacco shreds under the pillow, and yet Ingram's waistcoat, empty of everything that could interest anyone, lying on his chair. The inner secret pocket with its fastening...Did they all belong together, or were they but shattered bits of many circles? He was thinking them over as he left Appleton, left without any inquiry as to Tark. Let Appleton think himself unobserved, his next step in that case might be a helpful one as to settling his own status in the death of his brother-in-law.

CHAPTER 13

WHEN the chief inspector had left him, Appleton fell back into a chair looking as though he were half-fainting. For a long minute he lay passive, breathing hard, then he got better, and sitting up, dived into an inner pocket of his waistcoat, a pocket rather on the style of his dead brother-in-law's. From it he drew an envelope of oiled silk, such as is used by travelers to carry soap. From it he took another envelope and from this a paper covered with minute but very legible figures and writing.

He bent over it. So engrossed was he that he did not hear a light step come into the hall. After a minute his study door was opened, and his wife came in carrying some flowers in her hand. She turned with a start. So did he. The paper slid from his knee. In an instant she and he both swooped on it. He, being nearer, got it first. She turned, her face a dreadful, livid white, and, with her hand outstretched before her as though suddenly stricken blind, made for the door. But, again, he got there first.

He drew himself up, hand on knob, and thrust out his chest in his pouter pigeon attitude. "Ada!" came in round sonorous tones. "What do you mean by looking at me like that?"

"I think I knew all along," she said under her breath, her eyes now half-closed. "And because of the children, I have to stand by and do nothing. As you knew that I would!"

"Charles gave it me," Appleton said to that, "he gave it me himself."

She made a gesture of incredulity and despair, and seemed to walk through him as white fire will cut through any opposition.

Tark, meanwhile, had left the house in Markham Square immediately the chief inspector arrived, and returned to The Tall House. He was leaving that same afternoon, he said.

Now that the inquest was over, the household was fleeing as though from a plague spot. Miss Longstaff asked for a word with him. She began about the inquest first, which she had not attended, then suddenly looked at him with that odd stare of hers.

"Mr. Tark, I have a conviction that you know the motive for Mr. Ingram's death."

He returned her stare with one as unreadable.

"You frighten me," he said, his tight lips hardly moving. "Next thing, you'll be accusing me of having caused his death. The inquest brought it in as 'Death by Misadventure,' you know."

"You were hunting all yesterday on the quiet," she went on as though he had not spoken, "for something definite, too. A paper of some sort. Look here, why not take me in as a helper? I'm desperately keen on solving this crime-if it was a crime."

"You evidently think it was, from the position you've taken up with regard to Gilmour," he replied indifferently. And his indifference was real. This man did not care whether Ingram had been shot by accident or of deliberate intention. She saw that.

"It's the only possible position until things are clear," she retorted, but without heat. "Come, Mr. Tark, why not let us work together?"

There was open derision now in his unmerry smile that for a second just loosened those closed lips of his. "I'm afraid I shall not be able to help." There was no attempt at concealment of the mockery in his tone. "I'm leaving for my home tonight."

"Is Mr. Haliburton going with you?" she asked.

"Possibly. Possibly not. We occasionally leave each other's side, Miss Longstaff. May I ask you why you thought he might be coming with me? Did you think Miss Pratt and I were eloping, and he would want to be the third?" The man's manner was courteous enough, however jeering his tone, or his words. He held the door open for her with almost a bow as she walked towards it. Miss Longstaff looked at him, but not even the chief inspector could read that face above hers, except that he now showed intentionally a sardonic amusement at her effort to read it. He said good-by, still in the same key, and then went in search of Haliburton. That young man was pacing to and fro in the drawing-room, evidently on the watch for Miss Pratt. He looked up hopefully at Tark's light footfall, a step almost inaudible even on creaky parquet.

"Oh!" he said lamely, and again Tark permitted two lines to crease each side of his mouth.

"I'm saying good-by." He came in. "I'm going back home tonight. This sun makes me long for the real thing."

Haliburton nodded. He was not paying much attention.

"Who would have thought that she would take it like this!" he burst out suddenly. Anyone less suitable as a confidant for love's vaporings could not be imagined than the leather-faced Tark, but he only nodded.

"You never know how the cards will run," he murmured. "By the way, Haliburton, care to make a speculative investment? 'Big Profits probable, Small Loss possible' sort of thing?"

"What do you mean by big profits?" Haliburton spoke as though a trifle bored.

"Four hundred per cent." Tark's voice was low. "This is entirely confidential, mind you. Even the offer, I mean. Even the existence of the offer. But if you like to let me have five hundred, I can promise you two thousand in three months' time, to the day."

"You can have the five hundred," Haliburton said after a moment's thought. "But as a personal loan. To be used in any way you like. And I want no interest on it."

"Thanks," Tark said briefly. "But you've missed a chance. As a matter of fact, I wouldn't have made the offer to anyone but you."

As is human nature, when the offer was not pressed, it tempted more.

"Then you did have your talk with Ingram?" Haliburton asked. "You told me that if it was successful you'd have a magnificent proposition to offer a friend."

"It turned out not to be necessary," Tark said, and for a second a corner of his lifted lip showed his teeth.

"Well, good-by then, and thank you for getting me in here as a guest."

"I'm afraid that's hardly a pleasant experience." Haliburton did not smile. "Well, come in before you go. I'll have my check ready for you. Unless you would rather have it in notes?"

"I would rather," Tark said.

Haliburton replied that in that case he would go round to his bank of which a branch was very near and cash a check himself.

Again Tark said that he would prefer it like that. "Best of wishes about Miss Pratt," he said as he moved to the door again.

Haliburton's face looked sad. "It's no use, Tark, she's bewitched. She's entirely wrapped up in pity for Gilmour."

"Who wants none of it," Tark finished callously, "and I'd give you back a fiver to know why."

"Why what?" Haliburton looked like a man holding himself in with difficulty, who has resolved, however, to pretend to feel no pricks.

"Why he won't have her pity. What he sees in that Longstaff girl. There's a crabbed filly, for you. She'd love to see him hang. Well, she may yet." And after this, for him, amazingly long speech, Tark went upstairs, and rang for his suitcases to be packed. That done, he went in search of Gilmour for a last word. But Gilmour was out. He was in Moy's office, and that was the reason the solicitor had not stayed longer with Mrs. Appleton. Just now the two young fellows were both looking tremendously stirred up. Gilmour was speaking.

"I appreciate your reason for trying to dissuade me, Moy, but I've stumbled on something very odd...You know, I've been certain that Ingram died just as I described it. But—" He stopped and seemed to fall into a brown study. Moy stared at him expectantly. "Well?" he asked, as the other said nothing. "Well? Have you told the police about it?"

Gilmour shook his head, and Moy wondered if the clue led to Appleton, for Gilmour was a sort of unofficial uncle to the two Appleton children.

He waited in great anxiety for the next words.

"It's nothing they could deal with," Gilmour said slowly. "It's not a clue-yet. It's only existence-so far-is in someone's recollection of something. Well, they're hardly likely to go all out on such a foundation. But as it happens, a chance word has made me remember something too, that half fits...might fit..." He broke off again.

"Whose was the memory that jogged yours?" Moy asked.

"Miss Longstaff let slip something-oh, she had no idea of any importance in what she said-but it fitted most oddly into something —" and again to Moy's impatience, Gilmour stopped.

"I hope you're going to let me in on whatever it is," Moy said promptly. What could Alfreda Longstaff know? But Gilmour went on to dash his hopes.

"I don't want to talk about it to anyone. But I wish you would take charge of this envelope" — he took one out of his pocket —"and if I don't turn up by this time next week, or you haven't heard from me over the 'phone, I want you to hand it in yourself to Chief Inspector Pointer. Look, it's addressed to him. Now I'll enclose it in this blank one, on which I scribble your name." Gilmour proceeded to do so. "Have you a candle and some wax?" Moy had. Gilmour sealed the covering envelope and handed it to the other. "Everything is in that. It tells what I'm after, and why. But for heavens' sake don't let any one read it unless I don't come back, for I'm quite frank in it, and say precisely to whom my information points. Someone who may be perfectly innocent."

"Well, if you don't come back, the likelihood is that they aren't innocent," Moy said reasonably enough.

"By God!" Gilmour spoke in a tone of passion that startled the other, "I'd be willing enough not to come back, if that would be a help!"

Then his voice became calm once more. "I want you to explain to Miss Longstaff tomorrow." He looked at Moy with rather a hangdog look. "You know, I think it's very fine of her, I mean, not being willing to marry a man whom she thinks capable of murdering his friend. That she does think me that, isn't her fault. I know whose tongue has dropped sweet poison into her ears! But about Alfreda, there aren't too many standards in the world, and it's up to the women, the young women, as I see it, to keep their flags flying."

"Unless like Miss Pratt they believe you incapable of murder," Moy said to that. "Frankly, since you've brought the subject up, I must say that's the attitude I prefer in a girl."

Gilmour was not listening. He was intent on giving the other very careful instructions connected with that letter.

"I said to hand it on, unless you hear from me over the 'phone. Well, I want to arrange with you about that. If you get a message that sounds sensible enough, but as though it referred to something about which you know nothing, then I want you to take it as an S.O.S. and hand that letter on as I asked you just now. What I mean is this: Suppose you hear me-undeniably near the end of the wire saying something like this: 'Fraid I shan't be able to come down with you to the Smiths' cocktail party tonight' or 'You'll have to count me out for the box I promised to share' or any other excuse about my not being able to be, or go, somewhere of which we've never spoken, then you'll understand that it's an appeal for the Yard's help. You see, if I were in a tight place, I might spoof the people who had me there into letting me telephone you some perfectly innocent sounding excuse as to why I couldn't turn up with you, but, as I say, you'll know what it really means, and will act at once."

They discussed it for fully another minute. Moy rather shrank from such a frightful responsibility, but apparently it was the best thing that Gilmour could arrange in his own protection, flimsy though it seemed to Moy. He begged Gilmour to be more open with him. Gilmour thought it over for a while, then shook his head.

"I think it would only arouse suspicion. But I'll tell you this: I shouldn't be surprised if I had to leave England to follow the clue I'm after, or rather to get hold of it. More than that I can't say. But I assure you you couldn't help half as much by knowing what I'm going to try to do, as you will by sitting on that letter. I may not need it, in which case when I'm back I'll either ask for it again and burn it, or let you open and read it. But should I be on the right track, and should that track lead me into a hole, it'll be a wonderfully pleasant thought to know that you have it and will pass it on at a word from me. No, I won't say more. And I won't even tell you how I mean to make what the Hollywood films call my getaway. Which is a pity. For I'm fearfully proud of it-my plan, I mean. But you'd much better know nothing."

In that much Moy agreed with him.

"You won't get clear," he said confidently, and warningly, "and for your own sake, as I've said a dozen times in this interview already, you mustn't try it. We both know you're being watched. Of course you are! You'd never be able to show a clean pair of heels to a Yard man, and the attempt would only be absolutely misunderstood. Seriously misunderstood. And frankly, well, you know yourself you can't afford that! Which is the sole and only reason why I don't insist on coming with you."

Gilmour only gave a little confident laugh. "Wait and see!" was all he said as he finally left the other.

He went back to The Tall House, his head full of his plans. There he asked if Miss Longstaff were in. She was, and he found her in the library putting some books back in their place. It was amazing how popular the library was with three at least of the women connected with The Tall House and two of the men.

"Alfreda, I've come to say good-by —for a little while." Gilmour tried to hold Alfreda's long, rather bony, fingers in his, but she drew them away quite sharply.

"Well, good-by then," was her calm reply. He looked at her in silence for a long minute, rather a pathetic look on his face, helpless and pleading. It softened her for one instant "I wish I knew," he said finally, and quite frankly, "what has changed you so. I thought-once-that you cared for me. I —I —was sure of it."

"Quite so," all softness had gone from Alfreda now, "quite sure of it, as you say! So sure that you thought you could come and collect me any old time like a parcel left to be kept till called for." Her tone was venomous.

"My mistake, I see," he said quietly. "You lived in a little village-we hadn't known each other long. How could you be sure of your own heart-or-or I of mine?"

"Well, we're both sure of our own hearts now," was her reply with a little laugh. "You of yours, and I of mine!"

"I don't believe it!" He spoke warmly now. "No, I refuse to believe it. You're vexed with me. Something has spoiled it all-for the moment, but I'm as sure that you'll yet come to look on all this as a momentary madness as I am of anything in life. And I wish more than I can say, I'm not a clever chap at words, that you'd trust me. And be again as you were those days at Bispham." His voice was very tender. Again for a half second she hesitated. Was she all wrong? Jaundiced? Unfair?

She shook her head. "I can't feel like that-not since what has happened here."

"You really think I had a conscious, intentional hand in that dreadful blunder?" he asked.

She did not reply except by her silence and that unreadable stare of hers fixed unwinkingly on him.

"If that horrible thought is all that stands between us, then I don't think it will stand long." He spoke in a low eager tone. "But I wish you'd be frank with me."

"I don't think you do," she retorted, her chin in the air. "Or if you do, you're mistaken. You wouldn't really wish me to tell you all I think about-us-Mr. Ingram's shooting-everything."

"If you would tell me why you have this awful suspicion," he went on doggedly, "supposing it's really yours and not just suggested to you by someone else then it might help me. Wait!" as she would have spoken, "you said something the other morning-oh, no, if you won't be frank, neither will I be now, which —" He fell silent, gazing out of the window with wide open eyes and a sort of breathless look to his face. He stood like that for a full second before he went on quietly. "Which fits in with something I know which I thought of no use, no importance...but as we're not to be friends-yet —I won't say more. When I can clear myself I shall speak again Alfreda, and again ask you to marry me, and if I'm successful in what I'm going after, I don't think you will refuse me next time. Tell me, if I can clear myself absolutely-undeniably-of any suspicion of having killed Ingram intentionally, your answer would be yes?"

Again, in spite of herself, Alfreda was touched by tone and look, and by his words too. Supposing, just supposing, that her suspicions were all wrong, what an utter beast she had been, was being. She drew a deep breath.

"I don't think you could ever forgive me for acting as I've done," she said in a voice which, for her, was quite faltering, "and I don't think I should care to be forgiven and have to live with my forgiver —" Her smile had real mischief in it for once, "but if you can explain Ingram's death, the puzzle of it all, why, of course, I should be more than glad! More than thankful! But how are you going to set about it? How can you hope to solve this puzzle?"

"I have an idea where to look and what to look for," he said guardedly. "I can't be franker now, but when I reappear, you shall hear everything."

"Oh, you're going to disappear?" The old tone was back now, the old look in her eyes.

"Take that as confidential, please," he spoke almost sternly, "that much at least I have a right to claim from you."

"You have no right to claim anything!" she retorted hotly.

"Oh, yes, I have. That much of loyalty." And his tone shamed her.

She put out her hand swiftly. "I wish I could feel differently. I think I haven't a heart-just a sort of onlooker's interest in life...but I do honestly hope you'll succeed in clearing yourself. Not just because of what I think of you, but for" —she faltered under his steady gaze —"for humanity's sake," she finished almost shamefacedly. And she watched him go with a sudden feeling of ridiculously illogical remorse. Supposing he did-could — —clear himself absolutely, which both knew could only be done by bringing the guilt home to another-how she would feel! How small, how mean, how shriveled of heart.

She was still standing there, lost in thought, when Moy came back from his talk with Mrs. Appleton, and was still standing there when Mrs. Appleton herself was shown in. The butler thought that Moy was in the library. Even in her mood of intense preoccupation Alfreda noticed the look on the other woman's face, and in her eyes, a look of blank despair, of utter misery.

It startled her. Coming just after her talk with Gilmour and his words, it seemed to open a vista to her of something which might be in his mind...but surely she, Alfreda, could not be wrong in what she had hitherto called her intuition about the identity of the real criminal in this case?

Mrs. Appleton barely nodded to her. She wanted a word with Mr. Moy, she said, very urgently. Moy hurried in to the little parlor where she stood nervously playing with her gloves. She refused a chair. She wanted, she said, to see him about her brother's will.

"I want you to arrange for endowing scholarships at Pembroke-that was his college, and he loved it-and perhaps a couple of scholarships at his old school, Clifton, if the money will run to it. I want everything that remains, after putting aside all that may be necessary to safeguard Mr. Gilmour, to be used in one of these two ways or both. I don't want my brother's money. I know he really would have liked to do this himself, and only left me the money because he thought I might need it. I don't."

Moy looked at her in surprise. What a whirlwind way of doing things people seemed to be developing just lately.

"But what about Appleton?" Moy explained to her that, owing to the terms of her marriage settlements, she would have to have her husband's consent to any such proposal. "Not that there's any hurry," he said pleasantly, "you've no idea how long it takes to wind up an estate. And you've got to allow in your mind for the death duties, which will take about..."

He was prepared to go into detail, but she did not want to listen.

"I'm not interested, you see, in his estate," she said finally, "having no need of it —"

"But the children?" Moy knew that only Ingram's help had sent the two boys to the preparatory school at which they were just started.

"They won't need it either," she said resolutely with a twisted smile that left him a little alarmed for her sanity. And then she said a word about doing his utmost to help Gilmour clear himself, no matter where the trail might lead. Again she looked at him, and again Moy felt a little shiver at the look in her eyes. If ever a woman looked as though her sanity were rocking, Mrs. Appleton did. She left him after he had agreed to do as she wished, by which he meant to mark time until her nerves were in better trim. It was all very well to help Gilmour, he reflected with a smile almost as twisted as Mrs. Appleton's, but Gilmour was intending to help himself, and that by taking a step which, in Moy's judgment, meant disaster immediate and absolute.

As a matter of fact, he was wrong.

Gilmour's method of escape, as he called it, was simplicity itself, and like many simple things, it worked. He went to his club, and took a room for two nights, there, telling the chief inspector where he was going. Quite unnecessary this last, as both men knew. Then he went to bed and slept for the first night since the death of Ingram. Next morning at half-past six, a red-haired, shock-headed man in his shirt sleeves and wearing a green baize apron came down the steps swinging a brown paper parcel in one hand. Under his arm was a broom. The club was on the corner-he lit a gasper and walked round it, still dangling his parcel by its string. It was obviously a suit of clothes for the pressers. The watcher continued to keep an eye on the building as instructed. It was a languid eye, for the room had been taken for two nights, and nothing about Gilmour at The Tall House had suggested a passionately early riser. Once well around the corner, Gilmour took off his green baize apron and took out of the paper parcel a coat, rather a threadbare affair, which he now carried on his arm, leaving broom and baize apron around yet another bend. Down a street he hurried, and turning off it again, added a cap to his outfit, and arrived at that street's end looking like any of a thousand breadwinners walking to his job. He had paid a royal tip to the man to get apron and broom, a tip and a hint as to a most excruciatingly good joke to be played, and a bet to be won, through their means.

CHAPTER 14

NEXT morning Chief Inspector Pointer found a letter waiting for him at the Yard which he opened before any of the other correspondence in his basket. It was in Gilmour's rather sprawling writing and ran:

> DEAR CHIEF INSPECTOR POINTER,
>
> I am sorry if my going away bothers your inquiry in any way, and I know that, strictly speaking, I should not have tried to dodge your man, but a clue has come my way, or rather it has been in front of me all the time, but I have only just recognized it as what it is. I am on the right road, I know, but should I find things getting too hot for me, I may be glad of your assistance. In which case I will manage to get a message through to you. I only hope that you will not take my disappearance as a sign of guilt, but I must risk that.
>
> Faithfully yours,
> LAWRENCE GILMOUR.

Pointer docketed the letter and reached for another. He knew already how Gilmour had got away, and a certain watcher was even now sadly making for a provincial town where detection might be simpler an demand less keen wits. For the moment, there was no possibility of laying hands on Gilmour, and Pointer therefore dismissed him from his mind. He had many things to see to this morning. There was his-to him-engrossing hunt for a missing person who should fulfil the few stipulations that he had laid down. Town seemed to be half-empty, judging by the accounts that had already come in of people who were no longer seen in their accustomed places. Pointer flung most of them into the discard as soon as he glanced at them, but there were a few which he reserved for inquiries.

As for the party at The Tall House, it had broken up with a vengeance yesterday. Mrs. Pratt and Winnie were in a Dover Street hotel. Later on it was understood that the mother had accepted an invitation for both of them on Haliburton's yacht. Haliburton himself had left his usual club and home addresses with the police, but at this time of the year he generally spent a fortnight anonymously with one of his boys' camps at the seaside, acting, it was said, merely as a friendly scoutmaster, and hiding the fact of his being the provider of the camp from all but a few of the men helping him.

Mrs. Appleton was leaving as soon as possible for Capetown, where she had friends. Appleton would not be able to go with her, he had explained, but as he too needed a change, he was going over to Paris almost at once.

Tark had told the police that he was off for his home in Beausoleil and was likewise leaving today. Miss Longstaff had left The Tall House last night, giving an address near Hammersmith Broadway, where she had taken a room. She had no intention of leaving England.

Frederick Ingram had left last night by 'plane for Paris, and already Pointer knew that he had gone on at daybreak to Marseilles. The south of France is not often chosen in midsummer, especially by as poor a sailor as Pointer had learned that Frederick Ingram was, unless there is some strong attraction. In his case, since he still seemed devoted to Winnie Pratt, Pointer fancied that it was the green of the tables rather than of the waves that drew him. The chief inspector would have to see for himself if this were so or not, and also why Tark seemed to have such a sudden attack of home sickness just now. He had a word with the assistant commissioner before leaving.

"You think the case can breathe by itself, that you won't have to stay to apply artificial respiration?" Pelham asked him.

Pointer said that there was no reason why he should not absent himself for a short time, especially as all the wheels would turn just as well without him as with him.

The other shook his head. "Too modest, Pointer. Fatal flaw in an otherwise sensible man. However, perhaps you'll give me just a notion of what your merry men will be at?"

"Overcoming an osmotic reluctance to seeping through the cilia, sir," Pointer said gravely. One of the superintendents came in at that moment, and stared at him with a dropped jaw. Pelham burst out laughing, and gave Pointer his blessing. "Any special time limit?" he asked.

"Well, sir, there's something that may help us coming along shortly. And that's quarter day."

"Next week," murmured the superintendent mechanically.

"Just so, sir. Hitherto for some five years past Mr. Ingram had a thousand pounds to dispose of just after that date. It's possible some or all of it may come in to his estate...I'm rather counting on that...until then we must just seep, as I said," and he was off.

He traveled as plain Mr. Pointer, and went directly to Cannes. The air service has tremendously shortened that weary journey to Marseilles. In his case he flew directly to the little town itself lying in a half-circle around its Croisette. He had often been there before. Pointer was no lover of the Riviera. Many other parts of France have wonderful things to show, but Cannes, to him, holds all the vice of Monte Carlo, all its rapacity, its misery, its pitilessness, only with a little more gilding. He dined at the Casino where the prices, at our rate of exchange, made him decide to do a little slimming. Frederick Ingram was there at a table well in front of Pointer, who sat in a corner near the door.

Frederick did not order a long meal. He looked like a man in a sort of pleasant dream, but a dream which entailed a lot of looking at a little black note-book that he carried in an inner pocket. After his dinner, he made for the gaming rooms, greatly to Pointer's interest, for baccarat had been the young man's passion in former days. But he passed that great chamber, passed the Boule room and finally took a seat at a table at the end of the Roulette room. Pointer had learned from a word with the head of the Casino detectives that Frederick had played at that table and in that room last night, winning all the time, but playing for modest stakes, so that he came away with about ten thousand francs.

"It's not any system we have come up against before," the head detective added, "but it must have been one from the fact that in the beginning he noted every stake in a little pocket-book. As he did nothing but win he stopped his entries but he consulted it regularly each time before staking."

Pointer was exceedingly interested. There are several cast-iron systems of playing roulette, by which, in the long run, the player is bound to win. The trouble is that the run may be so very long that a fortune has to be spent to win a few francs. Had Fred Ingram got hold of a shorter, better one than any yet known? If so, where had he found it? Pointer thought of that dusty roulette wheel in a cupboard of Charles Ingram's flat. A system was just the sort of thing that a genius at figures might have devised. And apparently it had come into Fred Ingram's hands only after his brother's death.

Pointer watched Fred seat himself with a certain air of assurance. He staked, after consulting his little book with the same air, and took his winnings with a smile that said that all this was a matter of course. He won again and yet again, but he always staked low. There was a flush on his cheeks and a light in his eyes as he did so. The third time he lost, and then he lost in an unbroken sequence for the next couple of hours. Yet in all, Pointer calculated that he was only some thousand francs down when he jumped up, his face which had first seemed only a little troubled was now that of a man half beside himself with amazement. He pushed back his chair onto the toes of another waiting gambler, and hurried into the gardens, looking as though he had received the shock of his life. He fairly ran to a seat outside in the gardens under a lamp, and spread his pocket-book open beside him, before drawing out with great difficulty something from an inner pocket. It was a sheet of writing paper, which he laid down and began to compare with his notes, figure by figure.

Pointer came up behind him on the grass, fortunately the light fell so that he cast no shadow, and waiting until Fred had buried his nose in his pocket-book again, reached over, and snatched up the paper. It was covered with what, to his sharp sight, were Ingram's figures, those neat small figures of the dead mathematician's, which looked as though drawn with tiny wires.

Frederick whirled about with a shout, making a grab at his property. But Pointer held it high in the air.

"I'll have you broken for this!" Frederick was very white about the gills. "You've no more right to take that, than any footpad has. Hand it back at once!"

"I want first to know that it is yours," was the reply. "You see, Mr. Frederick Ingram, we are not satisfied that your brother's death was not for the sake of something that he owned. Say, a system of play. It might be considered by some people as much more to be coveted than jewels or securities. This sheet of paper was in your brother's possession at the time of his death. How did it come into your hands?"

Pointer spoke with such an air of certainty that no one, not even the assistant commissioner, let alone rattled Frederick Ingram; would have known that he was guessing.

Frederick Ingram turned blue.

"You mean that you think Gilmour shot him intentionally?" he asked, his eyes round and staring.

"That's just what you've maintained all along, isn't it?" Pointer asked.

"But I didn't really believe it!" burst out Fred, his face still shiny and streaked with red from his play in the hot rooms. "I didn't really think it!" he repeated.

Pointer, looking at him, thought that excitement had broken down the barriers of self-control as far as speech was concerned. It can act as insidiously as scopolamin on some natures.

"It's quite possible that someone intentionally changed a loaded for a blank cartridge in his little automatic," Pointer said slowly, "someone who wanted something that Ingram refused to hand him over." Frederick's eyes only looked excited, he said nothing. "Come," Pointer went on pleasantly, "leaving that on one side, suppose you tell me exactly how this paper came into your possession. And when."

"I've lots of my brother's papers, of course-and books. This was among some he handed to me a few days ago."

"You place yourself in a dangerous position," Pointer went on very seriously, "unless you can establish the fact that it was found by someone else-or that someone else was present when you found it." Frederick seemed to think that very likely.

"As a matter of fact, Miss Pratt and I were looking through Charles' books at my flat the afternoon of the day when he was shot. I knew that such a paper existed. She didn't. She dropped in to find something-any thing-that would prove that those cartridges of Gilmour's were all blanks. The receipt from his gunsmith was really in her mind, I think. But from the first book that she picked up, by the merest chance, out flutters this. She didn't know what it was, of course, and picked it up and put it back until she had gone, but knew that my brother had devised what he believed to be a unique system of winning at roulette. He was certain that it was so perfect that any casino would purchase it, if tried out at their tables." Here Fred Ingram gave a bitter laugh. "I thought he couldn't be mistaken, but, my hat!" Again he gave a laugh that was half a groan. "Fortunately, I tried it quietly, or should be in queer street. It's an absolute wash-out thought I must have made some mistake in copying out, but not a bit of it! Besides, I knew I hadn't."

Pointer was looking at the paper which he had just taken from him. At the top was written: System for Winning at Roulette. The letters were Ingram's, and yet...the figures were his, and yet...

Pointer himself could copy any writing with a lot of mechanical accuracy, such as had been at work here. But there is much more than that in a good forgery. Quite apart from the silly notion that forgery is always done slowly, for only a half-wit copies swift writing without at least equal speed, there is something that cannot be put down on paper and yet which must be imitated. A something much more subtle than accuracy of angle or length of stroke. The more Pointer looked at the sheet before him, looked at it as a whole, not into its details, the less did it convey the peculiarly firm, settled, orderly, almost sedate mind that the other writing of the dead man had done. He thought it highly probable that what he held in his hand was a forgery.

Another incidental confirmation was the fact that, as far as he had yet seen, Ingram always wrote with an ordinary pen, this was a similar nib to his, but had been written with a fountain-pen. One thing was certain, this system, as he had seen, was calculated to ruin anyone who staked high on it. Had Ingram intended this? Had he reason to suspect that his life was in danger?...Could this system be linked with those quarterly thousand pound increases in his capital? Had he sold the original system for a quarterly pension? This was a new possibility. But there was a more immediate one. Was Frederick Ingram by playing it, trying to place a shield between himself and any suspicion? Say he had the real thing, and was only pretending that he had been taken in by a worthless dud? Who better than he would know Ingram's writing? Who could easier place a paper where he wanted it found. Was it likely that Ingram the careful would have left such a paper lying in a book?

He questioned Frederick cautiously on this last doubt. Frederick could not but acknowledge the singularity of the place where the so-called system had been found. But he suggested that, as it had been devised some years ago, about five, he thought, Ingram might have mislaid it. The book in question was one of Arabic Equations which Ingram rarely opened. That, too, might explain, Frederick went on to say, why his half-brother had quite bruskly refused to discuss letting him have the system of which he had himself once spoken as infallible.

There still remained the possibility that Frederick, having openly played this travesty, would be freer, he might think, to produce what he might claim was his own improvement or revision of it, and play the real system devised by that brilliant mathematician, Charles Ingram. He had staked very small sums last night and tonight. He had lost only a matter of some fourteen pounds. Pointer broached that question now. Frederick looked awkward.

"It's odd. I'm generally a bit of a plunger. I meant to go all out on this. But-somehow-at the last moment, when I drew that pocket-book out and laid it beside me, I found myself only willing to try it for small stakes. I can't account for it myself." He looked genuinely puzzled.

Pointer eyed him closely with his seemingly indifferent glance. Fred Ingram was a good actor, if he was not honest. But then, if false, all this would have been carefully prepared, and mentally rehearsed many times.

"You aren't going to try the system again?" he asked.

Frederick said that he was returning to England at once. Having proved his half-brother's great idea to be a failure, he intended to forget all about it. "After a flutter at baccarat," he added with a smile. "I brought a hundred with me with which to break the bank, a lot of it still remains, thanks to my luck last night, which I thought was the system. And thanks to that unexpected wind of caution that suddenly blew on me when I sat down at the tables."

The baccarat room at Cannes is a noble hall. Vaulted ceilings, beneath which crystal chandeliers glitter like hanging baskets of diamonds, luxurious chairs for those who wish to sit on a central dais and watch the scene, while sipping cocktails or black coffee.

Two long rows of baize-covered tables at some of which people were standing three deep already. This is the Court of Midas. There was silence in the big hall. Only the clack of chips and the sound of the croupier's flat wooden rake as he called his "*Banco. Mesdames, messieurs, marquez vos jeux. Rien ne va plus.*" Frederick passed on to the next room, where the stakes were still higher. Here he bought some brown thousand-franc chips, others were playing with oblong blue chips worth ten times his, and many with white ovals which represented a hundred times his stakes. It was late. The hour of the real gamblers. The air of the room was tense in here. Within a few minutes it was tenser still. And when an hour was over Frederick Ingram was the richer by the equivalent of ten million francs, roughly eighty thousand pounds.

Pointer meanwhile had had another word with the chief of the Casino detectives. Could a man have a system at baccarat or chemin de fer? Impossible, the chief thought, as did Pointer. But they were puzzled. It is held not to be possible for a man to win at baccarat except by sheer luck, any more than he could cheat at that nimble gamble which may run to thousands of pounds on the draw of the all-important third card. The doubts of the two were soon answered. When another hour had passed Frederick was the poorer by some seventy-nine thousand eight hundred pounds. Finally he made way for another player, his face all streaked with the curious red that gambling brings out on a pale face. His voice shook a little as he drew a deep breath outside. "Well, I'm still my journey out and back in hand, and the hundred pounds with which I started." He turned in at his hotel. Pointer who was staying there too, asked him to his room. He did not think the paper a shield any longer. After his first run of luck at baccarat, Frederick would only have had to return to the roulette table and try the real system, if he had it, claiming that his luck was still holding. But he had left the Casino with no effort to get back again the ephemeral fortune which had been his.

Pointer left his own door unlocked, making an excuse to pop out and speak to Frederick as the latter was leaving, so as to make him aware of this, just as he had placed the paper taken from him on the mantel while he was still in the room.

No attempt was made on room, or paper, during what remained of the night. If Frederick really left Cannes in the morning, Pointer felt that he would have gone far to substantiate his story. Frederick did, repeating that, after all, he had had a change of air, and would be back home not a penny the worse, and with the charming memory of having been worth eighty thousand pounds for over half an hour.

Pointer stepped up into his compartment, which he had to himself. There was still five full minutes before the train was timed to start.

"Look here, Mr. Ingram, did you ever speak of your brother's system to anyone?"

Frederick seemed to think back.

"I may have," he said, looking up. "It's the sort of thing one's apt to mention."

"I very much want the names of anyone who knew of it, as well as you."

"Well, of course my sister and her husband know. Charles spoke about it once, before the three of us. Then, well, I think I once told Mrs. Pratt about it, not that she was interested...I think Miss Longstaff knew, too, whether from me or not, I can't say. Haliburton? No, he didn't know. Gilmour? I fancy he must have known, but I couldn't say for certain. You see, Charles never referred to it after the one week during which he worked it out."

Pointer saw him off, went back to his own room, and took out the paper again. He had brought with him several letters of Ingram's to Moy. He compared them all. Yes, he felt sure-though experts could be asked to pronounce on it if it should ever be necessary-that this paper was a forgery. It was empty of all significance, and Ingram's writing had plenty of personality. Who could have forged the paper, if it was a forgery, as he assumed it to be? Someone who wanted to stop Frederick's search? Therefore someone who knew both of that hunt's purpose and of the existence of such a paper among Ingram's effects? Someone had searched the bureau before Pointer first saw it. Mrs. Appleton had hunted for what might well have been just such a half-sheet as this...Appleton had been with Ingram on the night that he died...

One thing the chief inspector expected, and that was, that if someone had intentionally forged a system, the original was in his possession, for there had been no interest of late in Ingram's papers. Gilmour had never shown any. Nor had Haliburton. Nor had Moy, except for those papers with which, as a solicitor, he was expected to deal. Moreover, if the room had been searched after the murder, and the body was discovered, then Moy, Haliburton and Gilmour could all give each other alibis.

He could make a guess as to where that system was now. Before the day was over, he knew that his guess was being strengthened.

CHAPTER 15

APPLETON had crossed by the noon boat from Victoria, and gone on down to Mentone by air. That meant that he would have arrived last night. Pointer rang up the town police, and learned that rooms had been engaged for Ingram's brother-in-law at a comfortable but highly-expensive hotel there. He drove on out to it, along the beautiful Grand Corniche. The colors of sea and sky, the turns and twists of the road, are things of real loveliness. Mentone itself looked the usual arid desert of a Riviera town in the summer. And indeed, even in the winter its flowers and verdure are the result of money and art, not nature. Nature refuses to let even vegetables grow here, nor any fruit but the olive. In winter, when the mimosa and the heliotropes run from end to end of the main street, Mentone has its visitors who love its sunshine and its flowers, but in summer, like Beausoleil, it is merely a respectable name for Monte Carlo from which it is separated by but some ten minutes in the tram.

Pointer drew up at the handsome Palace Hotel. There is no fault to be found with the big hotels of the Riviera, provided you like that kind of thing. Not Arnold Bennett himself could have suggested better plumbing or bigger crowds. The chief inspector loathed them, but then his idea of comfort was an old, well-kept, quiet English inn, with cooking that can beat that of any other country in the world when at its simple best.

He arrived too early for even a French lunch, but the maître d'hôtel who used to be at Ciro's remembered him, and gave him the inevitable omelette and poulet en casserole in the big restaurant. Pointer questioned him about Mr. Appleton. The maître d'hôtel smiled. He would not be up for another four hours or so. "Look at that!" He indicated a table at the other end still littered with champagne corks. "The result of last night. At Monte Carlo they draped a table in the roulette room with black. Oh, yes, he broke the bank twice. Not difficult to do these days, you think? Still, he did it. Twice. Mr. Tark? Oh, yes, I know Mr. Tark quite well. Apart from his father-quite apart. He used to play incessantly, and with fair luck. He had one of these systems which do quite well if you do not force them. Losses and gains about equal. They have not seen him at the rooms for some time, they tell me, until last night." He went on to say that Mr. Tark had, in common with about twenty other people, had a sort of celebration supper with Mr. Appleton last night. They appeared to be but the merest of acquaintances. Mr. Tark, like the other guests at the supper, had followed Mr. Appleton's lead with, as a rule, great success.

Pointer drank his coffee and then took the little tram with its sensible division of first and second class on up to Monte Carlo. There are many things claimed for Monte Carlo which it is not, but it has an outstanding virtue, it is one of the cleanest towns in existence. When it rains, which it does more often than the papers will reveal, torrents of clear water rush down its streets like mountain rivulets, and add a charm of their own to the steep slopes.

At the Casino, he had a word with the head croupier who happened to be up, owing to the necessity of a visit to his dentist. He was a tall thin man with a white puffy face, and the curiously dead eyes of his profession, eyes which yet miss nothing.

"Yes, Mr. Appleton had won a great deal last night. He had played a new system, and it had worked. For that one evening," the head croupier added with a faint smile. "There are many such."

"Mr. Tark?"

"He had mostly followed Mr. Appleton's lead."

"Did they talk together?"

Not as far as the man knew. Both were well known in Monte Carlo. Mr. Tark lived at Beausoleil, of course, but he was never far from the tables for long. Mr. Appleton only came to Monte Carlo for about a fortnight each year. He used to play quite high, but of late years his stakes, and therefore his losses, had been slight. Last night he, the head croupier, had noticed only one oddity. Whenever Mr. Appleton lost, he had staked much smaller sums than when he won. That might, of course, mean nothing.

On the whole, Mr. Appleton had won four times out of six. Any good system would show the same results, provided the player had a run of luck. Tonight or to-morrow the money won would be sure to return to the Casino, probably with interest. Yes, the bank had been broken twice, which, as Pointer knew, only meant that that particular table had run out of its reserves of money. The usual farce of draping it in black, and sending for more money, which was brought in by a guard was gone through. It was a good advertisement. The head croupier shrugged. And in these days, *parbleu*, one needed advertisement.

Pointer put on his war paint that evening, and presented himself at the glittering palace of pleasure on the rocks which at night seemed built all of moonbeams and dewdrops and ivory. Lit up inside as superbly as outside, thronged with gorgeous flunkeys, it is still a spectacle to be seen, though the days of incredible toilettes are gone and makeshift evening frocks on very dowdy looking bodies abounded. There are seven hundred rooms in the huge building, though quite a quarter of these are secret little cupboards where, through artfully concealed openings, members of the *brigade de jeu* —the Casino's private detective force-can watch all that goes on.

One of these was put at Pointer's disposal. Inside he seemed to be separated from the roulette tables by a mere white grating. From the gaming room itself, nothing showed but rich panelled walls of stucco and plaster wreaths and flowers in very high relief. It was skilfully done. Pointer watched the garish scene. Appleton came in rather early. His step was jaunty, his head thrown back, his shoulders well squared. He had all the effect of a man with flowing evening-cloak and hat well on the side of his head. He sat down in a chair with almost a bang, and produced a note-book with something of a conjuror's flourish. Then he began to play. Tark was not far behind him, wooden faced, quiet, but as he looked around him Pointer realized that he was looking at a man whose only avenue of life was gambling. Only here, in scenes like this, did Tark really exist. He seemed to belong to the tables as some men belong to the fields, some to the towns, and some, Pointer among them, to the open spaces. Watching the two men, Pointer felt sure that they were not acting together. On the contrary, he had an idea from something that flitted across Appleton's face once or twice when he staked and lost, that he was amused. Tark was not. As a rule Appleton won, and Tark, following him, won too, but once when Appleton staked the maximum in the maximum ways, and Tark had followed suit, Appleton at the last fraction of a second altered his stake. Tark looked black murder down at the other's well-groomed head. His eyes for once showed his feelings. That time Appleton smiled openly. A swift grin of intense amusement. Watching him make his entries and calculations, Pointer saw that Appleton knew beforehand when he was going to lose. He had a chart by which he was steering. Tark knew it too, and all but showed his teeth each time that he, following, was led astray-deliberately astray. But outwardly there was no communication between the two players.

Again the bank was broken. Again the usual ritual followed of draping the table in crape, of bringing in great boxes of bundles of notes. The head croupier hovered about, but no one was much interested except those who were following Appleton. Pointer kept a careful tally of the man's winnings. In all he put them at around fifteen hundred pounds when he finally rose and let another have his seat. Tark stayed for a couple of chances, and lost, then he too went down to the station. Appleton was already in a compartment, Pointer bundled himself in, bearded and muffled and bespectacled. He drew out some Russian papers and seemed to lose himself in them as he took the farthest corner from Appleton. At the last second Tark jumped in, stumbled over a pair of elastic-sided boots thrust out, and apologized curtly. Pointer shrieked something in Russian, and nursed his toe, spluttering that he did not understand when Tark tossed him another negligent apology. Then he buried himself in his newspaper again.

"How much was it?" Tark asked, "we may as well divide up now. Tolstoi over there doesn't matter."

"Just over fifteen hundred of our money," Appleton replied, looking as though the words hurt him.

Tark gave a grunt of acquiescence. Evidently he too had made it that.

"Why did you stop playing?" he asked in a tone as though he had a right to an answer.

"Better so," was the reply. "Arouses less comment. Less risk of articles in the papers. Well, here's your half." And may it choke you was suggested by his voice as he handed over a thick wad of notes which Tark went through carefully, before stowing them away in an inner pocket with the briefest of acknowledgments.

"You led me up the garden now and again," he grumbled as he did so.

"I told you I would!" was the retort, and Appleton took up a paper and seemed to forget his companion.

The next evening Appleton did not play quite so long. But he again won over a thousand pounds. The fourth evening he won over two thousand, and this time the head croupier had himself taken the table after Appleton began to play. The man's eyes never left Appleton or Tark. Suddenly Pointer caught sight of Mrs. Appleton in the thick crowd around the table. He knew that she had left for Paris. That there she had taken a ticket to Mentone. Pointer, there-fore, expected to see her here tonight. She stood, a pale tired-looking woman where she could watch her husband's play, and not even the head croupier followed it more intently. Pointer had arranged with a member of the *brigade de jeu* to take his place if need be, and now he slipped out and drove back to Appleton's hotel in Mentone. He himself was staying at Monte Carlo. He wanted a certain corner in Appleton's little suite, one of the usual hotel arrangements, where a sofa was backed across the angle of two walls by a four-fold screen. For he had promptly inspected the rooms with the aid of a card from the Monte Carlo head detective, since showing which, he was allowed to do what he liked in Appleton's rooms. Just now, this was to insinuate a chair into one of the two bays made by the screen, draw it around him again, and wait. He might have an all night's vigil, but he thought not. There was that in Mrs. Appleton's face which would need privacy, he thought, to be spoken. What happened at the Casino after he left, he learned later. Mrs. Appleton got near enough to her husband to touch him on the shoulder. He looked up, and smiled a pale sort of greeting-very forced, very surprised apparently at sight of her. She only stared down at him with unsmiling eyes.

She bent forward as though to say something and Appleton rose at once. "Not here! Come with me to my hotel. I'll take the tram since you're always frightened of taxis abroad." He got up and lead the way out, those around smiling at what they fancied was the meek husband detected by his puritanical wife. "She'll be all right when she hears that he has won!" one man said cynically as he slipped into the vacated chair.

Tark, as Appleton afterwards learned, took a taxi to the Appleton's hotel, asked for him, was told that he was at Monte Carlo, showed a card of Appleton's on which was scribbled in what certainly looked like Appleton's writing, "Permit the bearer to wait for me in my room," showed it to the floor waiter, and had the suite unlocked for him at once.

Tark gave but a glance around the apartment. Pointer knew what was coming. Straight towards his screen refuge came Tark. Fortunately Pointer had taken the farther bay, just on some such off-chance as this. Tark drew out the sofa, slipped into hiding, and was just moving back the end of the screen against the wall on his side when the creak of the lift and steps sounded outside. He left the sofa's end where it was.

But the two people who entered together had no eye for the position of the furniture. Had the men hidden in the corner stood out in the middle of the room, they might have escaped notice.

Appleton shut the door behind himself and his wife and then turned to her quickly.

"Sit down and let me explain things —"

"No, no!" She shrank away from him against a table. "I don't want a confession. I only came on here with you to tell you that if you play again I shall go straight to the chief inspector. He knows, I feel sure, that I searched Charles' writing-room at The Tall House. And I think he guesses that I was trying to make sure whether you had left any of your cigarette ends or ash about. Oh, Edward, that you, you should have done such a thing." Anguish was in face and voice. "No, don't try to lie to me. You were never a good liar. And I know that what I'm saying is the truth. God help us all. God help Jackie and Bill."

"You're wrong——" he burst out imperiously, but she only shook a shuddering head and would not let him finish.

"Oh, don't pretend to me! I've known it, feared it, from the first. I who knew how wild you were to get his system. Remember, I heard you, and that dreadful man Tark, talking about it once. Oh, yes, I know that you told him that Charles might let a stranger try it out, where he wouldn't you, just because he knew what a dangerous gift it would be."

"Tark may have shot Charles," Appleton said, very white and set of face, "but I didn't, Ada. I know he got himself asked to The Tall House on purpose to get to know Charles better."

"He tipped Mr. Haliburton overboard probably for that reason," she threw in scornfully, "but it's you, not he, who is playing a system. You've got the paper, not he. Now listen, as I said, I don't want a confession from you, but I swear that you shan't profit by my brother's murder. If you play again, I shall give you in charge. I'll tell Chief Inspector Pointer the whole truth. How you badgered Charles for years since he let drop that unfortunate remark that he had devised a system that really was infallible. How he always refused to let you or anyone try it out, because he knew where it would lead. Or no, he didn't. He never thought that it would lead to his own death. Oh, Edward, to what depths have you sunk! To what depths!"

Appleton had had perforce to let her rave on. Something in her face said that to silence her you would have had to gag her. These words were too dammed up to stay behind locked lips any longer. But for the moment she was spent. She leaned against the table behind her, her hands now over her face.

"I see I must go into something I'd rather not speak of. No, you shall listen!" He towered over her. "You *shall* hear me out. I went to Charles that last night because —" his face twitched — "because we're ruined, Ada. Ruined. I've let my brokers keep my securities for me, as you know. They're bonds. Well, Graves pledged them with others to his bank to secure an advance to himself. He's gone smash."

Pointer knew of the big crash of Farral and Graves about a fortnight ago. Graves had shot himself, and many a man and woman wished that he had done it sooner.

"He's gone smash," Appleton repeated, "and now the bank, his bank, won't part with my bonds. My solicitors tell me that I can't force them to do so. Yet they talk of our Justice and our Law! We haven't a penny except the three hundred in the bank that I always keep for emergencies, and your two hundred which you have there for the same reason. Got that clear?"

"I don't care for your reasons—I don't want to hear them." She almost moaned the words. "I don't want to know the steps which led you down to Hell. But you did go down them. And you shall never touch the children or me again. Never. Nor shall you profit by your crime. Keep if you want to —" her lip curled —"the blood money you've won up to now. But enter a gaming place again, and let me hear of it, and you'll hang!"

"Will you listen!" roared Appleton, and by sheer volume of sound silenced her. "I was told, perhaps worry aggravated it, that I've got to have a major operation, yes, that old tumor again, within six months. The fees will run into a thousand pounds with Sir Rankin Rowbottom as surgeon, and he's the only man who can do it and give me a chance of surviving. Well, I caught Charles just as he was on his way back to The Tall House. Earlier in the evening he had told me that he wouldn't have a moment's time until midnight. There was something he had to finish and get off by twelve, to catch the midnight post. Well, I walked about, wondering how best to put it to him, wondering what would happen to you and the kids if he wouldn't let me have a try at that system. You see, no loan would help. It would have to be that system of his, or we were all beggars for the rest of our lives, though in my case the rest would only be a couple of years, but they would be years of increasing agony. I went home once, thinking I would try again next morning. But I didn't come in. I turned around with my key in the door and went back."

"I heard you," she said in a whisper. "I heard your step-your key-and your going away again."

"I caught a bus and by chance spied Charles just turning a corner close to that furnished house. I joined him, and we went back into the library there and had a long talk. I told him everything. I didn't want a loan. I wanted that system. In the end he handed it to me. I swear by God, I swear by Jacky and Bill, and my love for you, Ada, that I'm telling you the exact truth. He saw what an awful place we were all in. He got up, unlocked a despatch box beside' him, took out an envelope from the bottom, and handed it me. 'There you are. You've won-and you'll go on winning,' were his exact words. Then he added, 'I didn't think I could reconcile it with my conscience to hand that to any man, let alone to Ada's husband, but I give it you on one condition.' He made me give him my word of honor that if a casino offered to buy me off-as he said they certainly would —I would accept their offer, provided it was a reasonable one. He thought that Monte Carlo would offer me an annuity of two thousand a year for it. And the other big places even more. I had to promise that, and I did so gladly. Well, I went home as happy as a boy. I know what you felt about gambling-money, so I decided-Charles and I had decided that together-to say nothing about it...Then came the news of his dreadful end. I saw that you didn't think it an accident. I saw that you suspected me —"

"For the last month, Edward, you've talked in your sleep of getting that system. Over and over you would mutter that 'I must have it. He must give it me. It'll save us. I've a right to it...'" She panted the words rather than spoke them.

"I didn't kill Charles, but I was-afraid-of you-of the police-of the whole position. Then Tark accused me of murdering him for that paper. He offered to keep silence for a half share in all profits. It's my belief that if anyone murdered Charles, if it wasn't an accident, then it was Tark, before he knew that Charles had already given the system away. He guessed to whom then, because we had talked it over together. Oh, I knew Tark by sight as well as he knew me. You can't live at the Casino rooms as both of us did, without knowing one another perfectly by sight. But it was from Fred that he learned about the system. So he says."

"But you were the two who plotted to get hold of it," she said fiercely, accusingly.

"We talked of how to get it-of course we did. Once we knew of its existence. And as you know I thought he might give me a chance...Charles was so afraid I would turn into a desperate gambler...I didn't think he'd care so much whether Tark did or not. The chap only lives for gambling anyway...When he saw his chance of pretending to me that he thought I had shot Charles, I gave in...there was nothing else for it...And now, I swear again, Ada, that I've told you the exact truth. Look at me, look into my face, my darling. Surely you can read the truth there."

She fixed a haggard, intent stare on him, she half stretched out one hand, the other now tight pressed against her heart.

"Oh Edward, if only I could! I might, if you'll destroy-at once-that awful paper —"

Tark came out from behind his end of the screen. Mrs. Appleton gave a little cry. Appleton seemed too amazed even to gasp.

"Didn't know I was here, did you?" Tark said in his harsh, level voice. "Mrs. Appleton, I can't stand silent and see such a lie pass. Your intuition or suspicion was right. He shot your brother. I happened to see him at The Tall House, but until afterwards I didn't reflect just what it was he was at. No, Appleton, it's no use. I won't stand for it. You know that you shot Ingram, and unless you hand me his system-the right one, mind you-not the one we spoofed off Fred with, I shall go myself to the police. If you think it's worth while swinging for, keep it!" And Tark seated himself on the arm of a chair.

"How dare you repeat your lying accusation to me in front of my wife!" Appleton looked the outraged husband to the life.

Tark gave one of his short hard cackles. "Mrs. Appleton will be called as a witness against you, unless you're careful. I agree with her that it's a foul thing to kill her brother and use that money. Hand it over to me. I wanted to buy it from Ingram, as you know, not to murder him for it. You said that you thought you could get it without paying for it, if I'd put up five hundred to try it out with. Well, I got the money, and you got the system." His last words were full of meaning. "And now, hand me over that paper," he went on, his words suddenly cold and steel hard.

"Don't let him have it!" came from Mrs. Appleton. Her eyes were alight. She was quite undaunted now. "Never mind what happens. Burn it!"

"I haven't got it with me, Ada." He ignored Tark. Something in his face and eye suggested that there was no Tark, that it only lay between himself and his wife. His hand went to an inner pocket...

"You've got the copy," came Tark's hard voice. "I want that copy. Hand it over! Dare to go near those matches —" His body seemed to thicken, he was ready for a spring when Pointer stepped out from the remaining pocket of the screen. It was purest vaudeville, but no one in the room smiled. Pointer counted roughly on the surprise of his sudden appearance giving him just time to snatch a paper from Appleton's fingers. The man, with an ashen face, made a clutch at his hand.

"How dare you! You have no right whatever to be here...to take that. It's mine. Return it at once, or..." He choked.

"Or what?" Pointer asked coldly.

"Keep it!" Mrs. Appleton said suddenly, and her face looked younger and, in some deep way happier, than Pointer had yet seen it. "Keep it, chief inspector. My husband told us the truth as to how he got it. It is honestly his. Keep it for the time being. I lend it you-he lends it you on condition that you clear up my brother's murder, if it was one!"

"Bring it home to your husband!" sneered Tark. His eyes showed a curious red. Rather strange eyes had Tark. He looked a man most eminently capable of murder as he stood there, his thin small lips stretched away from his teeth in a sort of snarl.

Pointer turned to Mrs. Appleton. Her eyes, resolute and unwavering, met his. The two talked without words in a long look. He saw that she really did believe in her husband, that she was sure at last of his innocence, and that she was willing for him to run the terrible danger of being accused of her brother's murder, if need be.

But Appleton looked shrunken and withered. She crossed to him, and stood shoulder to shoulder beside him.

"Just what did you mean, Mr. Tark, when you said that you didn't know what he was at, when you saw him at The Tall House the night on which Mr. Ingram was shot?" Pointer asked. He dominated the room, as he usually did any room where he was. Tark shot him one glance from his calculating eyes that had now grown cold again, and answered promptly.

"I saw him in Gilmour's room when I went to my own-around one o'clock at night-doing something to the drawer by the door, just putting something back into it to be precise. Putting back the case that held the automatic with which Ingram was shot a couple of hours later."

"It's a lie!" burst from Appleton in tones of indignant horror and outraged truth. But the trouble was that, being a good actor, Appleton could assume that look and tone at will. Mrs. Appleton turned her head, gave her husband one look, and then turned away, her own face serene and tranquil.

"Is it? I think not!" came Tark's reply. If a liar, Tark was quite as good an actor as Appleton had ever been. "It's true. And you know it. And your wife knows it. Well, you've failed to pull it off. And now, I think I'll go home."

"What about being arrested as an accessory, Mr. Tark?" was Pointer's inquiry. "If you conceal information in a murder case —"

"In a murder case-yes. But this was not openly that," was the retort. "The coroner's jury brought it in as Death by Misadventure. How was I to guess the truth that Appleton was the real murderer?"

"Why else did I go halves with you but because you blackmailed me into doing it?" Appleton asked indignantly. "I agreed, because I needed the money and at once, and must at all costs avoid trouble. But make no mistake. Don't think that if I go to prison I won't take you with me, and if it comes to the rope-then to the drop with me." He spoke resolutely. Tark only lit a cigarette.

"Empty words! You murdered your brother-in-law, not I. I believed your account of the handing over by him to you of the system, and only offered to find the money with which to try it out. Naturally that being the case, I asked for half shares. I hoped, as I say, that Ingram would have sold it to me, but he was evidently not in need of money. You took a simpler and swifter way of getting what you wanted."

"Why were you hiding in this room?" came from Appleton.

"Because I rather thought your wife might want you to give up the system. That she knew the truth. In which case, I wanted it."

Pointer interposed. "And now, Mrs. Appleton, and you two gentlemen, I would like you to return to England."

Tark stiffened.

"You see," the chief inspector went on, "I particularly want to avoid any scandal, any calling in of the French police, and that can only be, if you all three voluntarily return to England, and stay there till things are clearer."

Tark looked for an instant as though he would demur but he thought better of it and when asked for his prospective address gave his former hotel. The Appletons would return to Markham Square, they said, and there place themselves unreservedly at the service of the chief inspector. One of Pointer's men in plain clothes would accompany them. Inspector Watts was staying at a quiet hotel ready for just such a duty. That done, the oddly assembled little group broke up.

Pointer waited until Appleton came back after seeing his wife off to her hotel. He had a long wait, but he counted rightly on the fact that Mrs. Appleton was too worn out to be capable of any further long conversations without a rest. At length her husband, looking some ten years older, returned alone and entered his sitting-room heavily, a night waiter carrying a tray following him. Pointer expected a protest at his own presence but on the contrary Appleton looked relieved. He offered the other a whisky and soda, which was refused, and helped himself, drinking as a man does who needs the stimulant.

"There's something been burning me all the time, chief inspector," Appleton began as he set the glass down. "About my brother-in-law. I tried to give you a hint that I thought his death wasn't accidental, but I was reluctant to mention his system. I was afraid that at the best I should get no chance of playing it, if I did, and at the worst, well, that what my wife thought would be your first idea. And one hears so often that what a detective thinks first he thinks all the time, that —" Appleton shrugged his shoulders and poured another drink. "There is something that I knew all along I ought to tell you-it's this. Ingram had had a fearful shock. He wasn't himself in the least. Which was one of the reasons why he let me have that system so easily. He was very pale and...I can't give you particulars, but his whole appearance, as well as manner, suggested a man who was fairly reeling under some blow.

"Now that had not been the case when I looked in and wanted a word with him before midnight. Nor was it the case when I met him on his way back from the post. Both times he was exactly himself, in looks and in manner. When we entered he didn't take me into the library, but into a little room by the door, a room which Tark and I used to signal to each other from, by the way-oh, just an arrangement of a signal each was to make to the other through the window should either of us have got the system-but to go back to Charles...He left me there for a moment, saying that he had a few papers he must see to before our talk, said he wouldn't keep me more than a minute...It was quite ten minutes before he came in and when he did, as I say, he was a changed man. However he led me into the library, though I think he had to force himself to take any interest in what I wanted to say, didn't ask me to have a drink, or a smoke, just stood by the fire staring at me from a white and rather ghastly face. But I couldn't afford to put off what I had to say...well, the rest I've told you...but even when we parted he looked just the same —a man who had had an awful blow, I thought."

"You don't think so now?" Pointer asked, in answer to his tone, rather than his words.

"Oh, I do still. But I'm afraid now that his shock was connected with what happened so soon afterwards. Whether he had caught sight of his murderer...and knew he was in danger...whether he had received the traditional warning dear to old-fashioned novelists...something of that sort was the cause of his appearance and absolute inability to really care for what I was telling him..."

"Had anything been burned in the hearth?" Pointer asked.

"Yes, papers. They were still smoking, but Charles said that he had burned the draft of the papers he had just posted, and he was a man who never told a lie."

"Do you mind telling me how he came to say that to you? Did you ask him what the papers were?"

"Certainly not." Appleton looked surprised at the question.

"Then did he go out of his way to tell you what they were?" Pointer persisted, and Appleton now saw the reason for the question.

"Now you ask me, he did. And now you've made me think of it, that wasn't at all his way. Excusing himself, explaining himself."

"I suppose you couldn't see what the papers had been? I consider this may be an important point, Mr. Appleton. You might have watched them smoking quite idly and without noticing them consciously, and yet, on reflection, you might be able to tell me now if they were letters, or printed papers, or bills..."

"The topmost paper looked like a letter. It was a sheet of the letter paper from the house that he himself used."

"Did Mr. Tark use it?"

"Certainly."

"And Mr. Frederick Ingram?"

Appleton nodded. "Yes, it was the house paper, with the headed address and telephone number and so on on it. Everyone stopping in the house would use it, I fancy."

"You couldn't see anything of the handwriting? Or whether it was in consecutive lines and so on?"

Appleton thought a moment and shook his head. "It was curled over, blank side up...underneath were other papers, quite a stack, I fancy, but of manuscript. All torn up small. The top sheet, evidently his covering letter draft, was a whole sheet."

"Could you see whether there was any margin or not to the writing?" Pointer persisted. "Even when turned blank side up, if still burning, you might have noticed that, the very fire might cause the writing to show as writing —"

"There was no margin," Appleton said slowly. "No, I recall that now."

"Mr. Ingram left a wide margin on the letters I've seen of his."

"Always. Yes, that's odd. I've never known him to write from edge to edge as was done on that sheet. Yet it was a letter...I mean there was, the usual short first line and the usual two very short last lines, one of conventional closing, and one a signature...Appleton was trying to picture again what he had seen without interest so short a time ago.

"Two lines, not three?" Pointer asked. "For a very formal, or a business note, would be likely to have three, including the signature."

"By Jove, now you've made me think back so closely, I don't believe it was Ingram's writing at all," Appleton said without replying to the question just put. "No, it was all over the page...and the signature was very short...Charles always had a long signature. His middle name was Augustus and he used it in signing, so that Charles Augustus Ingram made quite a little strip of letters on a page. Yet he told me he was burning the draft of what he had just sent off..."

More than this he had not seen, or could not recall. Again Pointer took him over each little item. Appleton changed nothing, and added nothing, except his growing conviction that the letter flung last of all on the torn-up scraps of white manuscript paper must have been a warning of his coming death.

Before returning to his own room Pointer went for a long walk. He wanted to think. First of all, there was the question as to whether Tark or Appleton could be the solution to The Tall House puzzle. Either or both might be, and yet...if so, it was a much simpler affair than he had fancied it...Putting aside all that had just been told him, for it was told him by a very suspect man, a man who might easily be the criminal himself, there was still the posting of that letter or package of manuscript...the last fitted in with the idea of ciphers...No one had so far acknowledged the receipt of a communication of any kind from the dead man, though the coroner had asked the public to do so. If Appleton's account was to be trusted, the way his brother-in-law had spoken beforehand about wanting to catch the midnight post suggested a man doing an accustomed thing...knowing just what post would be in time...Here fitted possibly the quarterly payments of a thousand pounds, a very large sum for a man to have without any note as to the services paid so liberally.

Judging by his well-known mode of life those services must have been written ones. Again came the notion of cipher reading or compilation. But Pointer could not see why, if so, the police had not been confidentially informed of the fact...some foreign power? Some distant business house? But if Ingram was earning four thousand a year, his services must be important; his death, published in the papers, must have been wirelessed or cabled, whether in one of his own codes or not to his employer...yet nothing had been heard in reply...

Well, much would depend on that search for a missing man-or a missing woman-whose disappearance the chief inspector thought might still be the shortest cut to clear up Ingram's murder, supposing it to have been a murder. As to the system being the motive, that was quite possible. In fact, but for the posting of something of which the registration slip was missing, Pointer would be quite willing to accept it as the motive. Appleton assured him that only four people besides its author knew of the existence of Ingram's system: himself, his wife, Fred Ingram and Tark. Appleton was quite sure of this. He himself had imparted the information to the last-named, and Ingram had told them, when speaking of it, that only they to whom he was talking knew of such a paper. Yes, the system did provide an adequate motive...Appleton's account of the change in Ingram on his return might be connected with that mysterious person of the post-office robbery...Appleton had joined Ingram some time after he had left the neighborhood of the attempt and of the escape, but Pointer thought there was a simpler explanation of Ingram's state of mind as described by his brother-in-law. He was going to test this explanation as soon as possible and in doing so a part at least of Appleton's account.

CHAPTER 16

MOY found the silence on Gilmour's part very hard to bear as one day followed another. He was not what is known as psychic at all, and yet he had a growing feeling that something was wrong.

Three days after Gilmour had left the letter with him, he rang up Miss Longstaff and asked her if he might drop in for a chat. She sounded quite willing. He found her sitting in a little basement room lit by what purported to be dungeon lanterns, a suitable choice he thought.

She was looking tired and dispirited, but the stare that she bent on him was as inscrutable as ever. She brightened up, however, after a moment.

"You've never been here before, have you?" she asked, waving a hand around. "Can you imagine a more naive attempt at deceit. That bookcase is supposed to be absolutely undetectable. Could anyone suppose it to be anything, but what it is, a bed on end? The manageress assured me that the wash-stand looks just like an antique bureau. It doesn't. It looks just like a wash-stand, from where it was bought-Tottenham Court Road. And do sit down on this Early English dower-chest, as she calls it, which screams aloud that it's a dwarf wardrobe. Now tell me why you've conquered your aversion to me, and actually paid me a visit?" She looked very wicked as she said the last words, and Moy fidgeted on his hard seat.

"You're joking," he murmured. She had a hard stare and a hard jaw but she was a young and handsome girl none the less.

"Look here," he said impulsively, "I dropped in to ask you if you haven't heard from Gilmour —" A shade passed over her mobile face.

"That's an egg that didn't hatch out at all as I hoped," she said with apparent frankness, lighting a cigarette. "Gilmour...I feel I've been rather a pig to him, but what's done's done. I hate turning back. It's always a mistake."

"Not in your case," he said urgently. "You see, I know how deeply attached to you he is-how much he felt your attitude. No other girl had a look in with him." He paused and repeated this last sentence.

"Well, perhaps," she said rather oracularly. "I mean perhaps I have been all wrong about him..." She fell into a reverie. Then she looked up.

"If he can find out who did do it, that's what he's gone for, isn't it? Well, I might go back to things as they once were. If innocent, he's had a rotten time. I wish you could tell him that. Can't you really get a message through to him?"

Moy told her that he could not. "Something you said gave him a clue, or rather set him off remembering something connected with it," he said, "and where he was, and when he's coming back, I haven't the wildest notion." Suddenly catching her eye, her intensity, he began to talk of something else, and asked her how she liked the house she was in.

She shrugged. "Beggars mustn't be choosers. I had hoped to be able to afford something better than this, but-well, my finances won't admit of it." She did not say that the post on the paper which she had secured was turning out to be a very weak reed on which to lean, if indeed she was allowed to keep it, for she had had a hint that a good many changes were being contemplated, and guessed that they would include her name even though, or rather because, her appointment seemed to be purely honorary-like her salary.

"Did you ever hear Mr. Gilmour or Mr. Ingram speak of a Mrs. Findlay?" she asked abruptly. Moy said that he never had. She sat very quiet at that, almost lost in the deep wicker chair which even the manageress could not say looked like anything but what it was.

"I hadn't meant to speak of it," she said slowly, and as though not quite sure yet if she wished to let it slip, "but I wondered once, and now I'm wondering again, if Mr. Gilmour's disappearance has anything to do with her."

"Who's she?" Moy asked promptly, all interest.

"This is confidential!" she said and waited for his "Certainly" before continuing. "I was with Mr. Gilmour one afternoon, we were going by tube, and stepped into the lift. Or rather were just going to, when he stepped back with a sort of jump. Now, I happened to be looking at him just then, and I could swear that he stepped out from the lift so quickly because he had caught sight of a rather odd-looking woman standing inside. Close to where we should have had to stand. She was a big woman, rather stout, with a floating black veil flung over the crown of her hat and hanging down behind. It was fastened on in front with a silver star." Miss Longstaff was speaking slowly, and Moy felt that she was watching him very closely. So much did he feel this that he wondered if she were telling him the truth, or merely testing out some tale on him to see whether it passed for true.

"Yes?" he said as she paused. He decided to make no comment. She looked disappointed, he fancied, and his distrust of her was not lessened by the notion.

"You've never met such a person?" she inquired curiously. "Never seen anyone who answers to that description?"

"I've never met a flowing black veil and a silver star," he assured her, "that's all you've described to me, except big and stout. What was the woman like besides?"

"Oh," Miss Longstaff looked almost contemptuous, "can't you see her from what I've said? No? Well, she had an earnest face, wore spectacles, and at the present moment has a fearful sore throat that makes her whisper."

"You know her then?" Moy was getting interested. Also puzzled.

"Yes and no. She lives or lived here in this house. But she's gone. And went without letting me know about it. But I'll go back, and as it's quite confidential I'm going to be very frank. You'll be horrified but I shall bear up." Again that wicked snap came into her dark eyes. "Well, I asked Mr. Gilmour why on earth he let the lift go up without us, and he asked me if I had seen two stout men standing by the liftman. One couldn't help seeing them-like the woman with the floating veil. I said that I had, and he told me that he wanted very much to dodge them. They were a couple of men who were collecting for some fund or other, and had badgered the life out of him so much a week ago that he had been weak enough to give them a half promise of a subscription. He regretted it the moment after, and wanted particularly to avoid them for a while. So he waited for the next lift and that was that."

"Well?" Moy asked again as she sat back. "What then?"

"Well, I didn't believe him, Mr. Moy. As it happened, both those men had been sitting in the same car on the underground with us, and he hadn't turned a hair. No, I knew then-as I know now-that it was the woman with the veil who kept him from entering the lift."

It was Moy who stared hard at Miss Longstaff this time. Was this true? Any, or all, of it? He waited.

"And just lately, since I've begun to rather waver in my ideas as to his accident with the revolver, I've wondered..."

"Wondered what?" Moy asked.

"Whether he hadn't an enemy after all. Which means someone who wanted to harm him. You know, Mr. Moy, I didn't believe his story at first-about shooting Mr. Ingram by sheer accident, but something in the way he spoke when he left me-when he disappeared-rather made me waver. And I've been thinking hard ever since, and bit by bit I've wondered whether there around that woman-might lie the clue to his disappearing so suddenly-she's left here too," she finished.

"How do you know her name, and that she lives here?" Moy asked.

"Mr. Gilmour met a friend, and I slipped away as soon as the lift got to the top, and looked around for the floating veil. Fortunately it was waiting for a bus just close to the tube entrance. So I waited too. And got out where she did. And came here after her, and took a room here and made her acquaintance. And all to no result!" She opened dramatic hands at the last sentence to show the palms empty. "She says she never heard of Gilmour, refused to recognize his description when I gave it to her. She swears that her life is entirely wrapped up in disarmament propaganda."

"Well?" Moy asked again, as she seemed to have quite finished. She hunched a shoulder. "It's not true, Mr. Moy. I saw Lawrence Gilmour's eyes fall on her and I saw the look of real uneasiness come instantly into his face and the look of relief when we stepped back and the lift shot away. She wasn't looking in our direction, but trying to get her purse back into her handbag. Now that's what's bothering me...I had to speak of it. At first, I thought it was connected with something underhand on his part. Something with which the death of Mr. Ingram was linked-if only I could find the link. But just lately-well, I'm feeling a little uneasy."

"Where's she now?" Moy asked, jumping up. "I'll have a word with her if you like."

"No one knows-or at least no one will tell me where she's gone to," Alfreda said to that. "I found it quite impossible to become friends with her in the short time I've been here. She was oddly distrustful of any overtures."

Not oddly, wisely, Moy thought, considering the motives which had actuated at least one maker of friendly advances. But he did not think Miss Longstaff had much sense of humor except a sardonic one.

"Perhaps I tried to hurry too much. Anyway she rather markedly held me at a distance. And then, one morning, I found her room door standing wide open and was told that she had gone. As a matter of fact I had borrowed a book just the day before, because I saw she was packing, and I wanted her to give me her address. But either she forgot about the book, or, as I now think, she wanted me to think she would let me know where to send it on, in order to get clear the easier. They tell me that she's been seen passing the house, so I have taken to haunting the streets lately because of a certainty that she knows more than she acknowledged of Gilmour, and therefore may know where he is now."

Moy asked if Mrs. Findlay had any other friends in the house. Miss Longstaff said that, as one would expect with a very dour-looking, plain, middle-aged body, she had no other friends whatever. "The manageress says she has no idea where Mrs. Findlay is. I suppose she's speaking the truth..." Miss Longstaff again showed that rather worn, dispirited look which she had worn when Moy came in. "But somehow lately I'm worried about Lawrence Gilmour. Uneasy. Almost apprehensive. He's cut himself completely off from all help. Anything might happen..." Moy saw what really looked like genuine concern in those bright dark eyes, and answering it, in return for what, finally, he believed was a true account which might help towards clearing away the shadows around Gilmour, he told her of the envelope left with him should an S.O.S. come. He did not tell her how the summons might come. She seemed very interested.

"He knew he might be going into danger," she murmured. "Oh, more and more I feel that I've wronged him."

"You changed the sheets, didn't you?" Moy said suddenly.

She looked at him with large eyes. "No," she said simply. "No. I drew out the sheet from under Mr. Ingram on which he was half-wrapped and half-lying. It struck me that the hole wasn't as far away from the edge as it ought to be, if the end had covered all of Mr. Ingram's face, and I pulled it out to have a better look...but I didn't change the sheet." Moy did not believe her, and his disbelief of this part of the talk swept over all that had gone before. He doubted everything that he had just heard, her change of mind, her tale about her first sight of the lady with the star. He rose and they parted on rather a forced note of concern for Gilmour. He wanted to think over what he had just heard, but an acquaintance buttonholed him and accompanied him nearly to his door, and Moy had to rush to be in his flat in time for Mrs. Pratt and her daughter, whom he had asked to have a look at his rooms now that they were finished. It would be a sort of leave-taking too, as they were going off on Haliburton's yacht so shortly.

It struck him, as he hurriedly put some flowers into water, that the steps outside sounded very heavy for two ladies.

The mystery was explained by the entrance of Miss Pratt, accompanied by Haliburton. The young man did not stop.

"He's coming back for me," Winnie explained. "My mother was detained by that dreadful chief inspector."

"Oh?" Moy was startled. "Detained" had a professional sound. Unconscious of it, Winnie bent over some canapes, and selected one with a sort of mosaic of egg and ham on it.

"I much prefer tea to cocktails, it's ever so much better for the complexion. Yes, my mother won't be able to get here after all. That dreadful man asked for a word with her, and I left them both looking very glum and busy. Fred Ingram is back," she rambled on. "I thought he was going to be away for weeks and weeks, but he says he tried a new system at roulette and got cleaned out. I'm glad he's back. He's so sympathetic...such a help to me these dreadful days. So is Basil. They're both such dears. Basil, of course, is simply wonderful. I do begin to realize that. But I can't forget poor Lawrence Gilmour...he might be dead for all we hear of him or from him."

At her words a little chill seemed to come into the room. She leaned forward. "Why did you let him do it, Mr. Moy, vanish like that?"

"How do you know he has vanished?" he countered swiftly.

"Miss Longstaff is beginning to worry too," she went on, without answering his question. "She's rung me up several times lately. I feel I haven't done her justice. I thought her so fright-fully hard, but, of course, if she doesn't love Mr. Gilmour, perhaps there was a certain honesty in saying so at once...I begin to think that she didn't care for him ever...and would have broken with him anyway. But speaking about him, Mr. Moy, didn't he leave any message, any address?" She was quite a charming sight in the plainly-furnished room, like a spray of lovely flowers all soft colors and grace; Moy's heart warmed to her. She was leaning towards him so that he could see the texture of her smooth pink and white skin, the sheen on the curls over her ears. "I believe there's someone who's his enemy," she breathed, "and who wants to harm him. Who hoped to have him arrested for murder, and still wants to harm him. He shouldn't have gone all alone, where no one can help him. He may be in some most frightful danger."

Moy could not refrain from a little comfort.

"He left an envelope with me that I'm to send on to the Yard should things go really wrong," he blurted out.

"How will you know if they are wrong!" she asked almost accusingly. Moy could only assure her that he would know, and explained.

"But you ought to have that precious envelope always with you! Think how awful it would be if he were to need your help and you had to waste time sending for it."

He assured her that no time would be lost.

Haliburton and Fred Ingram and Tark all came in together at that. Haliburton said he was sorry to bring the regiment, but they had all happened to meet and decided to go on together to one of the non-stop variety shows which had a really remarkable dancing turn of which all the town was talking.

Tark seemed as close-mouthed as ever, except that he shot Fred Ingram one swift look from expressionless eyes as he murmured that he had been home for a little visit which had done him a world of good.

He added something about being off shortly for Diamantino. Moy had no idea where that was, but it sounded as though it would suit Tark. Frederick and he seemed to eye each other so closely that Moy wondered whether each had come because the other was there.

Haliburton asked Moy whether he had any news of Gilmour, and Winnie, turning to the three visitors, passed on the information just given her before Moy could stop her. He had not bargained on that.

"He believes now that it was murder, and he's gone after whoever did it. All by himself. Isn't it splendid, Basil?"

For the first time since Ingram's death Moy thought she sounded insincere. Was it possible that Gilmour's distrust of her was based on some real foundation? A sort of panic seized Moy at the thought of what his tongue might have done. Then he reassured himself. He had not shown anyone the envelope. True, Tark's eyes and his had met when just a second ago he had glanced at his bureau to see that it was locked as usual. But Tark would not connect his, Moy's, swift glance, with the place where Gilmour's letter was kept. That letter lay heavily on Moy's mind. So much might depend on it. Of course, in all probability, it would never be needed, but...his visitors all began to talk at once. Miss Pratt absolutely insisted on Moy coming to the show with them. She said he was looking worried. He had already made his arrangements with the porter to answer his telephone, and, as always nowadays, left word with him where he could be at once reached, if asked for by Mr. Gilmour.

Moy found the entertainment dull. He excused himself after the first turn. Tark and Frederick Ingram had drifted out before it had properly begun. Back inside the building where his flat was, the porter came out to meet him as he made for the lift.

"One of your friends left his gloves behind him, sir. I let him in. They were lying on a chair. That all right? He said his name was Ingram."

Moy assured him it was and went on up. He remembered noticing Tark's gloves lying in a chair, as that silent man reached up to try one of the concealed lights in the dining-room. However, perhaps Frederick had left his too, at any rate there were no gloves to be seen now as he looked round his flat.

He felt out of sorts. Miss Pratt's words that Gilmour might be dead haunted him, try as he would to shake them off. Where was Gilmour? On what dark trail? His mind went to Miss Longstaff's odd tale about his reluctance, or rather his dread, of being in the same lift with the woman-Mrs. Findlay...but was there any truth in that story? If not, for what purpose had that astute young woman told him it? Was something about to happen which she wished to be able to attribute to the woman with the floating veil? Or...again a sort of chill swept over the young solicitor. Had she stuffed him with any story just to get him into a confidential mood, into a frame of mind to exchange his confidence for her rubbish? His account of the letter left with him for her account of a mysterious terror on the part of Gilmour? He went to his bureau, unlocked it and then the drawer where he kept the precious letter in another locked box. Yes, it was still there. That awful fear that had suddenly gripped him was absurd. Slightly comforted, but not at all pleased with himself, he returned to his chair and picked up a book.

The telephone rang. In an instant he had lifted the receiver. He heard Gilmour's voice, but speaking very, very quietly, as though anxious not to be overheard, saying:

"That you, Moy? It's me, Gilmour. Oh, I'm quite all right, thanks —" This in answer to a swift inquiry on Moy's part. "But listen, don't get worried if I don't drop in at the Eggs and Bacon tonight as I promised. I may not be able to get up to town. And as I promised you to look in and report, I was afraid you might do something silly if you didn't see me. Cheerio!"

"Righto!" came Moy's eager voice, "that's all right, old man." He heard the receiver dropped at the other end on to its hook, and sprang across the zoom. He unlocked the bureau with fingers that shook a little. The signal had come. He pulled out the envelope from its locked box, ran the paper-cutter carefully along the edge and drew out-four blank envelopes. Just such envelopes as were in his pigeon-holes always. He stared at the four, and felt as though his heart had stopped beating for a second. He had let Gilmour down He had let him down in what was perhaps his utmost need, his last extremity. That quiet in Gilmour's voice; was it fear, was it exhaustion, was it...

In a second he had the 'phone in his hand again and was asking for Chief Inspector Pointer, but Pointer was not at the Yard. His superintendent, however, took the urgent message that Moy almost stammered into the 'phone. That official seemed to know all about the case, and Moy was assured that the telephone call could, and would, be traced at once, and help, if possible, sent to the man who might need it so sorely.

Moy walked his room in an agony of horror and self-abasement. Someone had got in here, picked the locks protecting that which had been entrusted to him to guard, that which might mean life or death to the man who had given it him, and after getting the envelope, had taken out the precious contents and left him but the empty shell, as one gives a child a bauble to keep it quiet. He had only one hope-fingerprints.

CHAPTER 17

POINTER asked to see Mrs. Pratt. He could imagine quite easily what it was that she had written to Charles Ingram, the reading of which had so upset him that his brother-in-law thought that he had received some sort of warning note, but Pointer wanted facts.

Mrs. Pratt received the chief inspector coldly, with the look of a woman with whom the past is past, and who has no intention of being at the beck and call of Scotland Yard because she happened to have stayed in the house when a death had occurred.

"Mrs. Pratt," Pointer said, looking thoughtfully at his hat this time, instead of at his shoes, "I'm afraid I must ask you for some information which may be painful to you to give. But it's really important-in clearing up all the circumstances of Mr. Ingram's death-to be sure of what was in that letter which you wrote him. The letter which he burned after reading it in accordance with your own wishes. You say it was a rhyme of some kind, but I think that can hardly be this paper to which I'm referring. This one upset Mr. Ingram very badly. So badly that I can guess, we can all guess, what was in it. But I must have certainty before turning it down and passing on to other points."

Mrs. Pratt listened with an absolutely mulish face. But it had flushed. She had neither a mean nor a cowardly face, and that being so, he persevered.

"I do really beg you to be frank with me, as I say, until I know for certain that the letter in question only referred to Miss Pratt, was only written with the intention of preventing Mr. Ingram falling in love with someone who was going to marry another man. I can't disregard it. I must try to find out its contents."

"This is confidential?" Mrs. Pratt asked suddenly.

"Supposing it is something which has nothing to do with Mr. Ingram's death-absolutely." Pointer promised her.

"Of course it has nothing to do with his death!" But Mrs. Pratt was pale now, and her teeth set themselves after each sentence. "You've guessed rightly, Mr. Pointer. The letter you seem to've heard about was one in which I showed Mr. Ingram how hopeless it was for him to fall in love with my daughter."

"By telling him something about herself or her ancestry?" Pointer went on. The request of Mrs. Pratt that Ingram should burn the note suggested this, and her fear lest it fall into other hands-and its supposed effect on Ingram.

She flushed again and hesitated, then looked up frankly.

"In confidence I told him something quite untrue. I had to. I told him that Winnie had fits. That her father had had one when he fell overboard and was drowned. I knew Mr. Ingram was very strong about eugenics. It seems a horrid thing to have done-but-well, I had very real and dreadfully urgent reasons." Pointer waited. She had not finished. She was screwing herself up to say more.

"I'm tormented. I don't mind owning to you, and in strict confidence-by an awful thought, chief inspector. And that is that Mr. Ingram may have wanted to commit suicide and drawn Mr. Gilmour's bullet intentionally-after reading my letter."

Pointer listened very carefully now.

"You see, Mr. Gilmour was a very good shot, as was Mr. Ingram, I believe. And a good shot, when aiming a dummy cartridge at anyone, would aim it true, wouldn't he? He would shoot straight, thinking it was blank...nothing else would be natural. I've been tormenting myself with the fear that Mr. Ingram may have reasoned just like that and-and — —after my letter-thought that life wasn't worth living. Of course I haven't breathed a word of all this. And I should deny it if it came out," she flashed a glance of fire at the detective officer, "but between ourselves, and since there's still so much suspicion of poor Mr. Gilmour about, I'm afraid that's how it may have happened."

"That Mr. Ingram walked into the revolver, so to say, as another man might under a train, or a bus..." Pointer looked thoughtful.

She nodded. "I'm dreadfully sorry. But it had to be done." She spoke as a surgeon might have, after an operation which has cost the patient his life.

Pointer asked her a few questions, the drift of which she did not see. They were to find out if she knew, or could think of, any motive other than the one she had suggested. Then he had a word or two with her as to Miss Longstaff, and that young woman's probable feelings about the kindly interest which Miss Pratt took in Mr. Gilmour. Mrs. Pratt was a frank woman by nature. She seemed to be very open with Pointer.

"She's not in the least jealous, chief inspector, because Mr. Gilmour is entirely and most devotedly in love with her, and because of that he's quite safe from my daughter, however silly she may be. She's just crying for the moon because she's so tired of things that fall into her hands for the asking. But for Miss Longstaff my daughter wouldn't give Mr. Gilmour a second thought. As it is-well, it's passing off. I think I can even say it has passed off already. By the way, did Mr. Ingram burn that letter? Or did you find it? I was terrified of Mr. Tark getting hold of it and handing it to Mr. Haliburton. Of course he would prefer Mr. Haliburton to stay a bachelor. Mr. Tark won't have the run of his houses when he's married as he has now-just because of a lucky dip!"

"You may be quite reassured as to that. I believe that Mr. Tark can't show that letter to Mr. Haliburton, now or ever," and then Pointer thanked her and left. Supposing anyone knew or assessed Miss Longstaff's character, and attachment to Gilmour aright, and guessed the line which she had taken, the shooting of Ingram by Gilmour had removed two men from Miss Pratt's path therefore: Ingram by death, and Gilmour by making him no longer inaccessible to Miss Pratt. Pointer could see how anyone who knew the two girls and the two men might have expected just what had happened to happen.

This thought led to some reflective pauses in the chief inspector's brisk steps-he was walking to the Yard-but if so, this was one of those motives which can only be tested by elimination. Incidentally, Mrs. Pratt's confession as to what had been in the note which she had given to Ingram, and signed with her brief signature of *Ann Pratt*, bore out part of Appleton's story, and therefore practically dismissed the theory of an encounter with the third "post-office bandit." Yes, Pointer decided to drop that idea entirely for the present. He next thought over the woman's suggestion as to Ingram's death being really suicide on his own part. It was possible, but Pointer would have expected a man with such an intellectual side to him as had Ingram, to take refuge from any grief in the impregnable citadel of the spirit, like many another man and woman.

Pointer's mind passed on, as so many times before, to the posted papers. The *Of Von De* and the *Light Hell Claire* scraps belonged possibly to these. Yet if ciphers, or their deciphering, had played so much part in Ingram's income, one would have expected to learn of many, or heavy, postal deliveries at his flat. This was not the case. He had no office anywhere, as far as could be learned, nor did his infrequent and short absences from his study suggest this. Ingram seemed to have lived the quiet uninterrupted life dear to a man of letters. His half-brother and his sister claimed to have no idea that could assist the police in explaining the dead man's unexpected affluence. At The Tall House he had worked as one carrying out routine work. There was one other tiny detail. Pointer, in going over the proof-reading which Fred Ingram had done lately for his brother, noticed a great falling off in Ingram's output since a little before he went to The Tall House. Frederick said that his half-brother had spoken of being very busy on some work which did not need proof-reading. On Frederick expressing surprise, Ingram-according to the younger man-had said curtly that it was work for a firm who had all their proof-reading done by a member of their own staff.

What work would bring in four thousand a year without spreading the author's name abroad? And there was no known regular contribution of Charles Ingram's to account for the income paid him. Pointer felt that he ought to be able to think through this problem, as he had so many another. He dearly loved this part of his work. He stopped at a newspaper stall and, as so often before in this case, let his eyes and hands play over all papers spread out. Gardening articles weren't signed...but Ingram was no gardener...besides four thousand a year...Racing? Ingram had never gone to more than a couple of races, and had no books bearing on the sport of kings. Disconsolately, but doggedly, he turned the pages of a daily that he himself never glanced at, except from professional duty. A large square block caught his eye...held his eye...filled his eye...a crossword puzzle for whose solution three thousand pounds was offered. The author's name was not mentioned. He must be a clever chap, and possess a mind that was mechanical in a way, and yet extremely flexible...scholarly...mathematical...Pointer dropped the papers and walked on deep in thought. Ingram had wanted to catch the midnight post...quarter day was a week ago; the thousand had always been invested shortly after quarter day, would it again come to hand now that he was dead? It should have done so by now. Two days after quarter day had seen Ingram investing that thousand for the last five years. Could he test the possibility that Ingram was a crossword writer in any way? He himself did not go in for that amusement, but Chief Inspector Franklin did. He was known for his love of them. Pointer decided to go to his rooms at the Yard as soon as he had seen if there was anything important waiting for himself. But he found his superintendent with the telephone in one hand and two constables taking down notes in front of him.

"Gilmour left a message to be sent to you should he find himself in danger." The superintendent rapped out the news just received from the stricken Moy.

"The 'phone call has been traced. It came from a public telephone booth in Brixton. I sent Inspector Watts there at once with Evans and Ridgewell." The superintendent left the other to carry on.

Within half an hour Watts was telephoning from the box in question. There had been so many robberies from these public telephone boxes lately that a watch had been kept on them. None of the users had in the least resembled Gilmour. But Pointer had not thought they would.

Pointer set all wheels in motion, and then drove round to Moy's flat. He found him almost beside himself with worry.

"This envelope —I slit it at the top-but it still bears Gilmour's seal-his ring, you know-just as it did when he handed it me. Nothing shows to the eye-but what about fingerprints on it and on the bureau? There were no fingerprints on the blank envelopes. As for the one in which they were enclosed, Pointer examined the back with his lens. As he expected, he found so many of them that it would take the Yard's experts at least a day to sort them. It was a hopeless task. Moy again repeated that the envelope handed him had looked quite untouched when he took it out just now.

"I think we shall find that this seal has been shaved off with a hot knife, and fastened on with some form of spirit or gum," Pointer said finally. "May I keep it for fingerprints? It will be a long job. But some may turn up which will be of use-though, frankly, I doubt it."

Moy said he could keep it for any reason which might possibly help Gilmour.

"He's placed himself *hors la loi*, in a way," he went on, "but can't you save him? Can't he be reached?"

Pointer could only say that they were all working their hardest on the case and might yet come up with Gilmour.

"Not too late," came almost as a prayer from Moy.

"I hope not too," Pointer said very warmly to that, and asked Moy when his flat had been left vacant since the envelope had been handed him. When had it not, would have been easier to answer, it seemed. The flats were a simple form of service flat, the porter was a careful man, but he had four buildings to look after, and he could not, and did not, pretend to see who went in and out. If anyone had managed to obtain Moy's key, or had a similar one-it was not at all peculiar, Pointer found-it would be the easiest thing in the world to come and go unnoticed. Moy kept regular hours of a morning, and generally of an afternoon. He was seldom in of an evening from eight till past eleven. Altogether Moy's heart sank lower and lower, the more facts bearing on the matter he gave the chief inspector.

"And who knew of the letter?" The question he dreaded came at last. Dreaded and yet welcomed. For Moy was aflame to catch the person who had done this thing. He told the other of all those who certainly knew of the whereabouts of the letter, and added those who might do so.

"Fred Ingram and Tark both left the music-hall almost at once," Moy went on. "Tark first slipped out with a word about a forgotten engagement, and Frederick followed at once. I had an idea he wanted to say something to him."

"I should think that's quite possible," Pointer replied gravely enough outwardly, but with an inward chuckle. For that Fred Ingram, when he heard of Appleton's and Tark's successes at Monte Carlo, must have guessed that he had been spoofed was a foregone conclusion. Frederick was by no means a fool. Moy spoke of the incident of the gloves. Fred, when rung up just now, said that he had returned for his, and been shown in and out by the porter. Tark said that he had not left his behind, him. Leaving Moy to feel how inadequate is even Scotland Yard when confronted with some situations, Pointer went back to the Yard. After a glance in at his own rooms to make sure that nothing more had come for him to alter the lines of The Tall House puzzle, he sent for all the papers with crossword competitions running in them, beginning with the current month. Scotland, Yard has a well-stocked room, where papers and periodicals stay for a while, before being passed on to a sort of Home for Decayed Print in the suburbs.

CHAPTER 18

His colleague, Chief Inspector Franklin, had not yet come in, and Pointer had to work alone, sorting out on one side those Crosswords whose clues seemed to him of the kind to be written by such a man as Ingram, to be worth such a salary as Pointer believed might have been paid him for their composition.

Then he took these selected ones, discarded for the moment those with no money prizes attached, though he was not so sure of this being necessary, and concentrated on what remained. The fourth paper which he studied suddenly made his eyes sparkle. He was looking at the answers to the last week's puzzle, reading them along with the clues re-printed beside them. The first clue had read:

"Was called an idol, and whether one or not, contributed to the loss of an order." The solution was *Baphomet.*

A pamphlet rose before Pointer's mind, a nearly-finished article on the little copper image of a man with a beard and a crown found in every Chapter of the Knights Templar when their Order was broken up.

Ingram was one of those who believed that the name. Baphomet, or the little idol, as their enemies called it, stood for a cipher in which their True Rule and the Rite of Initiation had been written.

And then further down among the solutions was a word which again brought him up with a mental shock-the word *Devon* and further down still was an *Of.*

He thought of the so-called tri-lingual cipher OF VON DE and chuckled. From the first he had seen no reason why the letters might not stand for "Of Devon." He looked for *Hell, Light, Claire*, which also had seemed to him a fortuitous combination, but did not find them. He finished the clues and their solutions and sat back. The solver, the prize-winner, was given as a Mrs. Sampson of Lordship Lane, Dulwich. She must be a well-read woman to have solved this puzzle. A scholar had set these clues, and meant them to be tricky. The paper was the *Weekly Universe*, one which was pre-eminently a lottery paper, that is to say, its sales were influenced by the size and number of its prizes. This crossword for instance was a weekly feature it seemed, and always with a three-thousand pound prize for an all-correct solution.

He picked up the telephone and was put through to a news agency whose manager was a personal friend.

"Who is the writer of the *Weekly Universe's* Crosswords?"

"Lord Bulstrode himself," came the reply. "He's awfully proud of them. Some crosswords, aren't they?"

Lord Bulstrode was a man who, from the position of a cigarette salesman, had risen, first to be a tobacco merchant, and then to be the founder and editor-in-chief of the *Weekly Universe*, which had been running its sporting life for some eight years now. Lord Bulstrode...self-made if ever that adjective can be used...There was erudition in these puzzles...

He laid down the receiver and decided to try once more for Franklin. This time he found the other in, and with a minute to spare, while some fingerprints were being identified for him.

"First of all," Pointer began, "I want to say that I'm dropping your post-office robbery for the time being. I can't find anything to support it. But look here, Franklin, you're keen on crosswords; what about the one set by the *Weekly Universe*? The three-thousand pound prize one. Is it a good one?"

"Best going," came the unhesitating reply. "And the hardest. No initial letters or spaces to help you. And I don't say the clues aren't a bit too clever. Oh, none of your *Personal Pronoun* or *Japanese Coin* tricks, but for sheer difficulty, well, I've never known more than one person at a time to win it, if that. Often there's no correct solution. I got within two breaks of it myself once."

"I was wondering whether it would be possible to deduce the writer of a puzzle from his crosswords," Pointer said slowly.

Franklin was a man of quick apprehension.

"Easily. The difficulty would be to check one's guesses or deductions. As a matter of fact, we discussed the *Weekly Universe's* man at my Crosswords Club some time ago. And we think we've got him pretty well taped. You see, to win a really good puzzle, you've got to get yourself into the writer's skin mentally. We mean to capture that prize yet between the lot of us. But about the writer-he's one person. Has been for at least the last five years. He's distinctly a gentleman. A Cambridge, not an Oxford man. No great cricketer or footballer. Fond of tennis and fair at golf. Possibly a rowing man; we differed on that. No knowledge of animals. Traveled very little, if any. Well up in science. Personally I think he's a clergyman, but the others decided he was a schoolmaster, probably science master at some public school. He's unmarried. Post-war, of course. Rather young, I think. They say early middle age. Fond of John Masefield. Staunch Conservative. Member of at least one good London club. Lives out of town. Fair knowledge of flowers but hardly enough for a really good gardener. No good at music. Fond of a good play with a weakness for Ibsen. Loathes Strindberg. A first-class knowledge of chess. And one of the men of our Crosswords Club, a very brainy chap, says he's an authority on the Knights Templar or at least on their Order. I don't quite follow him there...but it's possible. There, that's the outcome of five years' close study-very close study."

"I'm told that Lord Bulstrode writes these crosswords himself," Pointer said innocently.

"Rot!" was the reply. "You mean that he wants it thought he writes them. That's true enough. So keep my opinion and that of the club to yourself. But what have crosswords to do with your murder?"

"Have you had any clues lately that *Hell* or *Light* or *Claire* would fit?" Pointer asked.

"*Claire!*" Franklin said in a tone of anguish. "*Claire!* I never thought of that. Well, it's not too late yet. That one has to be sent in this week. Half a minute —" He dived into his pocket and out with his letter-case. From it came a folded note-book, and opening it at a page, he jotted down on a printed Crossword square *Claire*. Pointer looked over his shoulder. He saw no words among the other's solutions that interested him. But four of the words found on the scattered bits, four of the so-called "tri-lingual cipher," had turned up already. The others would doubtless follow, for none of them fitted here. He was still studying the squares and making quite sure of this, which was not so easy as it sounds-for the clue to *Claire* was "Means light in some places, and yet may mean much more" —when Franklin was called away by his superintendent. He picked up his note-book and ran for it, with a murmur about having no time to waste as *he* was not on a murder case.

Pointer stood a moment quite still, looking down at his shoe-tips. That Ingram was the writer of crosswords for which he was paid a thousand pounds a quarter, each of which carried big prize money, explained several things...that inner pocket with its special fastening...the folded waistcoat under his pillow...supposing he had some notes or memoranda of the solutions...still in it, or even a notification of where he had sent his registered letter. His refusal to help with crossword solutions, or even to hear them discussed in his presence. And the crossword puzzle with Claire in it had only come out the day before yesterday, Sunday. And *Hell* and *Light* were not yet out. For they would not answer any of the clues published so far. That meant that Ingram had sent off several crosswords, not merely one on the night of his death. Probably, as he was paid quarterly, he posted thirteen puzzles. And if the murderer was out to get Ingram's most carefully guarded copy of the thirteen solutions which Pointer now believed was the real motive for Ingram's death, then the murderer would naturally have waited until the puzzles were posted. But not longer. The next morning might see Ingram taking his copy of the solutions to some safe, or Pointer was much mistaken. He judged the dead man to have been scrupulous down to the last detail in his work. He'd been in a hurry to get something-manuscript-to the post in time...He had worked as a rule with his door shut, if not locked. No one had been allowed to see at what he was working. No one, as far as Pointer could find, knew that he was a composer of crosswords. Thirteen puzzles possibly sent off in one batch. Thirteen times three thousand is thirty-nine thousand pounds. Quite a nice little sum. Yes, here was a motive which was quite as good as even an infallible system, and which explained all the actions of the dead man as well. It was a motive, moreover, which would not be as dangerous as playing the system would be. For that was known by at least four people to exist. It would have to be played openly. The solutions could be worked in secret. No one seemed to have suspected Ingram of being the author of these puzzles. Pointer went through the papers on his table, and made a list of the winners. The lady who had solved *Baphomet* interested him, for the clue set for that word had been all but beyond the allowable in sketchiness. The week before, the prize had been won by a Mr. Nevern, of Pawcett Road, Hammersmith. The week before that, there had been no winner. The week before that, it had been a parson...Pointer had his constable clerk write down all this year's winners. Meanwhile he picked up the telephone, and again talked to his friend of the news agency. How did people receive their money, if they won one of the *Weekly Universe* three-thousand-pound prizes?

He was told that if living in England, the winner had to apply in person at the *Weekly Universe's* office. If they lived in some impossible place, Bulolo for instance, the check would be paid into their account on receipt of a duplicate of the coupon sent in showing the claimant's writing and with a photograph of himself attached. The paper wanted advertisement, of course, and tried to interest the local press in the matter. As far as his informer could say, the prize had only once been won by a man outside the British Isles, and that had been a Remittance man who had died of drink two days before his check was sent him.

Pointer said he wanted information about the last four winners of this particular prize. He wanted some bright intellect sent along to secure it, while he himself made his swift way to the room of the Competition Editor of the *Weekly Universe*, whose name the agency gave him as Henry Orlebar. As he walked around to the huge white building only a stone's throw from the Yard, he remembered that Lord Bulstrode had got his barony for his financial aid to the Conservative party, that Ingram had done well when he stood as Conservative candidate for his university town, lowering the Liberal majority handsomely. That Bulstrode and Ingram were both members of the Junior Carlton Club, of which Haliburton was a member too. Could the link be political as well, supposing it to exist, between Bulstrode and that quarterly thousand pounds?

He found Henry Orlebar ready to see him immediately on his official card being sent in. Orlebar was a lean, horsey-looking man who might have sat for a painting of the horse prophet the world over. But his manners were good, and his smile very engaging.

"Circumstances look as though Mr. Ingram's death might be due to foul play, Mr. Orlebar, which is why I have called on you for a full account of why a thousand pounds has been paid him once a quarter from this office for the last five years." Orlebar let this pass, so Pointer had guessed right.

"It's really Lord Bulstrode's fine feeling," Orlebar began with a frank gaze bent on his visitor, as though delighted to clear up any perplexity. "Of course this is quite confidential, but Mr. Ingram was of such enormous use to him when he met him not long after starting this paper. I mean, by working out figures concerned with advertising and circulation which revolutionized all hitherto conceived ideas of such things. Bulstrode followed his advice-his system really-and the paper has advanced by leaps and bounds. Lord Bulstrode offered him a sort of extra post as Director of Circulation and Sales but Ingram turned the offer down quite decidedly. So Bulstrode insisted on his accepting a salary of four thousand a year, a mere one per cent, of what he saved the paper, thanks to his genius for figures."

It all sounded so straightforward. But apart from his preconceived notion as to what the payment was for, Pointer would not have believed a word of it. Such a sum, paid for such a reason, would have been sent in directly to Ingram's banking account, or posted him by check.

"And why has not the usual thousand been sent in this quarter day?" he asked.

"We're waiting for Lord Bulstrode to be back and give his directions as to sending it in," Orlebar said brightly. "Ingram's death, of course, alters the usual procedure."

"Why was it always sent in such a fantastic way?" Pointer asked next.

"Ingram's own wish entirely. He insisted on notes being posted him in a registered envelope. Whether he has any relatives who sponge on him...of course, it's not for me to say. But getting it in this way, it's obvious that he need not pay it into his account unless he wished to. Say it was overdrawn...he said something to me once —" Orlebar seemed to have a perfect spasm of frankness at the remembrance, his eyes looking positively infantile in their candor —"which rather suggested that. Though I've forgotten the exact words by now."

The one-hundred-pound notes looked to Pointer much more like Bulstrode's own preference, but Pointer thanked him, was assured that Orlebar had only been too delighted to be of use, as Lord Bulstrode would be, if he were not in South Africa getting some cool breezes instead of this heat. Of course, Orlebar went on to say, had he himself had any idea that Ingram's salary, for it was virtually that, was of any interest, he would have at once told the Yard all about it. But seeing that there seemed no question but that the poor chap had been shot by Gilmour-most unfortunate devil-he, Orlebar, had not even considered the matter.

"But now that you do know our suspicions, now that I tell you in confidence that we are thinking of murder as an explanation for Mr. Ingram's death, are you willing to put in writing what you have just told me, and swear to it?" Pointer asked. "I mean the reason given by you for his salary. I don't mind telling you, Mr. Orlebar, that what you have just told me does not square at all with certain information in our possession. Certain written information."

Orlebar no longer beamed frankness and candor. His thin face grew stiff. He rubbed his chin.

"Umph...I couldn't do anything like that, of course, without consulting Lord Bulstrode," he said promptly. "I might be mistaken...I wouldn't care to swear to anything without consulting him."

Pointer said that he thought that just as well, and inquired when the editor-in-chief would be back. He was expected next week. Pointer said the Yard would try and wait for his return, leaving Orlebar looking as though he would like to chew a straw, and meditate a while. Pointer quite understood his silence. The position was one which only Bulstrode himself could clear, up. Fortunately, the Yard would insist on having a full acknowledgment from him of the exact work done by the dead man, for that work-the concoction of the weekly crossword puzzles set by the paper, would, Pointer now felt sure, be the motive put forward by the prosecution for the murder of Charles Ingram.

Back at the Yard, Pointer was deep in his notes, when a clever-looking young reporter was shown in. He was from the agency.

"Here you are!" He pulled out some papers from his pocket. "Mrs. Sampson, winner of The *Weekly Universe's Great Crossword Competition*. Very little but that is known about her. Here's her picture, and I'm told it's a very poor one." He showed a grim-looking, middle-aged woman wearing a rather obviously false fringe that came down into her eyes.

"I got on to the *Weekly Universe's* reporter who had been sent down to break the glad tidings to her and interview her. He said she refused to tell anything about herself except that she was a widow, and was fond of crosswords. She claimed to have solved this one with the help of a friend. Friend to remain anonymous. The paper wanted to give her a reception, but she said she had a sore throat, and must not expose it to the night air. She really did seem in pain, and could hardly croak, the *Weekly Universe* man said, so they let her off the function, as she said she was leaving for a trip around the world as soon as it could be arranged. She was handed the check last week at the newspaper office, thanked them in a way that suggested that she was only getting her deserts, and cashed the check at once at Cooks, as had been arranged at her request by the paper. One of the editorial staff went along with her. She paid for a tour round the world, which took close on five hundred pounds, and had the rest handed over to her in French franc notes."

Pointer looked at the date of the payment. It was the day preceding Ingram's death.

"I went on to her address myself," the reporter continued. "It's a small house which lets out rooms. She had taken hers for a fortnight, the time just covering the reception of the news that she had won the prim and the receiving of the check. She had left there, though her tour is not due to start for another week yet, but she looked in at Cooks twice since then, once three days ago, once this morning. Only to pick up some folders. She's the sort of vision not encountered by the dozen. Corkscrew ringlets, and a black veil floating down her back pinned to her hat by a silver star in front. She didn't dress like that in Dulwich, and therefore it doesn't show in her picture. The *Weekly Universe* chap thinks she put them all on in honor of the great occasion of coming to the office."

Judging by the fortnight for which the rooms were taken, it almost looked as though Mrs. Sampson had known that they would cover just that particular period. Which, Pointer thought, was extremely likely.

"Now as to the winner of the week before," went on the reporter, "he's a chap called Algernon Nevern, and lived off the Hammersmith Broadway, a retired schoolmaster. Pawcett Road, No. 21, is the address. He was given quite a reception at the Hammersmith Town Hall a week ago, has left his room in Pawcett Road, and has vanished. I can't find anyone who has seen him since."

So Nevern had vanished. That brought things looping back again to Pointer's idea of a disappearance being connected with Ingram's murder. He would look up Mr. Nevern at once, otherwise the lady with the obviously added fringe, would have had his first attention.

He felt in his letter case for a fragment of wall paper which had never left him since he picked it up in the passage where lay Ingram's dead body, a piece of wallpaper which, so far, he had not been able to match. He was now going to see fresh rooms. One certainly, and probably two. He would not be at all surprised to learn within a few hours where this scrap came from. Since it was Nevern who seemed to have vanished, he would expect it to match Nevern's paper, supposing as he did, that it had been dropped in the corridor by the merest mischance, and had not been noticed by the person dropping it.

CHAPTER 19

POINTER went first to Lordship Lane. But the house in question neither knew, nor cared to know more, of the taciturn Mrs. Sampson, who had lodged with them so short a time, had won such a fortune, and had not distributed it among the inmates of the house. He learned no more than what had been told to the news agency reporter. They claimed to have no idea whence she had come to them, except that they fancied it was out of town. She brought in flowers on occasions which suggested a garden some distance away, as they were always drooping and flagging. She had had no luggage except one suitcase. Now, she had spoken to Cooks of luggage for the hold, and had the right labels for big trunks given her. Where was that luggage? Had she no friends, he asked. No, none. No letters had ever come for her until she had won "all that money," when the house had been swamped with communications for her, 'phone calls for her, telegrams for her, visitors asking for her. Had she had no 'phone calls at all before? Pointer had tipped the elderly housemaid well, and she was inclined to thaw. He explained that it was a question of wanting Mrs. Sampson as witness to a street accident. It was most important to get into touch with her. The housemaid said that Mrs. Sampson used to get a telephone call almost every evening. Always the same voice speaking. A man's voice. Dreadfully difficult to make out what he was saying. He never gave his name, not that she would have understood it, probably, if he had, but only asked for Mrs. Sampson, who seemed to expect the call and was always ready to answer it. Had the housemaid any idea of where the speaker at the other end came from? She had not. Did Mrs. Sampson ever ring him up, and if so, had she heard the number. Mrs. Sampson often did. She couldn't remember the number, but it was River something or other...That meant Hammersmith.

He was permitted to look into Mrs. Sampson's rooms. They had been let again, and did not interest him after one keen look around:

He asked about Mrs. Sampson's throat, and learned that she could hardly speak aloud, and could be heard gargling morning and evening with maddening thoroughness. Mrs. Sampson usually wore corkscrew ringlets and a floating veil on her hat, didn't she? The housemaid stared. He must be thinking of another woman. Mrs. Sampson wore her hair right into her eyes, straight untidy hair it was. As for hats, she lived in a black felt hat of severest cut while at the house.

Pointer drove to Hammersmith. Mrs. Sampson fitted the idea which he had had at the back of his mind all along as a possible solution to the puzzle at The Tall House. A rather unusual looking woman, large and full of figure, who seemed to have no relations or friends to inquire about her...she had, moreover, presumably had at least two thousand five hundred pounds in francs in her possession, and whatever other money she owned...But she had not disappeared. And Nevern had.

Pointer stopped at the house in Pawcett Road, a dingy place.

"He's gone!" the untidy but good-natured looking maid said promptly as soon as Pointer mentioned his name. "You mean him as won all that money? Said he couldn't stand 'the no-triarty.' I asked him what he meant by that and he says people coming cadging all day long." She flushed. "I mean —" she began awkwardly, "I mean-well, of course I don't mean —I wasn't intending nothing, sir, in repeating that. Not in your case."

"I haven't come about the money he won," Pointer said reassuringly. "I only want him as a witness in a street accident. How did he win his money? Horses?"

He heard all about the crossword competition, and interspersed the hearing with questions which gave him a very good idea of Mr. Nevern's appearance and habits.

"Any friends who might know where he is now?" he asked finally.

"He had a lady friend. She used to ring him up ever so often on the 'phone. She's had a bad throat lately. Said it hurt her to raise her voice. Oh —" in answer to further questions —"she was ever such an old friend. They used to telephone to each other nearly every day. She did crosswords too. Wonderful to think that there's all that money waiting for you if you only guessed right, isn't it!"

"What was her name? You mean Mrs. Sampson, don't you?" Pointer said easily.

"I never heard her name. She never gave it. 'Just ask Mr. Nevern to step to the telephone please,' was what she used to say, or 'Please tell Mr. Nevern that I think I've solved it myself,' and when I would ask who was speaking she'd just say, 'He'll know who it is.' She never even so much as gave her number."

"And didn't you hear him ask for it?" Pointer said with real curiosity.

"He had a telephone of his own put into his room. It's been taken out when he left, of course. That's why he never had no letters or hardly ever. He said he liked 'phones best and always used them himself."

Pointer asked if Mr. Nevern's room had been taken? It had not. Could he see it? He was often asked by young men if he could tell them of pleasant inexpensive rooms somewhere central. She took him down a passage and up a flight of stairs to what was evidently the best room in the house. And on the wall Pointer saw a rather pretty but faded wall paper of dun and blue and heliotrope, the same pattern as on the little piece in his pocket-book. Over the mantel-shelf a long strip had been torn away. He pointed to it now.

"What a pity! Spoils the room," he murmured.

"Mr. Nevern did that just at the end. He always kept piles of books there and caught it up with one of them. It had been loose for ever so long. I saw him do it. He was hurrying out, and came back in a rush, snatched up two books, and ran for it. That was when he did it."

How long had Mr. Nevern lived here? Nearly a year, it seemed. Had he always had this lady friend who telephoned him? Not till about three months or maybe a bit more, the little maid thought. No, there wasn't no one in the house who could tell the caller more about Mr. Nevern, because he hadn't any friends. "Nice old gentleman he is too," she went on, "if only one could understand him. Cleft palate he told me it was. Made him talk so funny!" She giggled. "Not that he ever tried to talk much. I liked him. He made you sort of sorry for him, no friends nor nothing, and always so easy to please."

Pointer took the room at once for a Mr. Jones. He did not want that wall paper removed. Mr. Jones was moving in at once, he told her, though he might not always be able to sleep there. "He often has to take night duty," he finished up.

The little maid said they had had a reporter once in the house and once a couple of girls from a dance club who were just the same. The main thing to Pointer was that the room was taken and the paper safe for the time being. His next move was to find Mrs. Sampson. Since Nevern was linked with The Tall House by that piece of wall paper and his disappearance, then the winner of the next crossword prize was equally linked. For from Nevern on, Pointer believed that all the next thirteen prizes were destined for one and the same person-the murderer. The trouble was how to find this so-called Mrs. Sampson, for he did not think that her name, any more than her fringe, was genuine. After a cup of coffee at a nearby Lyons, he returned to Pawcett Road. He hoped that the little maid would have either recollected something more or have talked with others in the house who might remember something more. As the taker of Mr. Nevern's room he was admitted at once. Wasn't Mr. Jones in yet? Pointer seemed surprised, but, as he himself had paid for a week's rent in advance, not dismayed.

"That lady who 'phoned to Mr. Nevern keeps worrying me," he confided to the maid, "she might be the very lady who had the street accident, and we particularly want to find out who she is. No name in her purse, poor soul. Nothing to tell where she lives."

"There's a charlady what helps once a week, Emmie," another maid listening near broke in now, "she says that she heard Mr. Nevern saying over the 'phone once in a funny voice, 'Ask Mrs. Findlay to come here to the 'phone, please. No name. Just ask her to come to the 'phone.' Well, that sounds as though it might be this Mrs. Findlay who telephoned him that often."

Mrs. Findlay! Pointer had seen that name written in a book which Miss Longstaff had among some of her books. Mrs. Findlay...and the address had been the house where Miss

Longstaff herself had taken a room since leaving The Tall House, a house of what are quaintly called American flatlets, the other side of Hammersmith Broadway from Pawcett Road. Miss Longstaff...Mrs. Findlay...Nevern...Ingram's murderer...Pointer walked on with a quickened pulse. The house in question was, as he knew from his men's reports, a most respectable one chiefly lived in by business men and women or professional people with small salaries. He found it without any difficulty, and asked for Mrs. Findlay.

"She's left here, sir. About three weeks ago. Gone down to her cottage in the country, before going abroad."

Along came a stout woman in black. This was the manageress. She took charge of the inquiries.

"The lady is wanted as a witness in a street accident," Pointer explained, handing her his official card.

"She's gone to her cottage in the country before going on a tour round the world. Thinking of settling in New Patagonia, or New California, or one of those places...She hasn't started yet, for I saw her only this morning passing the house."

"The address of her cottage?" he asked. The manageress did not know it.

"How about some friend who can tell me where to find her?" he suggested. "She doubtless has quite a number."

"Only one. An old gentleman."

"You don't mean a Mr. Nevern? To whom the accident has happened?" Pointer asked quickly. "Could you describe him?"

The manageress did. An elderly gentleman with curly gray hair worn rather long. The manageress did not know his name, and, though she had often seen him, had hardly ever really looked at him. "Personally I couldn't have stood his way of talking. He had a cleft palate. But there, I dare say he was ever so nice an old gentleman, really!"

"Has he called since Mrs. Findlay had left?"

"Yes, twice. But not lately. Just at first. He never gave his name, just walked to her room and knocked, if she was in, or asked for her and said he would come again if she was out."

"This is Mrs. Findlay, isn't it?" He showed a copy of the newspaper portrait of the winner of the crossword puzzle. It had been cleverly blurred to look like a snapshot. The manageress shook her head.

"Same sort of fat face and that, but Mrs. Findlay had hair going over so far back on her forehead, and long ringlets over her ears."

"Perhaps she's put a fringe on to be taken in," a maid suggested, looking at the picture in her turn.

"Catch Mrs. Findlay doing that sort of thing," scoffed the manageress.

"And where's her veil and her star?" asked the maid, laughing. "She wouldn't be found drowned without them, would she?"

Pointer obtained a very close, but not very useful description of the real Mrs. Findlay. The chief thing both maid and manageress insisted on was a floating black veil which she always wore fastened to her hair or hat by a silver star-the star of peace.

"How about a Miss Longstaff who lives here?" Pointer asked finally. "Does she know her?"

"She lives here, but she's not in at present. She knows Mrs. Findlay all right-in a sort of way-or did. I mean she knew her to speak to while Mrs. Findlay lived here, but they haven't kept it up."

"Mrs. Findlay wouldn't know who Miss Longstaff is, would she!" giggled the maid. The manageress shot her a reproving glance.

"She means that Miss Longstaff took her room under her pen-name, 'Miss Gray.' She writes as that, and we called her that at first. But now that she's really going to live here she gave us her real name. Lots of writers do the same." The manageress spoke defensively.

"Wouldn't she know where this cottage of Mrs. Findlay's is?" Pointer persisted. "I really do want to get into touch with the lady."

"Miss Longstaff wouldn't know!" The manageress was certain of that. She explained that certainty in the next sentence. "She asked me for it after Mrs Findlay left. But I hadn't got it."

"Did she too know the old gentleman with the cleft palate?"

The manageress thought that most unlikely, for Mrs. Findlay never let anyone into her room when he called. "On account of his infirmity, I think," she explained in her kindly way. She looked a good-natured soul.

Pointer asked about Miss Longstaff herself, and was told of how she arrived in the house. The manageress repeated that, "of course, as soon as she came here really to live she gave her real name."

Pointer returned to Mrs. Findlay and his desire for a word with her. Where did she generally have her meals? No one knew, except that she was never gone long. That finished his talk for the moment. He remembered the large Lyons where he had had his own coffee, and went back there. At this hour it was almost deserted. He again spoke of trying to find a lady-he described Mrs. Findlay with her floating veil-who was wanted as a witness to an accident.

"That's our star!" the manageress, a young and merry-eyed girl, said with a laugh. "We call her that because of the silver badge she always wears. She used to come here regularly twice a day, but we haven't seen her for-getting on for three weeks it must be now...Or rather, she passed here only this morning, so I've seen her, but not to come in. She's left us."

"And perhaps you know the old gentleman who had the accident. Nice old gentleman everyone says he was, cleft palate..." Pointer described Mr. Nevern.

"Oh, you mean him as won all that money-Mr. Nevern!" The manageress and a couple of waitresses were genuinely sorry to hear of an accident to him, "he's awfully short-sighted," one of them added. "Fancy having had an accident now!"

"They were friends, weren't they?" Pointer inquired, as though he knew that they were.

"In a sort of way," the manageress said rather hesitatingly, "they used to just exchange a word. Crossword puzzles was the hobby of both, you see. I heard him speak to her first of all. She'd been coming here ever so much longer than he had, oh, years and years, before I was moved here, and he's only been our customer for a few months. But he leaned across her table one day, and asked if she would pardon his asking it, but he saw she worked at crosswords too, and could she suggest a word of eight letters for Manifestation. And quick as quick she said 'Epiphany will that fit?' I was working on that one myself at the time in The People, so I've remembered it. She was quite right, too. After that they'd exchange a word or two, and then he sat down at her table once and they started talking in earnest. Not about crosswords. All about wars and killing men by thousands and so on. Made your flesh creep to hear them..."

Pointer said that apparently no one knew where Mrs. Findlay now lived. She had gone down to a cottage that she had somewhere —-

"In Buckinghamshire," put in a waitress. "I'm from there. I told her so, and she said as she had a cottage there. She didn't say where exactly."

That was all Pointer learned, but it was quite a good deal. He went back to the apartment house and asked for Miss Longstaff again. She was in and greeted him with perfect composure.

"I came to find out the address of a Mrs. Findlay, she's wanted as a witness in an accident case," he said easily. "Do you know where she is living now?"

Miss Longstaff said that she did not.

"How did I happen to meet her? Oh, hasn't the manageress told you?" She looked at him quizzically. "By the merest chance. I'm tremendously interested in disarmament, and when I heard that it was her life-work —well-of course, I was pleased to have as many talks with her as possible."

So she had had many talks, so many that she had thought that he, Pointer, would have been told about them. Pointer glanced at her, she stared back at him with that impenetrable stare of hers. A "Have you ever met an old gentleman in her room, with a cleft palate?" he asked.

With what he thought was genuine indifference, Miss Longstaff said that she had seen him once or twice through the glass side of the lounge, but had never spoken to him. Mrs. Findlay seemed to be afraid that he would be captured, she added dryly, and kept her door as good as locked whenever he was expected. Her eyes were on him all the time, he was sure that in some way his interest in Mrs. Findlay intensely interested this girl. Whether it did more, whether it disquieted her, even Pointer could not say.

"I understand that you borrowed a book from Mrs. Findlay," he went on, "how are you going to return it, if you don't know her address?"

"I suppose she'll write me about it, or it'll have to stand as a sort of farewell offering," Alfreda said flippantly. "Useful book, too. A thesaurus."

"Do you know if she had ever lent it before?" he asked.

She frowned, as though intrigued by this interest in the volume.

"As a matter of fact, this man you've asked me about, the old man with the cleft palate, had just borrowed it and brought it back. May I ask why?"

"Was there any kind of bookmark in it?" Pointer asked. "Frankly, Miss Longstaff, I consider that detail, though it sounds trifling, quite important."

"I like your 'frankly'," she murmured, eyeing him with eyes that almost glittered. "Bookmark...there were quite a lot of scraps of paper in it. Marking places II suppose. I think they're most of them still in it." She stretched out a hand and picked up a well-worn looking volume from a shelf that formed part of what looked like a Tudor dresser-in the manageress's opinion-and fluttered it. Nothing fell out. "Sorry, I must have lost them one by one."

"Could you tell' me if they were plain, or colored?"

She shook her head. "I don't think I ever noticed." A silence fell.

"Did you have that book with you at The Tall House?" he asked. She said that she had. Pointer knew as much.

"Anywhere where people could open it and read it-or lose the bookmarks?" he asked.

"I wish I knew why possible bits of paper interest you! But I had it lying out in my room for days, and I left it downstairs in the little Chinese room we used as a sitting-room more than once."

"Why?" Pointer asked.

She adjusted her skirt over her knees with care. "Just chance," she replied, then she looked up at him. "Frankly, just chance," she said, and smiled.

Pointer took his leave. Had that piece of wall-paper been among the 'scraps' in the book which she had borrowed? If so, it confused the issue instead of helping to clear it up.

CHAPTER 20

IT did not take the chief inspector long to find out from the land registry that a Mrs. Findlay owned the freehold of a small cottage in Buckinghamshire near Hotspur. Its name was Cloud Cottage, and though it was on an A.A. Throughway, it was quite secluded. Lying in a sudden little dip you had almost to step on it before you saw it, and then its encircling hedge, which looked much older than the little building, screened it but for its one chimney. Pointer circled it in his car and then made for the police station. He had his bag with him, and in a few minutes a tall, lean, elderly man who would have looked like a jobbing gardener even without the spade and fork over his shoulder, hobbled along the road which led past the cottage. His drooping mustache, his eyes, the very slant of his shoulders, suggested one of those traveling pessimists whose worst prophesies as to the flowers they plant usually come true. Leaning on the garden gate, he had a leisurely look at the cottage. Four rooms, he guessed, which was one too many, well-thatched and neatly painted, with a trim garden. It looked the retreat of someone whose means were ample for its small upkeep. The diamond panes glittered, the curtains and gay chintz behind them were spotless.

Pointer made his way to the back. He stepped very lightly. He did not knock on the kitchen door but opened it without a sound by means of a curious tool he took from his pocket, not one usually carried by gardeners.

Should Mrs. Findlay, contrary to his belief, be inside, he would touch his forehead and mention that he had knocked for five minutes before trying the back door and finding it open. She was not in, and he was able to walk quickly, but carefully, over the charming interior. But dead flowers smelled from the jugs of old pottery and a dirty hand towel hung on the washstand in the bathroom. The bed was badly made. So badly that Pointer would have supposed that the owner of this cottage could not have made it, and yet...or was it that she was in some great preoccupation of mind?

He left everything as he had found it, and locked the kitchen door behind him, before, spade and fork on shoulder, he plodded off for the village shops. At the nearest one he stopped. Could they tell him where he could find a Mrs. Findlay? As he hoped, being closest to her, that lady dealt here. But Mrs. Findlay, he was told, had stopped living at the cottage some days ago. The woman gave the date. It was the day of Ingram's murder. Mrs. Findlay herself had told the boy that she would want nothing more for some time, as she was going traveling. She often ran down still, but not to stop-and not to order things in.

The jobbing gardener scratched his long dark hair which was thickly flecked with gray, with a workworn earthy forefinger.

"Yet she arranged with me to come and fork over her garden," he said in the patient tones of one used to employers' vagaries.

"Bit early for that," the shop woman suggested.

Pointer agreed that it was, but he rather thought she was going to make a lawn, and in that case, if you wanted the ground to be properly drained, and settle well...

"I suppose the pay will be all right?" he wound up anxiously.

"Anything she ordered she'll pay for," the shop woman said confidently. "Pays to the minute always. But Ronnie here says she told him she wouldn't be back for close on a year maybe."

"What about a little old gent who was with her when she gave me my orders to fork up the back garden?" Pointer asked. "Long-haired little gent, funny way of talking...I works for a man in Ilford where she ordered some bulbs as wants to be put in soon..." he added, to explain his own unfamiliar face.

"I seed a little old gent come in the day she left," the boy put in. "Drove her down."

"Ah, but did you see her leave?" Pointer asked. "I can't think she'd place an order for bulbs and for her whole garden to be dug over and then just go away and leave it. Doesn't seem natural. I don't believe she's gone away yet. For a day or two perhaps, but not really left."

"I saw her driving off with all her luggage myself," the shop woman put in, "but as I say, she's been back since. But only just in and out, as you might say, with her car. Not living down here."

"Might be another lady," the gardener said doubtfully.

The woman was amused. "Who else wears a silver star, and has side curls like my granny used to wear?"

"Well, she never said nothing at the shop about leaving." Pointer seemed irresolute but finally said that as his master had sent him down to do the work he supposed he had better do it. He asked the boy to come along and, show him the way to the cottage, he wasn't sure he mightn't miss it.

The lad carried his fork and spade for him since the gardener seemed to have a stiff knee. They chatted about the cottage as they walked slowly along. Pointer seemed most interested in learning what he could of the one time when the boy had seen the little old gentleman arrive.

At the cottage the two walked round to the back Pointer seemed to see it for the first time.

"Looks to me as though she had had someone working here already," he said sourly. But he had never been more alert. This garden in this secluded spot-Nevern seen to arrive, not seen to leave...He went on: "Something's been moved here. Yuss, something's been turned about t'other way too. I don't know what, for I never seed the garden afore, but you did ought to know what it is, son. What d'ye think yer eyes be for? Something in this yere garden's been moved. Now just you tell me what?" and the gardener filled a briar with shag and began to smoke, hanging his coat on the hedge and rolling up his sleeves from sinewy arms burned black-apparently-with years of sun and wind. His heart was beating a little faster than usual. Would his guess prove right?

The boy stood with knitted brows studying the scene intently.

"That there shed!" he announced triumphantly.

"Ah!" Pointer said equably, and yet as one pleased with a pupil, "and where was it afore?"

"Over in that corner!" The young voice almost squeaked now. "That's right! And where it now stands was a pit for manure, chicken manure, she gets it from our chickens. That's it, and Mrs. Findlay has cleared it out, filled it up, and put the shed over it. The old gent and she must have worked hard. She never has no one to help her with her garden."

"Ah, I knowed something had been moved," Pointer said, nodding his head sagely. "When did you last see it in the corner? It's no good raking over ground for at least a fortnight what's had a shed stood over it. Needs that time to air, or ye digs in the sour top-soil."

"When I delivered here larst, it stood in its old place," was all the boy could tell him, and that, it seemed, was about a week ago-just before Ingram's murder, Pointer finally made out.

"Well, here's a penny, son, and thank ye," and the gardener began in a leisurely way to light his pipe until the boy could no longer see him, which meant only until he had closed the gate, for the little path turned so abruptly in joining the road that the cottage was out of sight in a minute. Then the gardener had a look at the tool shed. It was locked, but what interested him most was that it was on a four-wheeled truck base.

Around the bottom ran some wire netting as though to keep rats out from the ground immediately below it.

It was this very ground that interested the chief inspector, once he had noticed that the shed had been recently shifted. Below the shed his flashlight showed him black soil, evidently sub-soil. He bent up the wire netting for half a foot or so all around and with a vigorous shove moved the shed a couple of feet farther on. All the time he kept his eye out for the big outline of Mrs. Findlay appearing round the corner of the cottage, wearing her hat with its floating veil, silver star and dangling ear curls. Of one thing he felt fairly sure and that was that it would never again be accompanied by the little old gentleman who talked as though he had a cleft palate.

On the whole, he thought it very unlikely that she would be back here again. Though you never knew...if she remembered that she had not left the cottage in what Pointer felt sure was its usual order...

He dug down with the spade, for a trial had shown him that earth, such as was now on top of this little patch of roughly seven by four feet, could be found two spades deep in the rest of the garden.

At his third attempt he felt the spade come against something. He moved it half a foot along the length of the patch and again felt something below. Very swiftly and carefully now, scooping with his hands, he burrowed until he came on something, until he cleared a coat sleeve...a hand...and finally, working with extreme care, a dead face. So he was right. And the murder of Ingram and the body lying under the shed were linked.

Miss Longstaff was walking slowly along Hammersmith High Street thinking of Gilmour. Suddenly she was roused from her reverie. A woman had come out of a shop farther down, stepped into a passing bus, and been whirled away. It was Mrs. Findlay. Her throat was evidently worse, for she held a fur stole well across her mouth. But the silver star shone as gaily, the silvery ringlets nodded as briskly as ever. It was a chemist's shop from which she had come. Miss Longstaff recognized the name over the door as one which her sharp eyes had seen on several bottles of throat medicine in Mrs. Findlay's room. She stepped in.

"Mrs. Findlay was in here just now, wasn't she? I've just missed her. And I particularly want to see her. I suppose she's ordered something for her throat to be sent down to her at her cottage? If you'll give me the address, I can take it along with me. I'm going down that way."

Alfreda Longstaff had one asset. She looked thoroughly respectable. The shop man did not doubt her. After a little delay he handed her a bottle and the address, which she tucked into her purse. Then she too caught a bus and arrived at Paddington Station just as a train was due to leave for Hotspur. Her luck was in, she decided, and settled down in a corner of an empty compartment to think over the questions she would put to Mrs. Findlay. She walked up from the station. Cloud Cottage seemed to be deserted, but she rang the bell. There was no answer. She waited, uncertain what to do. Mrs. Findlay had ordered the medicine to be sent her by post so as to reach her that night. So she must be going to run down...After a long wait a car could be heard. It was an open little two-seater, Mrs. Findlay at the wheel. Alfreda walked to the gate to meet it.

"Don't scold me for having found out your little retreat. I shan't bother you but this once, and I've brought your throat medicine along with me. May I come in and have a short talk with you?"

Mrs. Findlay stood quite still, not even looking at Alfreda, after the one swift recognizing glance. She tapped the ground with her umbrella. Then she nodded, pointed to her throat, and to the fur still around her mouth and nose, walked with her majestic stride up to the door, unlocked it, and motioned to Alfreda to pass in. In the hall she took her to a room on the right, and whispered that she would be down in a minute, as soon as she had gargled. She did indeed come down within five minutes or so. She had not taken off her outside things, nor her hat, or put aside her fur stole which she still held in the same way across her mouth...

"And now, what is it, Miss Longstaff?" she whispered over its top, seating herself and motioning her visitor to take a chair opposite her, facing the light.

"Mrs. Findlay, I want so much to ask you a question. What do you know of Lawrence Gilmour? I asked you once before, but please, please be frank with me."

"Never heard of him," the reply came instantly, and with convincing firmness. "Who is he?"

"He is the man who shot Mr. Charles Ingram-by mistake-as he maintains. I've been rather against him...and I wondered whether...but perhaps you know him under another name? This is what he looks like. Mrs. Findlay had not even drawn off her gloves. She scrutinized the picture very carefully, but finally shook her head.

"Never saw him. But I have heard the name before! Oh, not from you or the papers! One day in the tube, I heard one man nudge his companion, and say rather eagerly, 'That's Lawrence Gilmour-that man there with the girl. Let's try him again. He won't refuse when he's got a skirt with him.' I didn't look to see what man or girl was meant, but on that occasion I did hear the name."

"When was this?" Alfreda asked.

Mrs. Findlay thought back. "I think it was when I was on my way to the first of the Universal Sisterhood and Brotherhood addresses...that would make it —" and she named the date when Alfreda had first seen her in the lift and thought that it was because of her that Gilmour had backed out so hurriedly.

"That's all I know," Mrs. Findlay said, adjusting her glasses with her thumb, a trick of hers. "Sorry. Very sorry that you've had your journey down here for nothing. I'd offer you tea, but I don't think you ought to stop. My throat trouble is rather catching-and very painful to me, even to whisper."

That it was catching Alfreda, had learned from the chemist who had had a look at Mrs. Findlay's throat in the beginning. But that did not worry Alfreda when bent on getting information.

"Look here," she said impulsively, "I'm sorry to stay even another minute. But —"

This time Mrs. Findlay rose. "It's too painful," she murmured, her hand to her throat. It was all of a keeping with Mrs. Findlay's grim unfriendly character. Alfreda thanked her, excused herself, and closed the front door behind herself after the briefest of leave-takings. So it was all a mistake. And she had wasted a good many very dull hours on a will-o'-the-wisp. Halfway down to the station a sudden thought struck her. How on earth had Mrs. Findlay known her real name? And known it without any questioning or remarks as to why she had gone under the name of Gray. She must be in closer touch with her old rooms than she, Alfreda, had been allowed to guess. Why this deceit on the part of manageress and maids? She walked back. She would ask Mrs. Findlay herself? She might never have another chance of a word with the woman. The bell-push gave no results. It was evidently out of order. There was no knocker. Alfreda thought of rapping, and then decided that in all probability Mrs. Findlay would still be in the room looking into the garden where she had left her. The French window had been at once opened by the lady, incidentally throwing a still clearer light on Alfreda's face. She went to it now, intending to tap and call to Mrs. Findlay. She was on grass. The afternoon sun was shining into the room she had just left, shining on the overmantel —a tall, old-fashioned mirror.

In front of this, standing close against it, Mrs. Findlay was now staring at her own reflection with close scrutiny.

For a second Alfreda stopped where she was. It would be a trifle awkward to surprise the lady taking such an evident interest in her looks. Mrs. Findlay would step away in a moment, Alfreda would wait a short interval, and then walk up and knock on a pane.

But Mrs. Findlay now dropped her fur stole, and seemed suddenly to cease to be Mrs. Findlay...she smiled at herself in the glass, and with the smile she became someone else...but who? Who? The figure in front of her with the hat with its flowing veil, put her hands to her ringlets, patted them into position, laughing at herself the while. Alfreda stood rooted to the spot. Down went her handbag with a jingle of coppers at her feet. In a flash the figure staring at itself in the mirror had wheeled. For one awful second the two stood face to face, then there was a leap, Alfreda was seized and lifted within the room. She was flung with fearful strength against the farther wall, while the glass doors were shut and latched and the blinds snatched down, then the figure turned again, and Alfreda knew that if she was to leave the room alive, she would have to fight for her life, and knew, too, that she had no more chance of escaping than has a mouse under the paw of the cat. That grasp, that fling, that awful glare in the eyes staring at her had told her as much.

CHAPTER 21

ALFREDA tried to swing a chair up, but it was knocked from her grasp. As it fell with a crash, something the crashed too-the French window. The linen blind was torn aside. A rock struck full on her assailant, who fell away and slowly lurched to her knees. Alfreda did not wait for further miracles. Again she swung the chair up, and, however clumsily this time, brought it down full on the swaying figure. The next moment it was taken from her.

"You're safe now! Steady on-he's down!" came a well known voice as a hand was laid on her arm. But Alfreda's blood was up. She twisted herself free.

"Of course he is! That's why I'm going to hit him!" She spoke with passion, and Chief Inspector Pointer had to fairly shove her aside with his elbow, while he bent down over the hat and veil and lifted them off, showing a head of beautifully parted gray hair, and with little ring curls all around and long corkscrews over each ear. He felt the skull.

"Nothing broken," he murmured with inward relief. He had flung that rock with more of a swing than he would have done had not the circumstances been a bit pressing. Magistrates have a preference for undamaged prisoners, and Pointer himself was very sharp with his own men as to any rough handling of their captives.

"I'll put these on him," he clicked handcuffs around the neat lace cuffs and the man's hands protruding from them.

"What-what —" came thickly from beneath the matronly hair, in a hoarse voice.

"Lawrence Gilmour, I arrest you for the murder of Mr. Charles Ingram and of Mrs. Mary Findlay —" followed swiftly the caution.

Gilmour said nothing now. He set his teeth and gave Alfreda Longstaff a look that she never forgot, that would sometimes wake her up bathed in cold perspiration of a night.

Alfreda said nothing in answer to it. Something in the grave, stern, almost sad, face of the detective officer made her realize the tremendous moment that this was...She, a living human being, was looking at a man who might very soon be that no longer.

"You damned spy," he said now between his teeth. "Take your ugly face out of my sight."

Pointer spoke sharply. "Mr. Gilmour, I think you had better say nothing, unless you wish to make a statement to me."

"What motive do you intend to allege? Of course I'm innocent." He caught the direction of the calm gray eyes that just for a moment rested on the shed outside. Gilmour's face went white. Again his eye fell on Alfreda. Again she shrank from the look of it.

"What motive?" he snarled at the chief inspector.

"Crosswords," Pointer said briefly, and Gilmour after that said no more. There was a sound behind them. A man in blue came in. Pointer said a word to him and then took Alfreda into another room. He made her sit down there, for she was trembling violently. She was afraid that she was going to be sick.

"Badly frightened?" he asked.

He got the instant reaction that he knew would come.

"Not in the least. I'll telephone for you, if you like." But she would have found it difficult to unhook the receiver. Pointer took out a flat flask and unscrewed the cup. He filled it.

"It won't hurt you," he said. "I really advise it. I don't doubt your pluck. But you were within an inch of death, Miss Longstaff." Pointer had had to leave the cottage for a brief word over the telephone to the Yard. The constable had misunderstood Miss Longstaff's approach by the back, had thought her a friend of the so-called Mrs. Findlay, and only Pointer's return and his sight of the dropped handbag on the grass outside had saved Alfreda. That handbag left there did not suggest a confederate to his quick brain.

She swallowed the brandy obediently while he telephoned. Then he turned to her. Even as he did so a car whizzed up. It was his own men whom he had summoned from town just after first prodding that place in the garden under the shed.

"Suppose we go back to town together in my car," he suggested, and Alfreda was glad of the offer.

"Now tell me how you came to be down here, how you knew, after all, where to come?"

She explained. "And where is Mrs. Findlay? The real Mrs. Findlay?"

"Beneath that shed out in the garden we have just left," Pointer said truthfully. This was no nature that needed shielding. "Gilmour, in the guise of an old man he assumed the name of Nevern-became friendly with her, and murdered her. Strangled her and buried her in her own garden."

"You spoke of crosswords. Do you mean she won a crossword prize and he killed her just for that?" she asked in horror.

That was but a small part of Gilmour's intended haul, Pointer could have told her. But he did not. That would all come out at the trial.

"And why, why did he pretend to care for me?" she asked. "You know, Mr. Pointer, that's what started all my suspicions." She played with her gloves on her lap. "When he came down to our village, I was very much impressed with him. I went for him, they'll all tell you down there. I suppose I did." She spoke judicially, quite objectively. "He stood to me for opportunity-escape-and all that sort of thing. But he flirted with me, and then dropped me. Then he came down again. I was perfectly certain, as I say, that he was not in love with me, I was sure of it. And I decided that two could play at that game too. I would come to London and have a pleasant time while looking around for work that would lead on to something, and then I would drop Lawrence Gilmour just as he had dropped me. For, you see, Mr. Pointer, I knew that he didn't care for me. I couldn't think why on earth he should pretend to, but I did have sense enough to know it was only a pretense. Why did he do it? With that silly, beautiful Winnie Pratt willing to take him any day?"

"Ah, she might be considered as a motive, Miss Longstaff. When Gilmour shot Ingram, he wanted there to be no shadow of a possible motive. I think he could have murdered Miss Pratt with pleasure. She tried to spoil his shield of no earthly reason for killing his friend. But please go on —"

"There isn't anything to tell. I wish there was. When I met Winnie Pratt I was more than ever puzzled. Some real game must be on to make him pretend he cared for me with her at his elbow! Then came the shooting of Ingram. Poor Mr. Ingram. I liked Mr. Ingram," she said suddenly.

"So did everyone-but Gilmour," Pointer agreed.

"I had been up night after night listening, and waiting about-always expecting to come across something that would give me a clue to what the game was. I thought of Mrs. Pratt's jewels..."

Pointer did not tell her every one was paste.

"I didn't know what to think...and the one night when something really was on, I was asleep in bed! Worn out with being up so much!" She gave her head a toss of self-disgust. "But I knew it was a shot! Just because I was expecting something or other...anyone else would have thought it a burst tire...but I was too late to find out how it was done. Then I noticed the hole in the sheet which never could have been made by a bullet through Ingram's forehead if the sheet had hung down over his face, and I got into touch with the *Daily Wire*. I passed on that piece of news to their reporter."

She told how she had done this.

"I rushed down to the room Mr. Ingram used to write in, to see if I could find anything there. Any clue...you always do in books, you know."

"So you do in real life," Pointer could have said, but he only nodded.

"That's all, I think. I've told you about why I followed Mrs. Findlay and tried to get to know her...Then when Mr. Moy told me about Gilmour having gone off to find the murderer I —for the first time-weakened. I told myself I had been an absolute idiot...especially when Mrs. Findlay, as I thought she was, spoke as though she had never heard of Gilmour or seen his face before. Oh, she-he-quite took me in just now! But I knew he had stopped back at that lift door to avoid Mrs. Findlay!"

"Half involuntarily, I think," Pointer said. He wanted to keep her talking. It was the best way, in her case, to ease the shock that she had had, he rightly thought. "She only knew him as Nevern. But he probably also thought it just as well not to obtrude himself, his real self, on her."

"I saw him once, I mean as Nevern. Through the glass window of the lounge at the apartment house, and never recognized him! But I only gave him half a glance, and he slouched so, and wore such shabby clothes, and had a muffler around his neck and such a battered old felt hat turned down all around his eyes...You know," she went on at a half tangent, "I left the book I borrowed from her lying about at The Tall House, open at her name on the fly leaf, to see if it would catch his eye. But someone always shut it. So I got tired of trying it."

"Had it lain before him he was probably too concerned with his double murder to pay much attention to trifles," Pointer suggested, as he went on out to complete his own arrangements.

"She won't stay a reporter long," Pointer said to the assistant commissioner. "I heard that they're going to make her a very good offer to watch the case for them as it were...I think Miss Longstaff is bound to go ahead in the newspaper world."

"I suppose they'll get her to write what it feels like to be the fiancée of a murderer. What it feels like to suspect one you love..." Pelham spoke in a tone of disgust. He loathed the *Daily Wire*. "Let's hope they'll get her to do one on 'What it feels like to have the man you wanted to marry, hung,'" he finished, and Pointer hoped that the opportunity might yet come Miss Longstaff's way. It did, had she cared to use it.

"Did you suspect Gilmour from the first?" Pelham asked curiously. He himself had been rather favorably impressed by that astute young man.

"Well, sir, if Gilmour's story was true and the second sheet found was the right one, however intricate they might seem, the other knotty points surrounding it would untie themselves, as they always do if worked at. But if his story was not true, if he intended to kill Ingram that night, why did he choose that way? And why The Tall House? The locality and time might mean that he wanted to confuse the hunt, if it had been an ordinary murder. But he himself openly confessed to having killed Ingram —'by a blunder' If he was guilty, why did he take this dangerous step? He who would have, and had, such ample opportunities of getting rid of him quietly."

"Yes, that affair on Scawfell at Easter seemed such a certificate of good intentions," murmured Pelham. "Why not then, Pointer? But I see the answer to that. The quarterly thirteen puzzles weren't out then. Or didn't he know about them?"

"I don't think he knew about them until that accident, sir, which took place just after the last lot had been sent off. I shouldn't be surprised if it was while opening his clothes, to feel if his heart were beating, that Gilmour came upon some paper which made him suspect or learn what Ingram's secondary line was, financially his most important line. Ingram's climbing plus fours have just the same kind of a pocket made in them as have his evening bags...yes, I think the prosecution can assume that then and there he learned the facts which he-on reflection-decided could be of such great use to himself."

"But about your suspicions," Pelham harked back, "I want to see them at work again."

"Well, sir," Pointer said, looking at his shoe tips as though they were a diary which he was reading, "I could only say to myself, that if Gilmour was guilty, then time must be all important. That Ingram's death must be wanted to take place no sooner and no later."

"Not during the Easter rock climb, nor during the snow climbing planned far July," Pelham nodded. He saw the obviousness of this.

"This idea fitted in with first the belief, then the knowledge that Ingram had posted something for which I thought it likely that he had had that inner secret pocket made. Something of great importance, that meant. Shall I boil down the rest of my laborious thinking, sir?" Pointer would never have made a good lecturer, he was too afraid of boring people.

"Anything but!" His superior protested, "take me step by step with you."

"Well, sir, if Gilmour were guilty, it looked as though he, too, would want to be free as quickly as possible after the murder. I could think of no other reason for him to have taken such a risky course as he did but one. Because Ingram's death was not to have a long inquiry tacked on to it, which meant that no question of murder was to be attached to it. As Gilmour planned it, absolutely without a motive, it would look just what he said it was, a horrible accident. And it would further give a man a chance of disappearing utterly without arousing suspicion afterwards. What more natural than that the poor chap who had had such a misadventure should drop out of sight, go round the world-and never return?"

"Did your-to me-inexplicable idea of disappearances fit in here?"

"Well, yes, sir, it did at once suggest that he must have some other identity waiting for him into which to pass. And when he disappeared 'to look for the criminal' as he put it, I thought I could put the odds at ten to one on, his being the criminal himself. Though I began to fear that he wouldn't be easy to come up with. I had no motive yet...Of course as soon as I thought of Ingram as a writer of crossword puzzles with big prizes, obviously the character that Gilmour had turned into would win one, and ultimately, all of them. I expected, first of all, before making inquiries, that both the winners after Ingram's murder would be incarnations of Mr. Gilmour. But they were seen together. One had disappeared entirely after taking his prize money, and the other had left her usual haunts but had been seen about, a person whom I would have chosen myself in Gilmour's position. A strange, unfriendly, solitary woman whose outline would identify her, without a scrutiny of her features. Those ringlets, that floating veil, that star...no one would look closely under the big hat. And she had a sore throat...could muffle up."

"Bit of luck that, for Gilmour."

"Assisted by Gilmour," Pointer said, "I suspect he put something into her tea to make her throat sore. And be able to drop in-after she was dead-at the chemist's for the 'same throat medicine as you put up for me before.'"

Pointer was right. Gilmour had done just that.

"Where was Gilmour supposed to be when he was murdering the old lady?"

"With Miss Longstaff, sir. He constantly lately has taken days off, out of his leave, on the plea of his fiancée being up in town, and of course has had it made easy for him to do."

"All the world loves a lover," quoted Major Pelham with macabre relish.

"Her liking to have her mornings to herself suited him excellently, of course," Pointer went on. "Just as she tells me that he often excused himself after a bare half hour or even less, on the plea of a colleague being down with the flu, and his having promised to take his duty for him. As Nevern, he went down to her cottage with Mrs. Findlay the morning of the day on which Ingram was to be shot. Got her to send a message to a man she often employed, a stupid sort of half idiot to move the tool shed on the next morning to a place over the manure pit, and then killed her. Buried her and left the idiot to hide the spot next day with the shed, while he made up as Mrs. Findlay, went to town, changing on the way into Gilmour."

"Busy bee," Pelham said with a shudder.

"And the dislike of Miss Pratt?" he asked. "Got that combed out?"

Pointer had.

"Well, well! How hard is the path of crime," murmured Pelham. "Fancy having to turn a stony eye and ear on the lovely Winnie, and beam instead on the distinctly waspish Miss Longstaff. What about Miss Pratt, by the way? Does she talk of committing suicide?"

"Not unless you call marrying Mr. Haliburton that," Pointer said. "She and her mother and Haliburton have all agreed that the wedding is to take place at once and young Mrs. Haliburton will be on her honeymoon to Greenland or Finland by the time the trial comes off."

"Quite right," Pelham said. "She's much too lovely a butterfly to pin up in a law court for everyone to stare at. Did she care for the brute, do you think?"

Pointer thought that Mrs. Pratt was right, and that Winnie, having met a man who was not bowled over by her looks, who refused to be won by her blandishments, thought that she must, indeed, have met a demi-god, a being not of mortal clay. The shock of Gilmour's arrest had put quite another complexion on things. She now agreed with her mother that Gilmour was not "normal," and had allowed Haliburton to decide that there should be no more shilly-shallying.

"I suppose that note Gilmour left..." pursued Pelham, who liked to tie his bundles up with everything inside them, "was just to spoof Moy?"

"Exactly, sir, and explain his non-appearance...You see, things had gone so contrary that he couldn't just set off on a trip round the world as he had planned. He was more than a little afraid of us...Lord Bulstrode might reveal the real writer of the crosswords...Gilmour decided that he had better go...and turn into Nevern until he could become Mrs. Findlay. Once safely her, he would have gone on that world trip, and duly sent in correct solutions to the *Weekly Universe* as Miss Smith, Doctor Brown, Mr. Jones, Mrs. Robinson, as need be; appear in a different form each time and take the check..."

"Neat," Pelham said. "Pity is that these simple ways of grabbing what doesn't belong to you, rarely work out according to plan. Ingenious chap, I think, Pointer, though you don't seem to like him. And perhaps he was a bit careless to drop that scrap of wall paper. How did he come to have it in his dressing-gown pocket?"

"I confess I can't say, though I could hazard a guess. But, by good luck, a fragment of it stuck to the lining of the pocket, so that even our searchers didn't spot it, yet it'll prove the link between him and meek little Mr. Nevern."

"What do you guess?" Pelham asked promptly.

"From the way the paper has been screwed up, sir, I should say that he wrapped a ring in it. He only wears one, a fine scarab. My guess is that he forgot to take it off once when he was Mr. Nevern, decided to be on the safe side and wrapped it in a scrap of paper before dropping it in his pocket because of its very shallow setting. It is just a little loose."

"But why put it in his dressing-gown pocket?" Pelham persisted, "he hardly strolled across London wearing that when he became Mr. Nevern, did he?"

"A scarab is supposed to bring luck," Pointer said. "It looks to me as though he had put it in his dressing-gown when he murdered Ingram for luck. And when he dropped the cartridge case, picked up off the bedroom floor, in the passage, he must have dropped the paper out too, tearing it as he scooped out the cartridge case. He, or someone else, stepping on it, flattened it out on the cream ground of the carpet, and never noticed it."

"Quite a neat little guess," Pelham said approvingly. Later on, they both learned that it was the truth.

"By the way, what about the system?"

"I let Mr. Appleton have it, sir, or a copy of it. He's just worked it with such success in Ostend and the Casino has offered him three thousand a year for life to sell it to them. He's accepted. What with what he's made before I stepped in, and this nice little annuity, he feels quite comfortable about the future and is going to have his operation with a tranquil mind next month. Mrs. Appleton can't do enough to make up to him for her terrible suspicion. As for Appleton, he really did suspect Frederick Ingram-and a cipher motive."

"The trouble was Appleton always acted," Pelham said, "and it's deuced difficult to spot when an actor's real, and when he's playing a part. I'm glad that shark Tark won't get any of the spoils."

So was Pointer. "I went so far as to explain to Mr. Haliburton what I had happened to overhear once in Appleton's room abroad," he said gravely, quite undeterred by the grin of Pelham at the word 'happened,' "and he's dropped Tark. Definitely. I think he suspects that the ramming of his skiff may have just been part of a plan to meet Ingram under unimpeachable auspices. Tark, of course, is the type you meet in out-of-the-way places of the world playing poker for his boots-or yours. He must have been the one who hunted through the study before Miss Longstaff. That was why he had to go on and wake the servants. She cut him off from the main stairs. Tark has resource and a face of granite."

"Why not say he has a face like Gilmour's 'heart," suggested Pelham. "I suppose Gilmour put that second corrected sheet into the linen hamper himself, and then waited for Moy to think of looking there?"

"I think that's what happened, sir. That hole was a bad blunder. He shot Ingram in his bed, to the best of my belief, Ingram was an unusually heavy sleeper, we know. I think Gilmour drew the sheet up over his face when he lay on his back fast asleep, stood at the end of the bed, or the other side of the room with his automatic fitted with a silencer, and shot him dead, through the sheet and the center of the forehead. It was a very small caliber automatic. There was practically no bleeding. I fancy he would have changed slips had there been any stains. He twisted the sheet around Ingram and dumped him on the floor just outside his own door, then went to his room and fired out through the bedroom window over the gardens after loading with six blanks. So that the shot would rouse the household. He had previously, on his way to his room, dropped the cartridge case from Ingram's room on the carpet near his door. Along with that scrap of wall paper.

"After firing-with his door open-he staggered about in the passage and felt for the switch, put out of action by himself, of course. And so on..."

"All that upholding of Ingram's suit of Miss Pratt was so much eyewash, of course."

"I suppose every murderer who undertakes a premeditated crime paints a picture, sir, and wants the investigators to take the picture he has colored so skilfully for real life. It's just a case of seeing through it, or as your book puts it, of 'seeping through the cilia.'"

Pelham nodded, pushing a box of cigars across to Pointer. "The stance of the faithful friend, just so. He was a clever chap."

"Well, he made two bad breaks, sir. The hole too near the edge of the sheet, and then picking on Miss Longstaff to be his girl. I suppose the latter was hardly his fault, rather his misfortune," Pointer ruminated aloud. "When he found Miss Pratt upsetting all his arrangements by trying so hard to fall in love with him, he looked around for cover. He remembered how welcome Miss Longstaff had found his company, how she had, to use her own words, 'gone for him,' and thought that he would get engaged for a short time to a little trusting country maid who would be delighted to say yes, and never question his actions. Miss Longstaff did. He overrated badly what he fondly believed was her love for him, and underrated as badly her brains."

"Yours were the brains he underrated," Pelham said affectionately, "as everyone does who thinks they can get the better of you."

THE END

CPSIA information can be obtained
at www.ICGtesting.com
Printed in the USA
BVHW050811140223
658473BV00009B/301